BASE SPIRITS

Ruth Barrett

'Base spirit
To lay thy hate upon the fruitful honour
Of thine own bed.'

—*A Yorkshire Tragedy,*
Act I, Scene ii.

*In memoriam of two young brothers—
William and Walter Calverley.*

*And with love to Sybil Barrett
Look, Mom—we finally did it.*

YORK, ENGLAND, 1605

Sir Thomas Leventhorpe had failed the victims in life. He could not fail them now.

Though he longed to be anywhere else that August dawn, his choice was irrefutable. The noble family murders had left him as the village of Calverley's highest-ranking citizen, and he bore a duty to witness the conclusion of its history's most tragic chapter. It was his sacred charge to stand present for those innocent lives cruelly dispatched by the very man that should have loved them most.

He lingered in the stark main corridor of Clifford's Tower, waiting to accompany the killer on his final procession. There seemed to be a delay. From what Leventhorpe could gather, the entourage was incomplete. He glanced about the small, silent group and caught the eye of the anxious man standing at his side—the only other soul afflicted with first-hand knowledge of the horrors that had led them to the Tower. Leventhorpe ventured an encouraging smile at the murderer's former servant, but John's pale, scarred face was stony. Sir Thomas touched the younger man on the shoulder and felt him quivering like a nervous beast, his arms tightly wrapped about himself in a desperate embrace. The brutal April morning at Calverley Hall had shattered John. Withdrawing his hand, Leventhorpe wondered why the lad had come to this dread place to be reunited with his nemesis. Perhaps in his own way John had no choice but to see the tragedy through to its conclusion. Leventhorpe could offer him no real solace but to share the burden of bearing witness.

In the Tower's stairwell door, a grizzled magistrate stood lost in thought, tugging gently at his beard. The elderly head gaoler, Master Key, waited outside the prisoner's cell door. A younger, assistant gaoler tapped his foot loudly against the flagstones and glowered toward the doorway at the opposite end of the corridor, a sneer playing on his lean face. Turning to his superior, he grumbled in a low voice: "That idiot boy is late again—and today of all days! I say we have tarried long enough."

Master Key held up his hand. "Be thou patient, Jack. The magistrate is not yet concerned with the time. Hugh must be present to learn the proper order of how matters proceed."

Leventhorpe's skin prickled at the thought. He dreaded having to witness the 'matter' in question, and felt pity for the unseen boy who would today be taught the finer details of his trade.

Footsteps pounded up the outside stairs and—as if overhearing his cue—a scrawny lad of no more than twelve skidded into sight. White-faced and out of breath, Hugh blanched still further as the men turned as one and fixed him with expectant looks. Giving an awkward bow of his head by way of apology, he staggered as he took a halberd down from the wall hooks. Jack strode over to collect the apprentice and hauled him into place by the ear. Leventhorpe was close enough to hear the gaoler's hissed threats.

"Yer in luck, boy. The magistrate himself was late to rise, else ye'd be wishin' ye could trade places with our esteemed prisoner."

Master Key shot his underlings a sharp glance from beneath his heavy grey brows and they ceased their disruption. Key unlocked the door, and he and Jack entered the cell. Leventhorpe heard the muted clanking of chains and after a moment, Sir Walter Calverley was led out between the two men. Leventhorpe's stomach twisted at the sight of his former friend and neighbour.

He caught John by the arm, steadying him as the lad's knees buckled. Neither had seen Calverley for months—not since his hellish rampage. Although Calverley was thin and drawn, he held himself with dignity. He wore a fine black doublet, and his lace cuffs and collar gleamed in contrast to the gloom of the corridor. Leventhorpe couldn't help but think that Calverley was very well dressed for a dead man: he must have set this outfit aside in anticipation of the occasion. Calverley did not so much as glance in their direction.

Master Key cleared his throat and nodded to the magistrate. The procession began its descent into the bowels of the Tower, the close quarters of the stairwell making for an awkward single-file progress. The stately magistrate set a careful pace for those behind. Leventhorpe and John followed next, with Master Key leading Calverley. Jack and Hugh took up the rear to prevent any chance of the prisoner's escape.

Time of day carried no meaning as they moved down into the still depths of the Tower. No one spoke: the only sound was the scuffling of heavy-booted feet. Flickering torches from the wall sconces lit the way, casting long, dancing shadows on the muted grey stones. Leventhorpe had the sensation of being buried in the earth as they moved ever deeper. He kept his eyes lowered, mindful of the uneven stairs, eroded by countless footsteps over several lifetimes. Suddenly, a rush of iridescent green-and-black beetles scattered out of the men's path. Leventhorpe felt a brief flash of delight to see something so lively—these animated jewels—existing in such a bleak place.

At the foot of the tightly coiled stone staircase lay a narrow, low-ceilinged passageway. Leventhorpe glanced along a seemingly endless succession of closed doors and gaping antechambers. Today's method of execution—*'peine forte et dure,'* less elegantly known as 'pressing'—could take several hours. His throat constricted. Already he found the dank air putrid and hard to breathe. The clammy walls, coated with an orange mildew, gave off a pungent odour. Here and there between the cracks in the stones grew a strangely pretty fungus with pale yellow flowers. Leventhorpe touched a curious finger to a cluster of the petals as he passed by. They disintegrated instantly and left a lurid smear on his fine lace cuff.

Lord, I pray this ends quickly—

At last, the magistrate came to a halt and peered around to catch the eye of Master Key. Jack and Hugh stepped ahead to replace their Master's hold on the prisoner. Hugh's hand clearly shook as he tried to get a firm grip on Calverley's arm, but he was met with no resistance: Calverley kept his manacled hands clasped before him in the manner of a clergyman and focused his dark eyes into the shadows at the far end of the passageway. Leventhorpe was again struck by the man's poise. Of those present, he seemed the least moved by what was about to take place.

Fumbling at his belt for an oversized key, the old Master slipped to the front of the group to unlock the low, windowless portal. He heaved his stooped shoulder against the recalcitrant door and swung it inwards. The magistrate ducked his head as he entered the chamber, followed by the others. As Key lit the torches in the iron wall sconces, Leventhorpe blinked and looked about the room. A wide plank of coarsely hewn oak leaned against one wall. Beside it was a heap of stones, each roughly the same size—twelve to fourteen pounds in weight. Four iron rings were set into the flagstones in the centre of the floor. The room was otherwise barren. Once the condemned man was safely inside, the door was shut and bolted. Leventhorpe felt trapped.

"Make him ready," said the magistrate.

As placidly as a docile horse, Calverley allowed himself to be taken by his chains and roughly stripped by Jack. The assistant gleefully assessed the clothing as he folded each item. Handing the garments over to Hugh, he winked at the boy's dumbfounded expression.

"For safe-keepin', lad. A boon for me. They're about my size—and he won't be needin' 'em in Hell now, will he?"

Leventhorpe was shocked by the outrageous theft but no one else seemed fazed. *It must be routine in such matters*, he thought. Perhaps it was considered part of the assistant's payment.

Calverley was made to stretch out face up on the

cold floor. A jagged stone was placed underneath the small of his back. His ribs standing out in sharp relief, he arched his body upward to accommodate the work of Master Key's calloused hands. The prisoner's long limbs were pulled into a cruciform position and shackled to the iron rings. At a quick count of three, the two gaolers heaved the plank from where it stood. With a grunt, they laid it over top of Calverley's naked torso. The strain showed immediately in his breathing.

From where he stood, Leventhorpe had the clearest view. Only the doomed man's face was visible at the top edge of the plank. Leventhorpe looked closely at his one-time friend. Calverley's full lips were parted as he gasped from the burden already on his chest—and the anticipation of what was soon to come. Beads of perspiration dotted his moustache and beard, and sweat soaked the thick waves of his dark hair. Leventhorpe felt sick with pity. For all that Calverley had so brutally performed to visit this fate upon him, his serene determination from the outset to lighten the work of his own executioners gave him the aspect of a martyr.

Perhaps he hath repented. Will he at last speak his mind to the Law?

Leventhorpe could not catch his eyes to ask this silent question. Calverley had disconnected. He fixed his unblinking gaze on the grimy ceiling, entombing any emotion he may have felt deep within and unreachable.

The magistrate stepped forward from the corner,

where he'd been absorbed in the examination of loose threads on the hem of his cloak. He had paid little attention to the tasks of the others. Master Key pulled his apprentice out of the way and made him drop the bundle of clothes he'd been hugging to his chest.

"Ye'll need to keep yer hands free now, son."

The nervous boy leaned his halberd against the wall, where it slipped along the moisture and clattered to the floor. Already skittish, Leventhorpe and John started at the racket, and John pressed up against his back as if to be shielded from the very Devil. The magistrate clenched his jaw and waited for the echo to subside. He spoke in a strong voice that belied his great age.

"You had your chance to speak before the Assizes. You chose silence. I therefore put it to you here and now for the Crown, and before these good men: Sir Walter Calverley, how do you plead?"

Leventhorpe stood waiting by his friend's head. John's nervous breath was hot on his neck.

There came no reply from Calverley but laboured breathing.

"Very well—" The magistrate stepped aside and nodded to the gaolers. "Lay on the weights."

With a mason's ease, Jack handed the stones one by one to his superior, pausing to allow Master Key enough time to place each stone securely onto the plank. The harsh sound of the weights grating together set Leventhorpe's teeth on edge. He watched as the face above the plank turned a hot red and twisted into a grimace. Gasping, Calverley groaned involuntarily.

"Stop—" Raising his hand, the magistrate stepped forward and leaned over the tortured figure. "We can proceed quickly, or we can draw this out. The choice is thine. I once saw a man linger under the press for three days. Again: how do you plead?"

Calverley said nothing.

The magistrate sighed and signalled to the executioners. Master Key, worn out by his efforts, doubled over in a fit of coughing. Hugh thumped him hard on the back. It only made matters worse. The old gaoler shook his head and gestured for the apprentice to take over as he retreated, leaning against the far wall and catching his breath. Hugh looked unsure of himself as Jack thrust a heavy stone into his arms. All eyes were upon him. The boy hesitated. His knees threatened to give out as he squatted down and placed the stone so gingerly upon the plank that it had no perceptible effect on Calverley. The next stone shoved into his sweaty hands was a good deal heavier and the boy lost his grip, dropping the weight with great force onto the plank. A strangled cry erupted from below. The boy leapt back. John gave a low groan—almost a growl—as Leventhorpe's throat constricted with dry heaves.

"Hold!"

At the magistrate's command, man and boy paused in their work, and Master Key clapped a steadying hand on Hugh's shoulder. The magistrate stooped to assess the progress. Leventhorpe's sight blurred with tears. The tendons on Calverley's neck were so strained that surely they might snap at any moment. Veins protruded at his temples and his wild eyes bulged. Leventhorpe could no longer recognize his neighbour's once-handsome features.

"So? How do you plead?"

Calverley made a liquid gasping sound, but no actual words came forth to admit either his obvious guilt or impossible innocence. The magistrate lost all patience. His voice rang sharply off the chamber's walls.

"Do not be tedious, Calverley! Thy family's blood was seen on thy very hands by this good gentleman!" Leventhorpe winced as the magistrate jabbed a finger in his direction. "This man—thy servant—bears the scars from the vile attack!" John ducked his head down on Leventhorpe's shoulder, hiding his face. "Again. For these most foul of crimes, *how do you plead?*"

Calverley croaked out a few inaudible words. Leventhorpe felt a flutter of hope. Mercy in the form of a swift hanging would be shown if a plea—any plea—was made. The magistrate would then have the authority to seize the condemned's remaining property for the Crown, and the executioners' work would be made relatively simple. Leventhorpe could return home and leave this waking nightmare behind. Perhaps poor, broken John could come and work at his manor, and he made a mental note to put an offer to the lad... afterward. Leventhorpe bent down over the grotesque visage to better hear Calverley, whose lips were moving weakly and running thick with bloody spittle. The magistrate encouraged the prisoner in a gentler tone.

"Very good, Calverley. Speak again. Your plea?"

Calverley gave a terrible wet gurgle and repeated himself in a faint rasp. John gathered his nerve and peered over Leventhorpe's shoulder. Calverley's eyes rolled and came to rest on John's face.

"They—that love Sir Walter... lay on—a pound—more weight..."

Leventhorpe felt John's fingers dig into his arm at the sound of his former master's voice, then the lad leaned in closer to the man who had caused such grief for so many. Calverley's words were no more than a whisper. All held their breath.

"I swear they shall—have nothing—more—of me—but my skin—John."

The two men exchanged a look of mutual understanding, and John's manner transformed. All signs of fear were gone. Releasing the grip on Leventhorpe's arm, John stepped away from the nobleman, drew himself up to his full height, and loomed over the dying man. Somehow, through his death's-head grimace, Calverley smiled.

"Good man. Ever-loyal—to me."

In the presence of the young man's intent focus, no

one was sure how to react. John raised his boot and calmly set it on the plank. With a huge final effort, Calverley nodded. John obeyed the silent call to duty and began to lean his full weight into the wood, never breaking his gaze from that of his master's.

"No, John!" Leventhorpe grabbed the servant and tried to pull him away. John roughly shoved him aside, determined to perform this ultimate mad act of service.

"Will someone not control this cur?" the magistrate bellowed.

Leventhorpe desperately cast his eyes about for help, but both Hugh and the formerly brash Jack both seemed equally frozen by shock. Master Key stepped in. He could not hope to bodily remove the strong youth from his task, but perhaps words could sway him.

"Do not be a fool, lad. True, 'tis meet to see him dead for his crimes, but not by your doing. 'Tis my charge to fulfill—mine and my brethren's. Heed me: fair or no, in the law's eyes this deed is as much murder as those he hath committed, and thou shalt be made to pay the price. I beg thee—stop."

Sweat dripped from John's brow as he redoubled his efforts.

A sickening crunch echoed through the chamber. With a final surge of blood bubbling up between his cracked lips, Calverley's rattling breath ceased. His eyes glazed and rolled back in his skull.

No one spoke. As Hugh threw up in a corner, the

senior gaolers recovered themselves enough to step up, take John by the arms and pull him back from the press. John met Leventhorpe's look of astonishment with a triumphant half-smile.

"Sir Thomas, do not judge me." John's lip curled as he turned his reddened eyes back to Calverley. "Tis blood for blood. Now, I am content."

PART ONE

'Bad turned to worse…'

—A Yorkshire Tragedy,
Act I, Scene ii

CHAPTER ONE

It was identical every time.

Out of the blackness, the familiar parade of images flickered into a hazy half-focus. First, the cage. The watcher drifted in for a closer look. Within its tight confines was the same faceless, huddled form pressed up against the bars. No matter the angle, its features could not be made out—no way to tell if it was a man or woman, young or old. Was the blurred figure even alive? The watcher dared not reach through to touch the hunched shoulder—dared not speak to it for fear of hearing an answer.

Then came the accustomed pause of a heartbeat or two.

The shadowy figure in a gown entered from stage right. Colourless, noiseless, the action played out like a silent film as the shadow made a slow and jerky progress to the edge of the cage. Its arms were raised upward stiffly, holding out a shapeless object to the prisoner in a gesture of offering... or perhaps of threat.

It was always at this point that all motion ceased. The picture jolted and became skewed, dissolving into a blank white screen as the watcher's voice shrieked out—

"Damn!"

The car brakes slammed on. Clara Ravenscroft lurched forward and her nodding head thumped into the back of the driver's headrest, jarring her awake. Muddled, she peered out the window and saw that they'd pulled over sharply to the side of the road and were on the verge of toppling into a ditch. A motorcycle roared out of sight over the crest of the next hill.

"That blasted fool darted out in front of us without even looking!" cried Martin Thornbury from behind the wheel. "Are you all right back there?"

Clara managed an affirmative grunt. She was so tightly packed in by luggage in the cramped backseat that no damage could possibly have been done.

"Huh. Welcome to England," said her husband, Scott Atkinson, from the front passenger's seat.

Martin laughed and pushed an unruly fringe of ginger hair out of his eyes. "No harm done. We're nearly there, anyway. With a little luck, I should get us the rest of the way to Calverley Old Hall without killing you."

He winked at Clara in the rearview mirror as he shifted gears to pull back onto the busy Bradford Road.

"That's the nearest bus stop for Leeds," he noted as they turned into the village proper. "Just over the way by the churchyard. That's old St. Wilfred's—predates the twelfth century."

Clara felt queasy. Despite her love of England, she'd been keeping her eyes shut against the sight of the West Yorkshire countryside whizzing by her window as they careened along the rolling green hills and dales. Somehow she'd managed to drift off. Scott and Clara had been in constant motion for what felt like days: the drive from Peterborough to Toronto with stop-and-go traffic through July rush-hour to the airport, the trans-Atlantic flight and—at long last—their old friend Martin's powder-blue Fiat speeding along on the wrong side of the twisting, hilly roads. Enough was enough.

Once we get to the guesthouse and settle in, Clara silently vowed, *I am staying put.*

"Here we are, folks."

Clara felt the car slow to a crawl and stop. She cautiously opened one eye to see Martin beaming at Scott, who frowned out the window.

"Well?" asked Martin as he swept his hand across the unremarkable view of the building before them. "What do you think?"

"What's that?" asked Scott.

Martin chuckled. "That, my jetlagged friend, is the Hall. Calverley Old Hall."

"*That's* what I've rented?" Scott's voice was edged with disappointment. Clara sat up for a better look at the guesthouse. Even her sleep-deprived eyes saw that the place was no Blenheim Palace: just a sprawling architectural mongrel made up of an awkward mixture of styles spanning several different time periods. The grey stone facade was begrimed with dark patches of Yorkshire soot, and the uneven slate roofs of each of the four or five visible wings sagged with age. Newer village terraced houses snuggled closely on either side of the structure and—except for Gothic casements on a small chapel jutting out at the front corner of the Hall—there was little to distinguish the building from the commonplace.

"So?" prompted Martin.

"Uh… it's not very isolated, is it?" asked Scott.

"It's kind of big for just the two of us," said Clara.

"Oh no," said Martin quickly. "Only one wing is the actual guesthouse. I just thought you might find the front overview interesting. Most of what you see is empty and awaiting renovation. Don't worry—the work's on hold until the rest of the council funding kicks in. You'll have plenty of quiet and privacy. The guest wing is around the back."

He pulled the car around to a narrow side lane between the rows of houses, giving a nod toward a tidy-looking wing nestled down into a sunken lawn. "That's the north wing guesthouse," he said. "Your home for the next two weeks."

The tires crunched on the crushed stone of the rear car park as they came to a final stop, and Clara sighed with relief to be at a standstill at last. Martin unfolded his tall frame from the car and flipped the seat forward to excavate Clara from among the heap of luggage. Scott was already out, and she hung back with Martin as her husband walked ahead with slouched shoulders into the shadows at the back of the Old Hall. He stopped, shoved both hands deeply into his pockets, and stood staring in through a dirty window.

"Here we go…" said Clara under her breath.

"What's wrong?" asked Martin in a whisper.

"Oh, you know him. He's just in one of his moods," Clara said. "Just don't take it to heart if he's grumpy with you. It's been a long journey."

"Right then," said Martin, offering her his arm. "Let's try to cheer him up." "How's it look, Scott?" asked Clara as they joined him.

Together, they peered through the grime into a cavernous room with an uneven dirt floor scattered with rubble. An open cellar yawned blackly from beneath a haphazard covering of a half-dozen rough planks. The vaulted ceiling loomed high above. A stone staircase led up to the top storey: the floorboards had long-since rotted away or been torn out, leaving the upstairs doorframes and fireplace seemingly floating in space. Throughout, the bare stone walls were thickly coated in layers of dust and cobwebs. The one inexplicable item of furniture—a modern gas cooker—sat abandoned in the centre of the room, its white enamel standing out like a single tooth against the gloom.

"Hm," said Clara at last. "Very… atmospheric."

Scott said nothing. His shoulders hunched a bit farther until his neck vanished from sight. Martin glanced sideways at his old university friend's dour expression and laughed.

"Never fear," he said. "This part hasn't been renovated. The guest wing is around the other side. Landmark Trust did a grand job fixing up the place so far, but I'm afraid that the budget ran out before they could get to this Solar wing section. And through that way—" he pointed at another filthy door to the left of the room "—there's a Great Hall with a massive fireplace and a gorgeous vaulted hammer-beam ceiling."

"Ooh… could we take a look?" asked Clara.

Martin shook his head. "It's locked up, and there's no way to access it from the guesthouse." He shrugged. "Not much to see: it's being used by the Calverley village council to store loose paving stones. Apparently some rich Londoners will pay top price for authentic Yorkshire flagstones to pave their garden walkways, and some dealers stoop to unscrupulous methods. Thieves pry flagstones right out of back gardens in the dead of night. Some locals have taken the stones up themselves to store in here and wait out the trend." Martin shrugged. "Personally, I blame those insipid home design TV series."

"You're kidding."

"I wish I were. A friend on the council let me have a peek—flagstones from all over the county stacked up in great heaps halfway to the ceiling. Between the stones and all of the renovation equipment, there's barely enough room to get from one end of the Great Hall to the other."

"That's nuts," said Clara, turning to smile gamely at her husband. "Isn't it, Scott? Good ol' British eccentricity, eh?"

Scott grunted.

Martin hooked his left arm through Scott's and led him around toward the side entrance, towing the quickly fading Clara along on his right.

"I've picked up the keys for you, and Emma came by earlier with a few groceries." He smiled at the couple as he unlocked the kitchen door. "I think you'll find this part of the Old Hall much more pleasant."

They stepped inside the newly renovated wing into another world. English country charm pervaded: blue-and-white Willow pattern crockery sat in tidy rows along the open kitchen shelves, and owls and ivy cheerfully intertwined on the William Morris drapery around the sunny windows. The walls were a warm buttery yellow, hung with nineteenth-century prints, their wooden frames painted a deep red to match the woodwork. There wasn't a speck of dust or a hint of cobweb in sight. Martin's wife, Emma, had placed a bouquet of wildflowers and a bottle of wine in the centre of the neat pine table.

"There, you see?" asked Martin. "Take a look around. I'll go fetch in your baggage."

Left on their own, Clara turned to Scott and tried to catch his eye.

"So? Do I get a smile now, hon?" she asked. "It's really nice. Come on—let's have a look in here."

Clara grabbed him by the sleeve and dragged him through the front foyer into the main room. It was large and L-shaped, with dark red throw rugs scattered on the flagstone floor. In the sitting area, cozy-looking royal blue upholstered armchairs and a soft brown sofa heaped with overstuffed cushions flanked a simple stone fireplace. A beamed oak ceiling and mullioned windows exuded an understated period atmosphere.

"This is perfect, isn't it?" asked Clara as she wandered over to the dining area. "What a great old table!"

She ran her hand down the length of the dark wood table lined with mismatched antique chairs. Shelves displayed old earthenware jugs, pewter chargers and chipped wine glasses with air-twisted stems. A heavy oak sideboard sported the requisite pair of Staffordshire ceramic dogs.

Grinning, Clara pointed to an oil portrait of a jolly rustic gent holding aloft a long clay pipe and an overflowing glass of ale.

"Hey, Scott—get a load of this guy."

Scott grumbled under his breath as he paced around the perimeter of the room. Clara sighed, eyeing the realistic foam on the painted glass of beer with a pang of longing. A drink seemed a great idea about now.

"Okay, sulky-face—what's up?"

Scott kicked at one of the throw rugs. "This place. It's not at all the way I'd pictured it."

Clara flopped down into one of the armchairs. "What were you expecting?"

"Something grand! The brochure Martin sent didn't have photos, but it went on and on about it being *'an authentic manor house once possessed by a noble Yorkshire family.'* Just the name 'Calverley Old Hall' put me in mind of something... stately. I wanted formal knot gardens and commanding views of windswept moors, not some ramshackle dump squashed up next to a 1950s row house with a dead lawn and droopy hollyhocks."

Scott met his wife's amused expression and clammed up, sinking into the chair opposite. Clara smiled, and he finally ventured one back in return. *He can be such a little boy!*

"Well, you have to admit that's clever marketing," she said. "They never actually promised you anything other than it's old. Your romantic imagination did the rest."

"I wanted this to be special. The way Martin was waxing lyrical in his e-mails, you'd think it was Hampton Court. Maybe I could book us something better."

"I don't *want* Hampton Court, Scott. Anything grandiose would be distracting. I just need a quiet place to get my writing done—and this is halfway between your conferences. It's the perfect home base."

He perked up a little. "You do look settled over

there, Mouse."

"I am. Now cheer up before you make Martin cry."

Scott finally laughed.

"How's that?" asked Martin from the doorway.

"Oh, I was just saying how fond you seem of this place," said Clara.

Martin dropped their suitcases by the stairs in the foyer and came in to sit with his friends.

"Isn't it splendid? My cousins lived down the other end of the village when I was a lad. I grew up playing football in the side yard out there. My family even held their annual Thornbury reunion here last Christmas. We were the first ones to use it as a guesthouse since the renovations. Actually, you two may well only be the second booking—but I dare say the word will soon spread. It's such a dear, comfortable old pile."

"How old is it?" asked Clara.

"There's been a Hall on the site since 1300. This is the new wing: 1640, or thereabouts."

"'New'?" Clara laughed.

Scott smiled. "Looks like the Old Hall has another fan," he said.

Martin stood up. "Shall I leave you alone to settle in? You must be knackered."

"No rush," said Scott. "We're fine. We got plenty of sleep on the plane."

"You mean *you* got lots of sleep," said Clara through a tremendous yawn. "I was wide awake the entire flight."

"Don't exaggerate. You slept."

"How would you know? You were dead to the world."

"Every time I looked your eyes were closed."

"Scott, please. You know how I feel about this whole trip. I've been too wound up to sleep properly for a week."

"Jesus. I hadn't noticed."

"No? So what else is new?"

"I really ought to be going," said Martin, edging back across the room to the doorway.

Scott bounced up onto his feet. "Hang on—I'm starving. Those airline breakfasts are pathetic. Anywhere good around here for lunch, Martin?"

"The Thornhill Arms is just down the road. They do the usual pub grub—pie and chips, bangers and mash."

"Sounds good to me. Shall we?"

"Why not? I don't have to be back in Leeds right away."

"Great," said Scott. He turned to Clara, who was nodding off in her chair. "Coming?"

"Not hungry."

"Don't you at least want a pint of real Yorkshire bitter?"

Despite the allure of beer, Clara shook her head. "I just want to sleep." "You? Turning down a drink? You must be tired!" Scott grabbed her arm and tried to haul her onto her feet. "Come on. You should stay awake."

"Scott! Let go—"

"If you go to bed now, you'll throw your system out of whack. Then you'll be even more of a misery than usual."

"Oh, cheers! Why do you need me with you every single minute of the day? Can't you just leave me alone?"

Clara pulled her arm away and flopped back against the cushions. Scott loomed above her with his arms crossed over his chest. She closed her eyes against the sight of him, hoping he'd just go away. Martin cleared his throat.

"Leave her to rest, Scott," he said, trying to sound jovial. "We'll only bore her to sleep anyway, nattering on about Romantic poets and our conference presentations. Right, Clara?"

Another huge yawn was her only reply. Scott stalked out through the kitchen and banged the side door shut. Jolting in her chair, Clara opened her eyes and met Martin's look of concern. She shrugged and gave him a weak smile. "Like I said before—he gets moody. It's no big deal. Just buy him a pint or three, and all will be well with the world again. I'll be fine here on my own."

"Are you sure you're all right?"

"Positive. See you tomorrow at supper, okay?"

Clara closed her eyes again to signal an end to the discussion. She felt Martin hovering for a few unsure seconds before he followed after Scott, leaving her alone at last.

* * *

Clara's head fell to one side and she jerked awake. Wondering where she was at first, she blinked around at the room and wiped off her chin with the back of her hand. Apparently, she'd been drooling from the corner of her mouth after she'd dozed off. How attractive. Time to find a proper bed. Her leg was asleep. She hauled herself to her feet after one-two-three false starts and rubbed at the pins and needles in her calf before she staggered out to the foyer to grab the smaller of her two suitcases.

Pulling herself along by the handrail, Clara plodded up the stone stairs and found the bathroom. She stared at her reflection in the mirror with morbid fascination: dark circles stood out under her grey eyes like bruises against her pale skin, and her nut-brown hair hung in limp strands.

"What are you doing here, Clara?" she mumbled.

This was all about Scott and his work: two academic conferences and some meetings with prospective publishers for his new book on Keats. Clara had willingly come along on his working trips in the past, but she'd had nothing better to do at the time.

However, this summer she had her own work to do: a commission to write a play for the Stratford Shakespearean Festival's next season. It was Clara's big, career-making break... and she hadn't even started.

Best not to think of that just now.

She dismissed the idea of a bath after a long, yearning look at the deep claw-footed tub. If she submerged herself in warm water in the state she was in, she'd probably fall asleep and drown. *It would never do for Scott to come back and discover a floating corpse: that would throw him completely off his game.* Instead, Clara stripped and stood at the sink for a half-hearted scrub of her face, armpits, and crotch. Feeling slightly less grungy, she peered around a couple of doorways into the smaller bedrooms and briefly considered the idea of sleeping in one of the twin beds. Knowing that Scott would only wake her up to move in with him, she found the master bedroom at the far end of the creaky hallway.

It was a large, airy room, plainly furnished in the restrained manner of the rest of the guesthouse with an oversized wardrobe, an oak chest and a pair of heavy old dressers. The decoration scheme was minimal: windows curtained with cream muslin, and the bed sporting an unadorned virginal-white coverlet.

King-sized, she noted. *Good. Lots of room to spread out.*

One whitewashed wall had exposed timbers and an imposing eighteenth-century portrait of a periwigged man with impossibly wide shoulders. His eyes seemed to watch Clara's naked form. She popped his moon-shaped face a salute with her middle finger and turned her back to him, draping her discarded clothes over a faded mustard-yellow wing chair. As she crawled at last into the expansive bed, the smooth cool linen felt like a welcoming caress on her bare skin. Clara's muscles tensed. Naked would be viewed as an invitation, and she was too tired to deal with the demands of Scott's libido. She threw off the covers and slipped back out of bed to dig a long, white cotton nightgown out of her luggage.

It was stuffy in the room, so she opened the window. A strong breeze outside brought in a gust of fresh air. As she lay back and listened to the old house creaking around her like a ship at sea, she hoped that she'd be too tired to suffer from her usual nightmares. Briefly, she floated on waves of half-formed images and slid off into a deep and dreamless sleep.

• • •

It was dark when Scott returned to Calverley Old Hall.

After a late lunch with Martin, he'd hung around the Thornhill Arms long after his friend's departure to soak up the typical country pub atmosphere and down a few more pints. A few elderly locals were scattered about in ones and twos at the dark oak tables or perched on stools at the brass rail of the bar for a quiet afternoon drink. The old men peered curiously at the solitary young stranger in their midst, but none did more than nod at him in greeting. Scott nodded back from his corner table and steadily drank, breathing in the beery tinge in the air left over from past patrons and feeling quietly festive.

Professor Scott Atkinson had high hopes for this trip. The first conference in Oxford was the most important of the year for Romantic Literature, and he was determined to make a splash with his Keats lecture. He had—he was sure—the most exciting new research of any of the other scholars, and some of them were the biggest names in academia. Ever since he'd unearthed them, he'd kept his discoveries a jealously guarded secret. Triumph was in sight: he could not wait to reveal what would earn him his proper place at the top of the ranks. The new, dark horse star academic from tiny Trent University was poised to take Oxford by storm! The second, smaller conference up north in Durham would be worth his putting in an appearance since he was already in the country; and in the meantime, he'd set up meetings with a couple of the better university presses about publishing his revelatory findings. Calverley Old Hall had been chosen—with Martin's dewy-eyed sentimental guidance—as a 'convenient' base approximately midway between the symposiums.

Scott frowned at the thought of the Old Hall. His other, more personal plans surrounding his marriage had depended on the place being grander and more isolated. It would be difficult to play at being lord and lady of the manor in that homely place. He'd wanted to get Clara completely away and escape from the real world so that they could be alone and talk: there was a great deal between them that needed to be said. He'd hoped a fantasy setting would appeal to Clara's imaginative sensibilities and loosen her up, emotionally and sexually. He needed to make her understand that he would always take care of her—that she should turn her energies toward starting their family. Enough time had been wasted on her pointless dreams of a playwriting career. One minor success years ago with a Fringe Festival hit, and she just wouldn't let it go. It was unhealthy and misguided.

Well, he'd just have to make her see he was right; then they could both be happy again. Scott picked up his soggy beer mat and tore it into small pieces, methodically piling up the scraps in the centre of the table.

"G'y-up, Taylor! It's yer round, mate."

The early evening crowd of local businessmen started to crowd along the bar, calling out loudly to their pals and filling the air with friendly, foul-mouthed insults. It was making his head hurt. Time to get on his way.

In a drunken mood to explore, Scott wandered around the village, quickly locating three other pubs. They were all similarly busy with the after-work mob, but Scott thought it only polite after he had made an entrance to have at least a pint or two at each pub before moving on. Being in his cups made him feel peckish all over again. Finding a take-away place, he affected a comically bad Yorkshire accent and ordered fish and chips. The stony-faced girl at the counter did not notice—or else was not amused by—his making fun of her kind and served him without uttering a word. He took a weaving stroll about the twilight village streets as he ate his greasy feast, until he eventually stumbled back across the Old Hall. Calverley was not large enough for even a drunken stranger to lose his way for long.

The Old Hall was dark and silent. Scott groped his way upstairs and took an almost-endless piss before he joined Clara in the master bedroom. Undressing, he tossed his clothes over top of hers on the wing chair and stood at the side of the bed watching her sleep. Despite the huge amount of beer he'd consumed, Scott felt a stir of desire as he pulled down the covers and crawled naked into bed.

"Clara? Are you awake?"

Clara didn't answer. She was on her side, facing away from him, her nightgown tucked up firmly between her legs as she hugged an extra pillow to her chest. Experimentally, Scott stroked her arm and pressed himself into the flesh of her buttocks, but she did not respond. Her breathing remained slow and even. He sighed and rolled over, too tired and drunk to feel any real frustration. Very soon he was snoring. Clara—for once—was too deeply asleep to hear.

* * *

In the early dawn, Scott was awakened by the sounds of weeping and he turned his head sluggishly toward Clara. There was just enough light for him to see her tucked into a tight ball with her arms in a protective circle around her head, her shoulders shaking with the violence of her sobs. Scott felt helpless. Clara looked so very small and childlike in the throes of her nightmares, but his attempts to offer comfort were not welcome of late. He rolled onto his side and placed a tentative hand on her shoulder. Though the air in the room was hot and stuffy, her body felt cool through the thin fabric of her nightgown. She flinched under his touch like an abused dog waiting for the next blow to fall.

"Shush," he murmured. "It's all right, Mouse. Just a dream…"

Scott was dropping off again, his heavy eyelids closing. He felt her shift and unclench her body, turning over to press herself up against him and accept his gesture of solace. He folded her into a sleepy embrace.

As she placed a hand softly on his bare chest over his heart, Scott felt a bolt from her touch shoot into him like a hot blade searing flesh. Exquisite pain flashed along the nerves of his limbs and out through his fingertips in electric shock waves. Scott's eyes snapped wide open.

A strange woman was lying in his arms.

The face was rounder and fuller than Clara's, her frame curvy and voluptuous. Long, dark hair pooled in a loose coil onto the pillow. The wide brown eyes staring unblinkingly into his own as he felt a depthless emotional agony coursing freely from her hand and through his soul like quicksilver.

Scott was invaded by despair down to his core. He slipped into a trance-like state as the foreign suffering threatened to overtake him completely. He could not tear his eyes from hers, her intense gaze at once both loving and condemning him. Guilt twisted in his stomach. A confusion of bloody images flooded unbidden into his mind: his own hand wielding a knife, the bone handle dripping red as it struck frenzied blows into tender human flesh, heedless to the victim's screams for mercy. False, horrible visions overshadowed his own memories… shoving his consciousness roughly aside… crushing him out of existence in order to fully possess him—

"No!"

Scott lurched back across the bed with a thin cry. He flailed blindly at the hands reaching after him, his eyes squeezed shut and leaking hot tears.

"Scott?" Clara's voice asked. "Wake up—are you okay?"

He stopped fighting. Chest heaving, Scott opened his eyes to see his wife half-sitting up beside him with one hand resting on his shoulder. He blinked hard and looked again. It was still just Clara.

"You're only dreaming," she said, using the same mildly annoyed tone employed whenever his snoring woke her up. She patted the bed beside her. "C'mon—it's over now. Go back to sleep."

Clara was already rolling away from him to the far side of the bed.

Scott took a few minutes to catch his breath. His chest felt tight, but the sharp pain was gone. His skin was tingling and he felt giddy and light-headed: no matter how he grappled to try to make sense of it, he could not remember the details of his vision. The images receded as quickly as they had taken form. All he could recall was the feeling of absolute misery and terror emanating from the strange woman—and the relentless fury in his own mind. He ran his hand over his sweaty brow and rubbed his fingertips at the headache starting to throb anew in his temples. He got up to find a tissue and blow his nose. Clara gave him a disapproving grunt. The closed-up room was stifling, and it was hard to breathe the hot, dry air.

Why the hell is the window shut?

Scott opened it wide to let in some fresh air, and went back to bed.

CHAPTER TWO

Clara did not get back to sleep after the nightmare. Scott was flat on his back and snoring in his inhumanly loud fashion. She tried prodding him into rolling over onto his side, but it was pointless. He was too heavy for her to shift, and the smell of beer coming off him with every breath was repulsive. She didn't like to touch him after he'd been drinking.

Sighing, she lay there with a weary smile studying her husband's profile—his gaping mouth, the blond stubble of his unshaven cheeks as they puffed out with each snore, his recently formed double chin. They'd been together for six years, and married for five years in October. Lately, it seemed a lot longer.

After another thunderous snore, Clara gave up on the idea of more sleep. Sunlight was glowing through the muslin curtains and the birds were competing with Scott with their raucous morning chatter. There was no sense in her lying there any longer listening to his racket, so she eased back the covers and slipped slowly from the bed, taking great care not to jog the mattress and disturb Scott. She tiptoed about, gathering up her toiletries and clothing and silently cursing the unavoidable creaks in the ancient floorboards. One spot beside the wardrobe gave a particularly clamorous *honk*, and she froze in place, casting a look back at Scott's hulk for signs of wakefulness. He didn't move. Whatever had shaken him so badly in the night, he now seemed carefree. Clara envied him his ability for finding sleep so easily. Once she was awake, that was it; there was no getting back to oblivion no matter how tired she felt.

An attempt to quietly pull the warped bedroom door shut behind her failed. Clara left it ajar. Forcing it would only create the exact kind of noise she wanted to avoid.

As the bath water ran, she found her box of pantyliners and dug out her secret stash of birth control pills concealed at the bottom of the package. With a little thrill of relief, she popped that morning's dosage before tucking the pills back in under the pads and sitting the box out in full view on the countertop. *Stayfree*. Scott wouldn't be caught dead touching it.

* * *

Soon in the kitchen, Clara warmed the teapot, then poured water from the kettle to let the tea steep. Normally she was a coffee drinker in the mornings, but it was her first full day in England, so… *when in Rome.* She set the coffee maker going for Scott and put in an extra measure of coffee. Judging by the strong alcohol stench wafting from him last night, he'd require a serious jolt of caffeine. Clara could hear him thumping around overhead. It sounded like he'd come through the floor any second. *The man's incapable of walking without driving his heels into the floorboards.* He was on his way down, hung over, to destroy her precious hour of peace. Clara was rarely left alone anymore. Scott had been working from his home office a lot—even holding two of his fourth-year tutorials in their living room! He claimed the casual atmosphere made for better group dynamics. All Clara knew was that it utterly messed with her writing schedule. She needed solitude or nothing got written. And now, instead of getting some precious time back this summer, he'd bullied her into the trip.

Ah well. He'd be leaving for Oxford in the morning and she'd have the Old Hall all to herself for the rest of the week. Once she had a draft of the play under her belt, she could afford to let him know what she really thought.

"'Morning. Your brew's almost ready."

Scott grunted as he made a beeline for the coffee maker. His matted blond hair was standing straight up at the back of his head as he dug around in his bathrobe pocket for his glasses, then gave them a half-hearted polish with the corner of a crumpled tissue while he waited for the machine to finish.

"Still alive?" asked Clara.

"Against all odds, yes."

As he massaged his temples with his fingertips, Clara rummaged a bottle of painkillers out of her purse and set it on the table. Scott poured his coffee, and with a stale, beery yawn, he plunked himself down onto a chair.

"How'd you sleep, Mouse?"

"I sort of napped on and off. I got some rest, until you had that bad dream. I couldn't get settled back down after all the fuss."

Scott regarded her blankly.

"Bad dream? That's weird… I don't remember a thing."

"Oh, yes—you were being highly melodramatic. Tears and everything." Scott gave a weak laugh and shook out three capsules into his palm. "How ridiculous. I never have nightmares. That's your department."

"Must have been all the pints."

"Argh… don't remind me."

"Want toast? There's bread."

"God, no. I can't face food." Draining his mug, he headed over for a refill. "Have you seen a phone around anywhere? I want to call Martin and Emma and double-check what time they're coming for dinner."

"We don't have one," Clara said, pretending to be absorbed in a *Country Life* magazine she'd found in the living room. "There's a laminated list of guest information on the counter. Says the nearest call-box is at the pub."

"Christ. Is there no end to the period charm of this place? I knew I should've brought my cell phone."

"The roving fees are extortionate—remember the crazy bill you got last year, just for checking messages while you were abroad?"

"Yeah, yeah... but for God's sake, there should be a phone. What if there's an emergency?"

"Scott, please try to relax. This'll be no fun for either of us if you don't stop nitpicking."

"Fine. I think I'll go take a long hot shower until I feel human again."

"Hate to tell you, but there's no shower. Just a tub."

"No shower?"

"And you have to flick on that immersion switch on the wall and wait for the hot water. Takes about half an hour."

"Shit. How fucking quaint."

"Hey, you chose this place. We could have easily booked in somewhere modern. It's all the same to me."

Scott topped up his coffee and headed for the stairs.

"Yeah. Well, I'm gonna go lie down while the water heats. And try not to make so much noise, huh, Mouse? You woke me up with all that crashing about this morning."

"What? I thought that was you—"

But Scott was halfway up the stairs and didn't hear.

Guess it must have been the floors settling, she thought. *Old houses are full of strange sounds.*

• • •

Martin and Emma were due at six o'clock.

At four-thirty, Clara began a drawn-out ritual of getting ready. This second bath was unnecessary, but it was a good way to further avoid Scott. She'd disappeared upstairs when he went out to make his phone call, then feigned napping most of the day while he'd sequestered himself in the living room going over his Keats notes. Clara only wanted to get through this evening without having a scene; then she'd finally be rid of him and get some work done.

She poured a healthy dollop of foam bath under the taps and settled in for a long, rose-scented soak. The bottle was courtesy of Martin's wife, Emma. Clara had only met her a handful of times over the years, but they were fast friends. She smiled at the thought of seeing her again. *Such a warm, generous woman.* Besides leaving a week's worth of food and a case of wine in the kitchen, Emma had scattered small treasures throughout the Old Hall for Clara to unearth during her stay: a bottle of ruby port in the living room, wildflower bouquets in every room, a dish of pastel candy-coated almonds by the bedside. In the unlikely case that Scott appreciated the thoughtful gestures, he never said—though he did polish off the almonds over the course of the day.

Clara stuck with the port.

She stayed in the tub until the skin on her feet whitened and puckered like the toes on a drowning victim. Once the water was cool and the last of the bubbles evaporated, she shifted to pull out the plug, sloshing water over the rim. Her fumbling hand toppled her empty port glass from its precarious perch on the edge of the tub. It landed unbroken onto a heap of towels on the floor.

At the mirror, she assembled her pale face with care. On the few other social occasions with Emma, she'd always felt comparatively mousy. Years spent around theatre types had taught her a few tricks: a bit of artful make-up and Clara would be ready for tonight's command performance. Dabs of foundation hid the stubborn dark circles under her eyes. Careful application of lip-liner and lipstick made her thin mouth appear full. As a final touch, blush added the missing roses to her high cheekbones. The real challenge was her hair: it hung to her shoulders in a damp, unlovely clump and she had no blow dryer. After a thorough towel-dry—

and much coaxing and swearing—she tamed it into a bun and pulled a few tendrils loose over her ears, softening her sharp features so she wouldn't look so much like a spinsterish schoolmarm.

Now for the costume—

In the bedroom, Clara donned a long off-white dress of crinkled Indian cotton and noted that it hung more loosely on her frame since last summer. She stood back to evaluate her appearance in the full-length mirror on the wardrobe door. The overall effect was downright Merchant-Ivory. The demure Victorian look would appeal to Scott—she could have stepped from the pages of one of his beloved Romantic poems. It did not please her. Somewhere along the way, she'd lost her own style: her former downtown Toronto Queen Street West edginess—mostly black, with a touch of leather—was gone. Sighing heavily, she considered changing outfits, but there wasn't enough time.

As Clara topped up her port, she heard Scott's feet pounding up the stairs. She tried to pour the port back into the now near-empty bottle and spilled an angry red splotch on the skirt of her dress. Hiding the booze on the floor by her side of the bed, she stepped behind a chair to shield the stain just as Scott pushed the door open.

"Oh. You look nice."

"Thanks."

"I guess I'd better hurry up and get changed." He

started to undo his belt buckle.

"I'll go downstairs and listen for the door," said Clara. She slipped past Scott with her body half-turned away, her left hand casually concealing her guilt. Once in the kitchen, Clara hiked her dress up into the sink and flushed away the port as best she could. She was still sporting an obvious pinkish damp patch fifteen minutes later when she answered the door, but no one made any mention.

"Clara, darling!" Emma swept her into a fragrant embrace. "So good to see you again! Look here—we've come with all the makings of a feast. Be a love, will you? Help Martin and me shift some of this stuff from the boot."

Out by the car, Martin was already heading into the kitchen with a box in his arms, pecking Clara on the cheek in passing. Emma handed Clara a foil-covered platter.

"Hope you don't mind the idea of a stay-in dinner party. Martin thought the best plan would be to stay overnight and leave together for Oxford in the morning. That way no one has to be the designated bore, since we aren't driving tonight."

"Oh no, it's great—Martin mentioned it on the way from the airport. There's plenty of room."

Besides, thought Clara, *if they stay there's no chance of Scott and I getting around to our 'big talk' before he goes.* That was the last thing she wanted to deal with tonight.

All she wanted at the moment was another drink.

Scott met them in the kitchen, looking suitably casual-academic in chinos and a button-down shirt. Smiling, Martin held up a plastic carrier bag and dangled it enticingly from his fingers.

"Brought you a gift, old man," he said. "You're more than welcome to it, if you don't mind all of the undergraduate margin notes and coffee stains. I have my own copy back at the house."

"God damn!" Scott yelped as he pulled a huge volume out of the bag. "Do you have any idea how long I've been trying to get a hold of this edition? It's been out of print for fifteen years. I've been all over the Internet to no avail. Look, Clara—*The Roland's Edition of Keats*!" His eyes glistened like he was Indiana Jones discovering a lost horde of Egyptian gold.

"Honestly! Such children." Emma laughed. "Sweetie, pour us girls a drink and then scoot out there and set the table. Clara can keep me company while I work on supper."

Clara could have wept for gratitude as Martin opened a bottle and poured out two gloriously large glasses of Chardonnay. He and Scott obediently scooted into the other room and left the women alone. Silver bracelets jangling, Emma waved away Clara's offers of help with a smile—*'I've got it all in hand. You just sit and chat with me'*— and set about chopping fragrant bunches of fresh herbs. Clara leaned against the counter to admire Emma's ease at her tasks and tried not to gulp down the longed-for wine too quickly.

Everything about Emma was generous and abundant. Her large brown eyes were framed with naturally luxuriant lashes. Long hair spilled in lush mahogany waves over her shoulders like a Pre-Raphaelite artist's model. Laughter played about her mouth, her full lips curved into a constant smile. Draped in a flowing burgundy dress, she kicked off her shoes and moved about in an undulating barefoot dance as she took over the kitchen. Every gesture she made wafted breaths of spicy perfume. Clara felt drab beside such Gypsy exoticism. She tried to drape herself over the counter in a more languid pose to better mirror her visiting hostess, but felt she didn't possess the necessary curves to pull off the proper effect.

Emma topped up their wine glasses at frequent intervals. The alcohol worked its welcome magic through Clara's bloodstream, giving a warm flush to her cheeks. The edges of the world resumed the pleasant blur of intoxication.

Emma set a roast into the oven. "I've marinated that creature all day. I do hope you like lamb," she said in her rich alto voice. "Silly me—I never thought to ask if you were vegetarian."

"Oh, no. I eat everything."

Flicking her eyes over Clara's gaunt figure, Emma took the foil off a platter and pushed it across the blue tiles of the countertop. "Get stuck into that. Smoked trout terrine. It's divine."

Clara did, her appetite growing with her renewed drunken glow.

"Martin tells me that you're going to have a play at the Stratford Festival next season. How very exciting! Congratulations. You both must be thrilled."

Clara smiled and poured herself some more wine.

"I have an old school chum down at the Royal Court Theatre in London who might be useful to you. I'm sure he'd be glad to take a look at the script."

"It's... not quite ready to be looked at just yet—but yes, please. Thank you, Emma."

"Not at all. Just remember me kindly in your BAFTA acceptance speech."

Their husbands' barks of laughter drifted in from the dining area. Emma flashed an indulgent smile.

"It's lovely for Martin to have Scott over for a visit. He's forever going on about what a brilliant time they had rooming together at Oxford back in the day." She unpacked yet another box and tore lettuce into a wooden bowl. "It's just too bad you didn't feel you could stay with us. We've plenty of room, you know. It wouldn't have put us out in the least. I love playing hostess, as you can see."

Clara set down her glass.

"I didn't know that was an option."

"Oh? I'm sure Scott told Martin that you didn't

want to impose on our hospitality, and that you'd pressed him to rent a guesthouse instead."

"No... actually, *he* was the one who utterly insisted on the Old Hall."

"That's odd. I wonder why he said all that?"

"I have no idea. He's been making a lot of decisions on my behalf lately."

Emma stopped tossing the salad.

"Clara, are you all right?"

"I've been better."

"The move for Scott's job at Trent must have been hard on you. I take it life in Peterborough is a big change from Toronto?"

"It's... quieter than I'm used to, but it's not that bad a place. I don't think I'd mind so much if Scott would—"

"I've left your hubby with his new treasure," said Martin as he strode into the kitchen. "I hope we'll manage to pry him away from the pages long enough to join us for supper." He slid up behind Emma and wrapped his arms around her waist. "Anything I can help with, love?"

"No, you're all right. Everything's under control."

Clara watched as Emma leaned back into her husband's embrace with a slight wriggle of her hips. Martin lowered his face into his wife's hair, giving a little comic growl and nipping at her neck. She laughed and swatted at his nose with a wooden spoon. Clara felt a pang of loss twist inside her guts like a trapped bird. She drained the oaky contents of her glass in one long draught and pushed herself away from the counter.

"Excuse me a moment," she said. "Loo break."

* * *

Locked inside the bathroom upstairs, Clara perched on the edge of the tub and wept, careful to muffle her sobs with a bunched-up towel. When was the last time Scott had touched her like that? More to the point, when was the last time she'd welcomed his touch? Whenever he laid a hand on her now, there was an air of demand about it, or a feeling that he was marking out his territory. It was all she could do not to shrink away.

Too good to be true.

Clara stood at the sink and peered at her miserable face in the mirror. In the beginning, Scott had been a 'real catch,' as they say. Smart and charming, handsome and funny, great in bed with such sensuous hands… On top of all that, he had the added perk of money. (Or rather his father did, which came down to much the same thing.) They wanted for nothing. He'd been her ticket to escape the life of a struggling artist living hand-to-mouth. But the big changes with the tenure-track job offer, the sudden move to a small town and her subsequent isolation had all happened far too quickly. Scott seemed like a different man with his new job: formerly attentive, he was fast becoming a control freak. The growing demands that Clara focus on having children rather than a theatre career seemed out of nowhere, and she felt powerless to stand up for herself. The cracks in their marriage threatened the very foundations.

Clara realized she'd been in the bathroom for an awfully long time. She flushed the toilet and hurriedly repaired her blotchy face as best she could from her scatter of bottles and powder compacts. Frowning at the imperfect results, she was glad that the lighting in the Old Hall was so dim. She hoped they'd be dining by candlelight: with Emma's genius for details, she must have brought along candles.

* * *

As Clara lingered in the foyer at the foot of the stairs for a moment to give the redness in her eyes and nose a chance to fade, she heard whispers coming from the main room. Walking on the balls of her feet, she peeked in at Scott sitting in a chair with his back toward the doorway. He was hunched over his precious *Roland's* and reading under his breath with boyish excitement. She leaned against the wall and watched. His concentration was that of a child intent on his play, aware only of himself and his self-created universe. He looked sweet. Clara liked him best in such moments: it contrasted with his darker side and his too-caustic wit. Her heart lurched with a desire to have things back as they once were—if it wasn't too late. The wine was really starting to hit home. Clara could feel a slight swirl of weightlessness beginning to take hold at the back of her knees. She reached out to steady herself with a firm grip on the brass doorknob.

Now's my chance, she thought. *I should go in there right now and catch him while his guard's down. Ask him what he's trying to do to me. Does he even realize he's been making me miserable? Lord only knows I get myself down enough without his help—*

"Where are you two? It's time to eat." Martin and Emma appeared bearing food platters on their way through to the dining table. Scott didn't even look up.

"Scott," said Clara quietly. "Supper's ready."

He didn't appear to have heard, and Clara had to summon him back to Earth with a light touch on his shoulder.

* * *

"This is just wonderful, Emma," said Clara.

In truth, she was too drunk to really taste anything. She spoke little over the course of the meal, and instead concentrated on the challenge of carving her meat without dropping her knife. Burgundy wine flowed freely at the table to accompany the roast lamb.

"Your glass is nearly empty, Clara," said Martin from behind her chair. "Finish up—this is a different bottle."

Obediently, Clara drained her glass. Martin was an attentive wine steward. No sooner was one bottle emptied than he was at the sideboard uncorking another from the selection of reds he'd lined up awaiting their turn. Allowing someone else to pour her drinks had proven unwise for Clara. She quickly lost all track of how much alcohol she'd consumed and toppled over the edge from comfortably numb to quietly reeling.

"Here now!" slurred Emma, holding up her glass. "Don't let's forget the cook!"

Martin laughed and topped up his wife's drink. Scott waved away the offer of more and poured himself some water from a cut-glass pitcher instead. "Taking it easy, Scott?" asked Martin as he sat back down.

"Yes. I feel like I've been swimming in booze since we landed."

"I should slow down too, so I'm not muddle-headed for the drive in the morning. Gauging by the glow of my lovely wife, she'll be sleeping it off in the backseat of the car tomorrow."

"Oh?" Scott raised his eyebrows and leaned forward. "Are you coming with us to Oxford, Em?"

"I have a vacation week, so I thought I'd tail along for the ride. Maybe head into London for a day and do a bit of shopping."

Scott turned to Clara with a gleam in his eye.

"That sounds like fun, Clara," he said. "You'll just get lonely up here on your own all week. Why don't you come with us and have some girl time? There's plenty of space in the car, isn't there, Martin?"

"Always room for one more." Martin winced, shooting Emma a quizzical look as she kicked his shin under the table.

"Now, now," said Emma. "Stop tempting Clara. She has a great deal of work to be getting on with—haven't you, pet?"

"Yes," said Clara slowly, trying not to garble her speech. Her tongue felt like a small, sleeping animal that she was compelled to hold in her mouth without waking. "I have a strict deadline to meet. I'll be too busy to feel lonely."

"Oh, there's no danger of you being lonely," said Martin, winking at Emma. "Not here at the Old Hall."

Clara felt her heart sink. "Do you mean the neighbours? Oh, I hope not! I don't want to have to be rude to anyone, but I have so much to do—"

Emma laughed. "Oh, the neighbours aren't the problem. They keep themselves to themselves."

"What are you two going on about?" asked Scott.

"The ghosts, old man."

Scott's smile faded. "Ghosts?"

"Of course! Well, you can hardly expect a place as old as this to not have a ghost or two rambling about the corridors."

Clara was having trouble following the conversation. That last glass had sent her far beyond her outside limit, and her ears felt as though they'd been stuffed with cotton. The voices came to her as a collection of haphazard sounds and were barely audible above the deafening rush of blood in her head. Still, the story sounded intriguing.

"Did you... see something when you stayed here for your reunion?" she asked.

"Nothing too ghastly," said Martin. "Just a few items found out of place that no one claimed to have touched. The odd something going bump in the night."

"The sound of footsteps banging around when nobody was upstairs," added Emma.

Scott set his water glass down hard on the table.

"Stop it! You'll give Clara nightmares. She has enough of those as it is." "No, it's okay," said Clara, picking up her wine. "I think it's kinda neat. Who are—rather *were*— they? Does anyone know?"

"I'll tell you who they were," said Scott. "Martin's niece and nephew playing pranks on a bunch of half-drunk adults, that's who."

"I'm a little hazy on the facts," answered Martin. "There was some sort of household tragedy back in the early seventeenth century. Sir Walter Calverley went off his nut and killed most of his family in a rampage."

"Ooh! Tell me more," said Clara. "Maybe I could use it as writing material."

"I can't remember all the details—"

"That's a switch," mumbled Scott with a half-laugh.

"—but I do have a copy of a play somewhere that's based on the event—*A Yorkshire Tragedy*. I'll see if I can dig it out for you when we get back from the conference. It's a real potboiler, as I recall. Shakespeare's own acting company, The King's Men, performed it at the Globe in London, and he may have had a hand in writing it, though it's hardly on a par with *Hamlet*."

"Shakespeare?" asked Clara, perking up. *This could save my neck with the Festival.*

"Indeed! It was a notorious crime in its day. The family had connections by marriage to Sir Robert Cecil. There was a sensationalized account circulated in pamphlet form, and it proved such popular reading that ol' Bill Shakespeare and his players cashed in on it."

"Sort of the Jacobean equivalent to a TV movie-of-the-week about the O.J. Simpson murder trial," suggested Emma.

"Exactly," said Scott. For some reason, the whole idea seemed to make him twitch. "Historical or not, it's nothing more than a trashy scandal. Can't we talk about something else? Besides, Clara has an overactive imagination, and now she'll be dreaming up all sorts of weird things."

"Aw, Scott," said Clara. "This is *interesting!* It's good fodder for the muse—I want to hear more!"

"I can do you one better. Let's raise the ghost of Sir Walter!" Martin leapt up and started looking about the room.

Emma chortled. "What are you on about?"

"We used to do this out on the Old Hall yard on Bonfire Night when we were kids. First, we just need to give ourselves a bit of space." He cleared away a side table and an easy chair to make room in the far end of the dining area and then rummaged around until he found a jar of pins on the writing desk. "Perfect! Now, we just need some hats."

"How scientific," said Scott. He did not look amused.

"Hats and pins? Why?" asked Clara, snickering as she drained her umpteenth glass of wine.

"Dunno, really." Martin shrugged. "That's just the way it's always been done."

The women got up from the table and staggered about in search of headwear. They and Martin were having a blast.

"Hats, eh?" Scott regained his sense of humour as he caught the wave of jollity and finally entered into the oddball spirit of the moment. "I think I saw a rain hat and a couple of caps on the front hall coat rack." He strode out to fetch them. "Here we go. Now what?"

"We form a pyramid on the floor—just so," Martin scattered the hats and pins into a haphazard triangle shape on the carpet. "Next, everyone get in a circle and join hands."

Giggling, they did as instructed.

"Now: repeat after me." Martin cleared his throat and began reciting an intonation in a deep baritone voice.

"*Old Calverley, old Calverley, I have thee by th'ears…*"

Both women erupted into gales of mirth.

"Girls, please!" Scott tried not to laugh. "Get a grip. Raising dead spirits is serious stuff. Go on, Martin."

"Right. Everyone all together this time: *'Old Calverley, old Calverley, I have thee by th'ears—I'll cut thee in collops unless thou appears!'*"

"What the fuck is a collop?"

"Clara!"

"Sorry… "

Between snorts and giggles, they managed somehow to repeat the incantation three times in ragged unison.

"Then what happens?"

"Dunno, really," grinned Martin. "We kids always scarpered before anything could happen."

They stood in silence, still awkwardly holding hands and listening out for… something. Clara caught Scott's eye.

"Boo!" he yelled. Everyone jumped and started to laugh.

"Scott! You're a bloody terror!" shrieked Emma, wiping her eyes. "You need sweetening up. Who's for pudding?"

As if in a dream, Clara helped to clear the table for dessert. She silently coached herself through the familiar steps: *to pick up a plate, one must curl one's fingers under the rim, grip firmly and lift…* Veering dangerously off-balance as she turned toward the kitchen, her bony hip collided with the sharp corner of the sideboard. A quick peek around assured her that if anyone had witnessed her stumble, they'd politely affected not to notice. She was glad she'd kicked off her shoes halfway through the main course. In heels she would have toppled over sideways.

Coffee and pudding was served. Clara couldn't be sure if she'd helped to carry the cups and dessert dishes to the table or not. Whatever the sweet was, she was too far-gone to identify it—something heavily laced with brandy and drowned in double cream that she fruitlessly tried to scrape up with her fork. If she'd been alone, she'd have picked up her plate and lapped up the creamy booze like a cat—but drunk as she was, she knew it would be improper to indulge her feline inclinations in front of company.

"Shall we?"

In a haze, Clara followed after the others to the sitting area, avoiding the heap of pins and hats from the failed spirit-raising. She headed for a wing chair at the far end, but Scott grabbed her hand and pulled her down onto the couch beside him. Martin passed around snifters of Grand Marnier to the others before sitting beside Emma, who languorously sprawled on the two-seater opposite.

"My dear, I'll have to take you upstairs and pour you into bed soon," he said. "We have an early start tomorrow."

Emma gave a theatrical groan of protest and curled up at his side, one hand resting high up on his thigh and stroking in gentle circles. The wine she'd consumed made her movements languid and her alto voice even more relaxing in tone, like a cello. Martin dangled his hand over the curves of her ample breasts. One side of her dress had slipped off her shoulder, and Clara imagined she could hear the purring of some exotic beast.

Inspired, Scott flung his arm across the back of the couch behind Clara. She shrank up against the armrest and went to sip of her orange brandy. Nothing happened. Blinking down, she saw that the glass was already drained. Scott exchanged her empty snifter for his full one.

"I still think you should come along to Oxford," he said. His fingers were digging into the flesh of Clara's upper arm. "You're going to be too jittery here on your own now that Martin's filled your head with silly ghost stories. Who knows? There may be a time lapse required after the ritual in order for Old Calverley to make his appearance… you won't get a word written jumping at every shadow." Everyone was looking at Clara and smiling. She felt herself detach from her body and float high up over the room, watching the action from the beamed ceiling as Scott forced his plans toward fruition with a gleam of impending triumph in his eyes. Her thickened tongue was frozen to the roof of her mouth and she was seized by panic. Clara's eyes rolled toward her friend in a mute appeal for help. Straightening up on the loveseat, Emma pulled her dress back into place and flapped her hand dismissively at Scott.

"She'll be perfectly fine on her own. You're a big girl, aren't you, Clara?"

Clara nodded.

"Well, then: stay behind and get writing. Leave her be, Scott."

Scott glared across the room at Emma with hooded eyes and continued on as though she hadn't spoken.

"You can work in the library during the day and meet up with the rest of us at night." His voice was smooth and reasonable as he captured Clara's hand, crushing her bones in his grip. "Say you'll come. We all want you to. *I* want you to."

"But, Scott," said Martin. "It's such a waste for Clara to come with us and leave the Old Hall empty. You've paid a small fortune to rent it."

"It's only money," said Scott lightly. Clara felt her knuckles grinding together as his hand clenched hers like a vise.

"Your *father's* money!" Clara spat. Scott's hold faltered and she lurched to her feet and out of his reach. "How many times do I have to tell you that I need to be by myself? Why can't you just leave me alone for *five fucking minutes*?" There was a terrible silence as Clara tottered over to stand beside her friends who were now both sitting bolt upright on the edge of the sofa cushions. Scott's reply was icy. "In that case, you should have stayed at home and saved me the airfare." He drained her abandoned glass and banged it down onto the side table.

"I wanted to stay home, remember?" Clara's voice rose in hysteria. "But *you wouldn't let me!*"

Emma reached out to steady her.

"I think we're all getting tired and cranky," she said, giving Clara's aching hand a little pat. "Let's call it a night, shall we? Come on, you two. Kiss and make up."

Scott slipped his arm around Clara's waist with a squeeze. As he brushed her ear with his lips, he gave it a sharp little nip, indicating that in bed tonight there would be no escape.

• • •

Emma and Martin bid them goodnight and went straight into the other guestroom. Scott was having a quick wash before bedtime. Clara could hear him in there, splashing about and loudly humming—heedless of disturbing their friends' rest. *Foreplay*, she thought bitterly, as she sat fully dressed on the edge of the bed and waited. The last time they'd fucked had been over five weeks ago, and neither of them had made any sexual overtures since. After their ugly scene following dinner, she knew there would be no point in rebuffing her husband's advances. He'd be in no mood to be put off.

Scott was coming up the hallway. Clara reached for the port bottle on the floor and took a couple of swigs. The less she felt, the easier it would be.

Silently, he pulled off her dress and laid her out on

the bed. Clara passively allowed her limbs to be manipulated as he removed her underwear. The room lurched on a sharp tilt and she felt the mattress begin to rotate jerkily in quick circles under her back. As she'd done earlier in the sitting room, she disengaged and hovered near the ceiling to watch. Scott was not without sexual skills, but Clara's body had long since closed itself off to his touch, whether or not she was drunk. It had been ages since she'd last felt anything like authentic arousal. *Months? A year or more?* Scott seemed unaware of her indifference. Maybe it simply caused him no concern. He feasted upon her small breasts, kneading the flesh of her inner thighs with abandon as he pushed her hand down onto his erection. She played her role and pulled on him with mechanical strokes. To her, it was no more than a hazy dream. *At least he isn't being too rough this time…*

And anyway, he'll be gone in the morning.

He knelt over her, straddling her chest and pressing himself up against her lips. Clara closed her eyes and floated still farther away. She opened her mouth and drew him in, past all caring. Scott's voice came to her from a distance, instructing her what to do, describing what he was going to do to her: even in bed he had a need for running commentary.

"Oh yeah, that's right… suck it. Just like that. Get it good and hard."

One hand held her head firmly in place as his hips

pumped, dictating the tempo to best serve his own pleasure. Almost as an afterthought, he licked his forefinger and reached behind to flick around her entrance and get her primed. Clara felt nothing. Her jaw was tiring and her mouth was too dry from all the alcohol. She wished he'd get on with the next and final stage, but Scott was in no hurry. He'd always preferred to make a meal of it and take things slow.

"I know what you want."

Just at the point when she didn't think she could stand any more, he pulled away and settled himself between her legs. Urging him on, Clara writhed her hips a bit and squeezed her eyes shut in a false show of abandon. As he rammed in, he stuck his tongue into her ear like he was invading her skull. Clara twisted her head away and avoided his kisses as he began his usual stop-and-start build-up of momentum.

Not too much longer now...

Suddenly, his movements became urgent. Gone was his customary languid rhythm: the strokes pounded into her fast and furious. His habitual litany of pornographic sweet nothings gave way to harsh panting and short, wordless groans of pleasurable effort. Yanking Clara's hips from the bed, he forced a pillow beneath her and tilted her up at an angle to meet him, never breaking his stride. This was different. Her back arched and all of her nerve endings burst into life, the exquisite new sensations breaking down the wall she'd so carefully constructed. He redoubled his already fiery pace. Clara's hands grappled at the headboard to prevent the top of her head from striking. She bit into his shoulder and tasted a foreign, astringent saltiness.

Deeply aroused past the point of no return, Clara's eyes flew open. The face above hers contorted with excited determination, his sweat raining down freely onto her from his brow and chest. Clara shrieked as she was gripped by a sudden and powerful climax. He smiled at her triumphantly, grasping her thrashing hands and pinning her fast by the wrists. He tossed his head back with a shout and gave a few final stuttering plunges before he collapsed heavily on top of her.

Clara's mind whirled with the urgent need to get out from underneath the crush of post-coital deadweight lying across her chest. He seemed to be falling asleep. She tried—and failed—to take a deep breath. Panic set in. Clara pushed at him fruitlessly, slapping at the muscles of his sweat-slicked back.

"Get off of me!" she wheezed in his ear. He gave a sleepy, interrogatory grunt but didn't move. Clara heaved at him with mounting hysteria. Realizing that there would be no rest for him until he shifted, he grudgingly rolled off of her and onto his back.

Clara scrambled across the bed and lurched upright onto her unsteady legs, blinking down at the moonlit figure. He swiped a hand through his dampened waves of dark hair to clear it from his face, and yawned as he flung his arms wide on either side and settled in to sleep. Her eyes swept over his body, taking in the sight of the long, sinuous limbs and the well-furred toned chest glistening with beads of perspiration. The facial features were strongly defined as though they'd been sculpted: high cheekbones, arched and heavy brows, a long, straight nose. His smiling mouth was full and womanly, framed by a neatly trimmed Van Dyke moustache and goatee.

Very handsome.

And Clara had never seen him before in her life.

As her knotted stomach gave a menacing roll, she stumbled out of the bedroom and raced down the endless hallway. Smashing her knee blindly into the doorjamb, she just made it to the toilet and collapsed as the violent nausea hit. Wave after relentless wave racked her thin body. Tears coursed down her cheeks as she struggled to gulp a breath of air between the spasms. The cramps slammed into her like blows from a fist. It felt like she might die.

The overhead light clicked on.

"Mouse?" asked a husky whisper. "Are you all right?"

Hands draped a white terrycloth robe over her quaking shoulders and rubbed her back in gentle circles until the dry heaves subsided. Clara was afraid to look up. When she finally gathered the courage to lift her head, she saw Scott with his fine blond hair hanging limply over his blue eyes. His familiar smooth and nearly hairless body was hunched down beside her on his stocky thighs, his recently formed stomach paunch rounded in a slight bulge over his groin. Peering at her intently, his ruddy, boyish face was full of concern.

"Let's get you cleaned up and go back to bed before we wake Martin and Emma, okay?"

She stared for a moment longer before she nodded, sobbing in oxygen. Gently, Scott helped her rise and led her to the sink, keeping a steadying hand on her back her as she splashed water on her face and rinsed out her sour mouth. He steered her back up the hallway to bed, and sat by her side watching as she sipped delicately from a proffered glass of water.

"I'll always look after you, Mouse," he said, helping her to lie back. "Stop fighting me so much. Just let me take care of you."

Clara was drained and put up no resistance. She lay shivering in the coolness of the sweat-soaked sheets. The heady scent of the stranger rose from the damp linen to flood her nostrils, but she felt too heavy to move and clamped her eyes shut against the possibility of any further visions. The room was still spinning, though more slowly now—and the motion rocked her into a depthless oblivion.

CHAPTER THREE

The shadowy figure in a gown entered stage right and made its usual slow and jerky progress to the edge of the cage. Stiffly, its raised arms held out a shapeless object to the prisoner as an offering… or as a threat.

All motion ceased. The picture jolted and became skewed, dissolving into a blank white screen as the watcher's voice shrieked out—

Clara came to with a muffled cry. Her heart still racing from the effects of alcohol and her nightmare, she almost welcomed the familiar rumble of Scott's loud snoring from the other side of the bed. There was no way she'd get back to sleep. Clara dragged herself from bed and went to the kitchen to brew some lethally strong coffee. As she waited for the java, she popped a couple of painkillers, her head full of mental mud about the events of the night before. Only her recurring nightmare stood out with any clarity. Troubled, she sipped gingerly from a pint glass of tap water as she tried to conjure up details. There were fleeting glimpses of another, more incoherent dream, plus a vague recollection of a bedtime episode involving sex and vomit… but Clara pushed these images away, feeling soiled by the little she could remember.

Coffee's ready, thank God. She poured a huge mug—black, no sugar—and tentatively swallowed a gulp, her stomach complaining noisily at the bitter, acidic intrusion. She gave herself a minute until it seemed like it was going to stay down. No stranger to hangovers, Clara knew this one was bound to be a doozy. It would be a miracle if she felt human before noon. By then, Scott and the others would be long gone.

The thought of deliverance was enough to induce a weak smile. Pouring a second mug of coffee—double cream and two heaped spoons of sugar—she took it upstairs for Scott, stopping by the bathroom to flip on the switch so there would be plenty of hot water. These were not acts of kindness—but prompts to get him out of bed and on his way.

The other guestroom door opened as she passed. "Good morning," Emma whispered, her robe half off her shoulder. She looked almost as rough as Clara felt.

"Hi. There's fresh coffee in the kitchen."

"Thank God!"

"Hey—I hope we didn't keep you two awake last night when we were... in the loo."

"Didn't hear a thing. I was dead to the world as soon as I hit the pillow, and Martin could sleep through Armageddon."

Clara went back to her own room. Setting the mug down on Scott's bedside table, she retreated a safe distance and sat in the wing chair before she spoke. Her voice came out in a monotone and her tongue felt like it was wearing a dirty woollen sock. "You should get up now. It's nearly eight o'clock." She took another baby-sip from her coffee.

Scott grunted and yawned operatically before sitting up. He propped the pillows behind his back and slurped from his mug, licking the side to catch a dribble before it could fall onto his bare chest. He put on his smudgy glasses and peered at Clara with an expression of amused concern.

"So. How are you feeling this morning?"

"How do I look?"

"Like you died a week ago."

"Sounds about right."

"No wonder. You really outdid yourself last night."

He took another noisy gulp. "I don't think I've ever seen you that far gone."

"Yeah, yeah…"

"Not that I minded in the least," he said, his manner growing coy. "You were an absolute tigress when we got to bed. Remember?"

"No, not really."

"Oh, you were a wild thing, all right." Setting his coffee down, he cupped himself through the bedclothes at the fond recollection. "Come on over here and I'll remind you."

Clara's stomach roiled dangerously. "Please, Scott. Not now. I'm practically a corpse."

Following the direction of his leer, she looked down and pulled her gaping robe shut to conceal her breasts. He got out of bed and crossed the room. Shamelessly naked, he loomed over her chair. The musky, sour-milk smell of his warm body made her head reel.

"I'll make you feel better," he said, holding out his hand expectantly. Clara didn't take it. She wrapped both palms tightly around her mug and twisted her face away from his eye-level groin.

"Come on back to bed. We'll replay everything… step by step. I promise you'll remember it all this time."

"Scott, no! I feel terrible. I think I'm still a bit drunk. Besides, Martin and Emma are up. I don't want them overhearing us."

Bending down, he gripped both arms of the chair,

pinning her in place as she shrunk against the tall backrest. His lips twitched into a half-smile.

"Don't look so worried. I'm not going to force you." He crouched down on his haunches. "But, please—say you'll come to Oxford. Last night was the first time in ages when things felt the way they used to, and now I don't want to let you out of my sight. I think the change of scenery is having a good effect on us, Mouse."

Clara took a deep breath and spoke to him in the slow, patient tone one reserves for explaining complex matters to simpletons and small children.

"Scott, I've told you this over and over again. Please listen to me: I have to get this draft finished. I'm almost out of time. I know how you feel about my writing, but I'm not letting that stop me. I'm sorry."

Scott said nothing. His blue eyes lost their former bedroom allure and hardened into points of ice as his casual grip on the chair tightened. Clara swallowed hard, and affected a lighter note in her voice.

"Beside, you'll be too busy with workshops and lectures to miss me—and you've got to schmooze for your book. You don't need me there to do all that. Nothing says you're required to bring along your spouse."

"Emma is going with Martin."

"Good for Emma."

"You used to come to all of my conferences."

"Not every single time—only when I didn't have work to do. Stop pouting. Just go, do your best, and enjoy yourself. You'll be back here before you know it. We can do something fun together over the weekend before you leave for Durham—"

"Don't tell me you're staying behind again! I thought you'd come up North, since you won't go to Oxford. You said you would!"

"I've never promised you anything on this trip, Scott. At the very most, I said that I might be able to—if I get enough work done to justify taking a break."

Expecting concession, they both stared the other down.

"So?" said Scott at last. "What's it going to be?"

"If you leave me alone now—and only if I get my draft finished—then I promise I'll come with you to Durham. Happy?"

He leaned in closer until their noses almost touched.

"Then you'd better get busy—because I won't take kindly to any more of your refusals."

He pushed himself upright with a violence that nearly knocked both Clara and the wing chair over backward. Storming from the room to take a bath, his footsteps sounded like gunshots on the creaky floorboards. She hoped Emma was done in the bathroom: in his state, Scott was likely to barge right in on the poor woman. Clara clamped her hand hard over her mouth to suppress a new wave of rising sickness.

* * *

Clara went back down to sit at the kitchen table and

keep out of Scott's sight. Emma soon joined her, dressed simply in jeans and a black T-shirt with her damp hair pulled back into a single braid. Her face was pale without makeup, and she was unusually quiet as she poured coffee and sat down. That was okay. Clara didn't feel much like talking. Sharing some of her painkiller tablets with Emma, the two of them nursed their coffee and suffered their hangovers together in a comfortable silent tandem. Finally, Clara heard Scott upstairs handing the bathroom over to Martin, and inwardly prayed her friend would be quick. Mercifully, he was. Once Martin was clear, she slipped quietly back up the stone staircase for her turn in the tub. The door at the end of the hallway to the master bedroom was closed. Clara ran a lukewarm bath and climbed in, trying not to shiver. Scott's footsteps banged by and hesitated outside the bathroom as Clara held her breath and kept still. The lock on the door was broken, and she was at a great disadvantage if he decided to come in and have another go at her. After an interminable minute, Scott cleared his throat and thumped down the stairs without so much as a goodbye. Clara remained soaking neck-deep in the cooling suds until she heard the kitchen door close and the Fiat starting up out back. Only after she heard the crunch of tires on the gravel laneway did she allow herself to dissolve into tears.

• • •

The hangover abated into a dull throb at the top of her

skull by mid-morning. Clara could function with this invisible yarmulke of pain, just so long as the queasiness was gone. Her stomach had settled since Martin and Emma drove away with Scott. She was still muddle-headed, but there wasn't a lot of choice. Time to get to work.

First, she had to stake out her work surface. The main room was a disaster area—no way could she think straight until it was tidy. Moving slowly, she cleared up the last of the dishes and wiped the crumbs off the dining table. Every available surface seemed to have an abandoned glass or empty bottle on it. She swept through the sitting area gathering scattered brandy snifters, swearing as she nearly stepped into a pile of pins and hats on the floor. What on Earth… ? Clara thought hard through the hazy memories of the night before and vaguely recalled performing some dumb-ass Beetlejuice ritual to raise a ghost. Kneeling down, she picked up as many pins as she could find from the carpet and dropped them into an empty snifter, then cast an eye around the room to assess her cleaning job. Hardly sparkling, but it would do.

Clara performed her own, more serious creative ritual: setting out her writing gear. She sat down at the dining table and turned to a fresh page in her nearly blank notebook. Uncapping her blue pen, she stared at the naked white paper and chewed at the ballpoint's lid until she felt the plastic give way and crack between her molars.

"Okay, Ravenscroft. Get busy."

Her voice sounded hollow to her own ears. Nothing was coming to her by the old-fashioned freehand method: maybe if she tried composing directly onto the computer she'd have better luck. Clara flipped open the laptop and opened the 'Stratford Play' file. Leaning back in her chair, she read over everything she had so far:

Stratford Work in Progress: Title TBA
ACT ONE- Scene One:

Lights up, dimly revealing a black stage—blank but for a barred cage up-centre. It is six foot square, just tall enough for a man to stand upright. A FIGURE is huddled within on the floor, face obscured, back turned to the audience.

There is a beat of a few seconds. Silence.

A WOMAN enters from stage right. She is dressed in a nondescript gown of the period [?], and bears an object [a covered tray? a cup? a book? what IS it??] The WOMAN halts as though fearful of the caged FIGURE. It seems unaware of her presence.

Gathering courage, the WOMAN approaches the cage, her hands extending the object to the FIGURE as an offering [or a gesture of threat?]

WOMAN:

The cursor winked at Clara mockingly, waiting for the dialogue to appear. Nothing came. Her hands clenched in her lap. There was a cold sweat breaking out on the back of her neck: she touched at the clammy feeling, and her fingers came away damp. Clara had until Friday morning to write a complete draft of a four-act play. Four days.

An act a day was not impossible: not for Clara Ravenscroft, affectionately known among her theatrical circle as 'the Eleventh-Hour Lady.' Never had she let a deadline get the better of her. Part of her creative genius was her ability to use the build-up of last-minute pressure as a springboard to blast out scripts. True, there had been many an all-nighter pulled and not a few close scrapes over the years, but that had always been her style. Ideas for plots and characters bumped around in the back of her mind, like a pot of stew on a slow simmer, until they were ready and then—bam! Clara adored the urgency of this leap of faith. She actually revelled in riding the wave of panic, and delivering a script into a director's perspiring hands just in the nick of time. Like skydiving or bungee jumping, it could all go badly—but most of the time it was thrilling and life-affirming. It was this process that made her plays full of trademark spontaneity and quirky liveliness. The precedent was there: her biggest success, the Fringe hit False Fortunes, had been written in under a week, just in time for the casting call.

This time it was a death-struggle. She should at least have a bare-bones idea by now. And this was for the world-renowned Stratford Shakespeare Festival, not just the Toronto Fringe. The stakes were huge.

All Clara had was the cage, the hunched figure, the woman with the object and nothing else. Nada. Zilch. It was bad enough that the dream images had haunted her sleep every night for months: the mute woman and the faceless prisoner had broken the surface of her subconscious and taken a stranglehold on her creativity during her waking hours. In the past, she'd formed entire plays inspired by dreams, but this one resisted being manipulated into anything useful. Worst of all, it refused either to go away or make room for anything else. The fragmented dumb show replayed itself over and over on a loop. Clara was unable to rein it in—she could find no storyline or character to impose on the shadows in order to force them to life. It was like carrying around twin corpses in her womb.

But today, there was something new and hopeful.

Something Martin was talking about at dinner was sticking in her craw: the history of the Old Hall. Didn't he mention a play? Shakespeare? A deranged lord and master, financial ruin, murder... good stuff... and set in the perfect period for Stratford. Clara rubbed furiously at her achy temples trying to recall details. Nothing was forthcoming. Damn it. The drinking was starting to get in the way, more often than not. Maybe it was time to check out the AA meetings in the basement of the Lutheran church around the corner from their Peterborough house. She smiled wanly at the notion of sharing Styrofoam cups of bad coffee with strangers as they poured out their sad tales every Thursday at 7:00 P.M. Taped to the walls, Crayola portraits of Christ from the kids' Bible study class would bear silent witness, smiling down His beneficence upon their collective lost souls.

My name is Clara, and I am an alcoholic.

(An unhappy wife and a total fuck-up as a playwright.)

Or maybe just get a grip, girlfriend.

If only she had a copy of the Yorkshire play, she could use that as a starting point. Maybe an adaptation—or a modern retelling—would be the best way to go. There wasn't the time to start something this big from scratch so late in the game. She scanned the bookshelves on the off chance the Old Hall's caretakers would stock the dramatization of its sad claim to fame, but she found only well-thumbed magazines and pulp fiction paperbacks.

The tinny Westminster chimes of a mantel clock dinged four times and Clara stared in disbelief. Hours had flown by since Scott and the others left, and her mind was still as blank as the open page of her notebook on the table. She tossed down her mangled pen and shut down the computer. Her head was spinning. Too much caffeine and painkiller on an empty stomach. Maybe if she ate something she'd feel more up to the task ahead.

In the kitchen, she sliced some of Emma's granary loaf and made toast, noticing that Scott had left a volume of poetry behind in the middle of the table. He'd probably taken it from his bag and tossed it there on the way out to lighten the load; he hated being weighed down by too much stuff. Clara scanned the title: A Selection of Keats and His Contemporaries. He wouldn't need it—he knew most of the poems by heart. Most actors would kill to possess a fraction of Scott's gift for memorization. It was almost scary the way he could quote whole passages from books word for word, even if he claimed to have only casually skimmed the work.

The mere fact of the book being left out in plain sight annoyed Clara. It was as though Scott was reminding her that only his career mattered, and that he was not too far away: that he'd be back to invade her solitude before she could get herself on course. For someone who admired poetry and the English classics so much, he showed an ironic disdain toward her as a living playwright. Maybe he was right. Who was she kidding? Today was turning into another washout.

Clara could not get it up. Again. She was losing it.

And then there was Scott. The occasional dark moodiness that once seemed so compelling to her theatrical sensibilities was taking him over. He frightened her: not only was he clingy and manipulative, as of this morning he could be downright threatening. This was not what Clara signed on for when she married him. Maybe they were lost now too—and she lacked the energy to do shit-all about it.

On a sudden feeding frenzy autopilot, Clara headed to the fridge and pulled out the leftovers from last night's feast. She hovered before the open door for a moment, eyeing a chilled bottle of sauvignon blanc: she had no desire to repeat the out-of-control state of the previous night, but a cozy tipsiness might help to blunt the edges of today's disappointments…

AA be damned. I need this.

Her tender stomach gratefully accepted a toasted roast lamb sandwich. Lightly giddy after a couple of glasses of wine, she grabbed an apple and headed back out to the main room, bypassing her abandoned workstation and selecting a dog-eared Ruth Rendell paperback from the meagre selection on the bookshelf. Before she was through the first page, she realized she'd read the mystery before—but she granted herself permission to enjoy this one, final lazy evening to herself. The way Scott was acting, there was a great deal more to face up to than just getting the play drafted. Clara needed to let it all sink in and simmer away at the back of her mind. Even if she didn't sleep again all week, she promised herself that the remainder of her time alone in the Old Hall would be productive. It has to be—or else Scott wins.

Flopped on the couch, she read throughout the rest of the afternoon and evening, listening to the sounds of sporadic heavy downpours outside and the odd creak and bump from the house, sipping her way slowly through the rest of the bottle. Martin had left heaps more wine in the pantry. Without thinking, she opened a bottle of red and drained it as she ate the rest of the cold lamb and roast potatoes with her fingers, leaving greasy, garlicky fingerprints on the pages of the paperback.

It was ten o'clock when Clara finished the novel and set it aside. She decided to call it a night, get a good rest and get an early start in the morning. If she stayed up any longer, she'd be tempted to open a third bottle, and she could ill afford another groggy-headed lost day.

Feeling only the slightest buzz of drunkenness, she shut off the bedside lamp. There were no bed-spins this time as she settled in and went to sleep.

* * *

The dream—again.

As the mist parts revealing the caged shadow for the hundredth time, Clara's subconscious squirms and wills the vision to hurry up and play itself out.

The Woman enters.

Clara's attention is electrified: for the first time, she sees everything with perfect clarity. The grey fog shrouding the Dream Woman's form and movements into an unfocused blur has lifted, and the detail is exquisite. Encased in a stiffly corseted bodice, her breast heaves in apprehension. The ornate sleeves of her gown taper closely and end in a delicate, scalloped lace edging at her wrists. The voluminous skirts fall to the floor in waves and obscure her feet from view. The dress is of a lush, deep indigo damask shot through with silvery threads shimmering in the torchlight. Clara hears the whish of silk as the Woman urgently approaches the Cage.

The chamber itself is wholly visible: barren of furniture, there is little to see but iron torch sconces set into the damp stone walls. Clara can smell smoke in the dank air and—as the anxious Woman pauses—the scent of lavender wafts from a silver filigreed pomander suspended from her waist on a light blue ribbon. Framing her lovely face is a fan-shaped lace ruff collar, and her thick dark hair spills from beneath a pearl-edged hood. The object she holds in her pale hands is a small, red leather-bound volume: a book of prayers. Nervously, she touches a garnet cross on a silver chain at her throat.

The Woman's attention is focused on the cage in the centre of the chamber. Clara strains to see, but the Figure behind bars is still nothing more than a hunched dark shape, and seems oblivious to the Woman's presence. Stricken, she turns away from the sight of the prisoner and reveals her features to Clara the Watcher. Her large eyes are dark and wide-set, her face full and round, awash with unchecked tears. Full rosy lips, parted in grief, contrast against her translucently pale skin. A quiet sob echoes from the walls as the Woman looks up… and gazes directly at Clara. As she always does, she raises a hand—not toward the caged Figure as in the usual course of the dream, but to Clara the Watcher in a silent plea. Clara feels rather than hears a soft, strangely accented voice appealing to her from deep inside the back of her skull:

"Hear me. Bear witness to our story."

Clara's own loud gasp woke her up. The Jacobean woman's words replayed over and over in her mind like a bar of music, and she lay dazed for a few moments until she came fully awake. It was too hot in the room. She squinted at the window, puzzled to see that it was shut. She was sure she'd opened it before going to bed—maybe she'd have to keep it propped open with a book. As Clara struggled to unravel her legs from the twist of sweaty bedclothes, her nostrils twitched at the acrid masculine scent left over from the night before and she froze. In her mind's eye, she caught a sudden fleeting glimpse of a stranger's body pressing down and pinning her to the bed. Clara sat up and grappled to bring the image into sharper focus—but it flickered and receded beyond the edge of her memory. The smell of the sheets was making her queasy. Shuddering, she tried to recall where she had seen the clean linen supply and reached for the bedside lamp. The bulb expired with a cracking pop! and Clara emitted a thin shriek of surprise.

Her cry was echoed by a young child's voice.

"Mother!"

There was a hollow, frightened quality in its tone. Had a neighbour's child wandered outside in the night and found itself locked out from home? She got to her knees on the bed and peered out the low side window at the darkened side yard. All was still: nothing out there but moonlight and shadows.

"Mama! Mother!"

The voice came from downstairs.

Clara's entire body was racked by a violent jolt of fear, the mattress trembling along with her. Needles pricked along her every nerve ending.

Clutching a pillow tightly to her chest, Clara huddled in the dark and strained to listen, praying for silence.

"Help me… I am hurt, Mama—I am killed!"

The cry was one of pure agony. There was no ignoring it. Galvanized into action, Clara bolted from bed and tore across the room. Her knees gave out and she grasped at the doorframe to steady herself. Cocking her head, she tried to hear over the loud rasps of her own panting and pinpoint exactly where the child's voice was coming from.

It can't be in the Hall... can it? Oh, please let it be outside...

But no—there it was again. No more words this time: only a miserable, choked sobbing resonating off the floor down below. Clara steeled herself and groped her way along the dark hallway until her hand found the railing at the top of the stairs. A low moan emanated out of the pitch-blackness from the direction of the living room. There was no choice but to go down to investigate.

Blindly, Clara took a tentative first step. Her bare foot slipped in something wet and she staggered off balance, her hand shooting out to grab for the banister. Her fingers closed on empty air. Toppling onto her back, she careened down the entire length of the stone staircase.

Abruptly, the eerie moaning stopped.

Clara lay momentarily stunned in the front entrance foyer, afraid to move in case she'd damaged her tailbone in the fall. With luck she'd instinctively tucked her head forward into her chest or she could have split open her skull. She eased herself into a sitting position and ran her hands experimentally over her limbs. Nothing seemed broken, but her hands came away sticky and damp.

Clara couldn't see a goddamned thing. Crawling in the direction of a little mahogany table she remembered by the door to the kitchen, she felt around for the small lamp she knew to be there. Her hands shook so violently that she nearly knocked it to the flagstones before she snapped on the light.

Clara's nightgown was soaked in blood.

Her panicky self-examination discovered no open wounds—only the preliminary bumps and swellings from her tumble. Confused, she glanced back.

A long, dark streak of wet blood ran down the centre of the stone staircase. Clara's gorge rose in the back of her throat as her eyes followed the trail into the foyer. The smear continued on from the foot of the stairs, leading through to the main sitting room. Whoever was bleeding, they'd either crept or been dragged in there.

Clara hauled herself to her feet, staining the pristine butter-coloured walls with gory handprints. The close air in the Old Hall was suddenly frigid, and her bloody nightgown adhered to her body, chilling her to the core. She was so convulsed by shivering that she could barely walk. Taking slow, stiff baby-steps she made her way around the corner into the main room and swiped her hand over the wall until she found the light-switch.

A shocking amount of fresh blood formed a widening pool on the floor. It gushed freely as if from a gaping wound, but there was no body anywhere to be seen.

Clara froze in place. Around her—echoing both from inside her head and all over the room—the unseen child's screams redoubled. She could not block out the horror: even with her eyes squeezed shut, all she could see was the spewing blood.

Then as suddenly as they'd begun, the cries choked off. The child—she knew—had died. She'd felt it. The death released Clara from her enforced stillness, and she whirled around and flew toward the front door. Blinded by tears and terror, she pulled and twisted the doorknob, but her hands were too slick with the dead child's blood to get a solid grip. Flailing at the heavy door with her fists, Clara at last caught enough breath to scream for help, almost tearing her throat with the effort. No one seemed to hear in the nearby houses. At least if they did, no help was forthcoming. Martin's words echoed in her head:

'The neighbours keep themselves to themselves around here.'

Clara's strength was drained. Her unheeded cries gave way to hitching sobs as she sank to her knees, one hand still weakly grappling with the unyielding doorknob. She cast a wary eye back toward the horrors of the main room.

The blood was gone.

Clara blacked out.

CHAPTER FOUR

A new visitation—

Clara walks across the grounds toward Calverley Old Hall. Opening the door, she steps into the coolness of the front foyer as the door clicks shut behind her. She blinks to adjust her vision to the dim light. Two small figures slowly approach from the gloom at the base of the stairs.

Children.

The older child must be one she'd heard—and felt— die. He gazes up at her, his face pale, his dark eyes mutely pleading. At his side is a smaller child wearing an identical white sleeping gown. The children stand before her, holding hands and watching her expectantly. She cannot move.

The boys drift forward as one, and each boy reaches out his free hand to clutch at Clara. She wants to back away, but pity for them holds her in place. Clara glances down and watches their fingers sink into the indigo silk of her gown's voluminous skirts.

"Mama—"

A loud thud on the floorboards upstairs cause all three of them to jump. The boys' sad eyes stare up at the ceiling.

"It's Papa—" The familiar voice of the eldest child echoes in the back of her skull, just as the Woman's had in the clarity of her last dream. The children's fingers tighten on the folds of her dress.

"Stay with us. Bear witness."

Heavy footsteps pound toward the top of the stairs. A voice booms out:

"Are you there with thy bastards, whore?"

Clara yanks her skirts free of the boys' grasp and dives for the door. The abandoned children follow, their mouths open in silent wails. She feels sorry for them, but she does not wish to stay and face the man they call Papa. Wildly, she tugs at the door-handle, feeling the cold little hands reach for her, as the heavy boots stomp down the stone steps. The door holds fast. The children begin to scream. The man's voice is right behind her, shouting:

"Whore! Whore! Whore—"

"Wrroof! Woof-woof—"

A dog barking outside summoned Clara back. The

bright midmorning sunlight beamed through the windows into her eyes, and she groaned as she found herself still crumpled in a heap on the bare flagstones of the front foyer. Her head was like a block of granite and there was no part of her body that did not ache. After a couple of shaky attempts, she managed to raise herself into a sitting position. Getting the rest of the way to her feet proved a greater challenge: she braced her back against the door for support and slowly slid herself up by pushing with her throbbing leg muscles. The strains and bumps from the spill down the stairs shot bolts of pain through her with every movement.

Blearily, Clara looked around. No sign of any recent death struggle. Not a trace of blood—wet or dry—was to be seen: not on the stairs, the floors, the doorknob or her nightgown. The walls and door were bare of handprints. She hobbled into the living room and found it calm and orderly. The empty wine glass and her paperback were on the table by the sofa, just as she'd left them before going up to bed. The only difference Clara could discern was a barely perceptible coppery scent in the air and a faint metallic taste at the back of her throat.

Clara coughed and found her voice.

"Hello…?" she croaked through cracked lips, hoping to God that no one would answer.

No one did.

She staggered out to the kitchen and gulped two

glasses of water. Spotting the bottle of painkillers, she grappled with the childproof lid and spilled half a dozen tablets onto the table; scooping up four, she tossed them down the hatch. Clara kept a sharp eye out for phantom blood puddles as she hauled herself upstairs to the bathroom, turned on the hot water switch and waited in a daze. She soaked her sore muscles in the tub for half an hour, her ears straining all the while for any unusual sounds. Giving a bitter little laugh, she half-remembered the drunken dinner conversation—something about unexplained footsteps and misplaced objects—and the silly children's ritual they'd performed to raise the ghosts. Scott had been sure that hearing spooky tales would wreak havoc on her overactive imagination.

"Guess you were right, eh, hon?"

Her voice sounded small and strange to her ears as it rebounded off the tiles. The bath water grew cold, and she was shivering. Time to get out.

Clara limped to the bedroom and stood naked before the full-length mirror. Face-on, she appeared unhurt. She twisted around to inspect the rear view. Angry purplish-black bruises were coming up all over her back and buttocks, and a few nasty red welts stood out in bas-relief against her white skin.

"Now what do I do?" she asked her reflection.

What else? Leave. Get a safe distance from Calverley Old Hall.

Wincing, she dressed in her loosest jeans and a long-sleeved blue cotton shirt. The outfit might prove too hot for a warm summer's day, but Clara wished to conceal her marks from the view of strangers. If anyone noticed the full damage, she'd become the target of kindly meant questions—and she couldn't give answers that wouldn't make her sound off her nut.

"It was just a nightmare," she said to the mirror. "You were sleepwalking and you fell down the stairs. That's all. And Scott's right: you do drink too much. It's making you paranoid."

However reasonable this explanation sounded in the cold light of day—and as much as she needed to work—Clara had no desire to hang around and test the rationality of her theory after nightfall. The Old Hall had been peaceful all morning, but the thought of spending another night there on her own made her tender stomach heave.

Pain darted up her limbs as she stuffed enough into her backpack to see her through a few days. She scanned the local transit schedule Martin had left behind. According to the alarm clock on the dresser, she had fifteen minutes to get to the stop by the church and catch the next bus into Leeds. Good. She'd be out the door and well on her way into the city before that annoying little Westminster clock in the living room chimed noon.

Downstairs, Clara shoved her laptop, notebook and

a couple of pens into her backpack alongside her T-shirts and underwear. She'd have to find a quiet guesthouse if she had any hope of getting her work done by Friday. Given her present state of mind she might not get *anything* done—but she pushed that poisonous idea firmly to the back of her head and flipped through the British bed-and-breakfast guide her mother-in-law had presented as a bon voyage gift: *A Room with a Loo.* Scott's mom sure loved a good bad pun. Clara startled herself by laughing out loud. She half-wished the old twit were there to scold her about her drinking and ask pressing questions about her prospects for future grandchildren. Even that would beat being stuck in the Old Hall all alone.

After a quick glance through Yorkshire destinations, Clara opted to head up to York rather than hang around Leeds. Maybe she'd even luck out and find a copy of the Calverley play in a local library or a used bookstore: surely such a popular tourist city would have books of Yorkshire historic interest. She skimmed the long list of guesthouses with her finger and a twinge of renewed hope. With so many hotels and B&Bs, there'd be no trouble finding a room even at the height of the summer tourist season. It was a much more picturesque retreat than Leeds, and only half an hour away by train. Clara had fond memories of a family vacation there in her teenaged years. Tears welled up at the thought of her parents, and she suddenly felt terribly lonely. A rush of consolation came with the idea that she could call her mother from the hotel. The once-welcome isolation of having no phone at the Old Hall suddenly seemed very dangerous.

A final check through her wallet for bus fare and traveller's cheques turned up the Gold Visa card her mother had slipped to her last Christmas. Scott didn't know she had it: Mom had taken her aside and given it to her without either Scott or her father seeing. Clara had tried to give it back, but her mother waved her away with a wise look in her eyes.

"To use for emergencies. You know—in case you should ever have to fly home to us in a hurry. For whatever reason."

Clara kept it tucked it away out of sight behind some old business cards ever since. She didn't see her parents in person all that often, but no one knew her like her mom. Both of her folks were good to her: always had been. They'd supported her creative drive for theatre ever since she started doing plays with her friends in public school. They never once judged her life choices—just raised her to follow her heart. Clara wished she'd followed that parental guidance more closely. If she'd paid more attention to her inner voice's sending up early warning signs about Scott two or three years ago, maybe now she wouldn't be stuck in such a shit heap of problems. Mom always had her head on straight. This card *'for emergencies'* was her way of giving

Clara a means for a practical escape. This, she thought, definitely counted as an emergency.

Clara had every intention of being back at the Old Hall on Friday when Scott returned. The one thing she could be sure about in all of this insanity was that she'd never mention what did—or didn't—happen the night before to her husband. It would be tantamount to suicide if she admitted to seeing ghosties and ghoulies and long-legged beasties. *Did people still get committed to asylums?*

In case Scott got back before she did, she scribbled an undated explanation:

Hi—

On a quick research break—gone to York. Back by 7:00.

—C.

Clara sat the note on top of his poetry book on the kitchen table. Heaving her weighty backpack gingerly onto one shoulder, she went to take a farewell glance around the main room. Everything looked so perfectly ordinary by daylight. Her 'experiences' of the previous night were fading in her memory and seemed more and more likely to have been mere nightmares. Clara sighed, and rethought the idea of running away.

"This is stupid."

But even if it were only her nerves playing up, it

would still be a good idea to get out, even if she just went for one night. She wouldn't get much writing done if she kept on expecting to see spectres.

Clara turned to the front door.

The deadbolt would not work. She twisted and yanked at it to no avail.

"Oh, for God's sake—*come on!*"

It was stuck. Infuriated by the apparently indecipherable British lock, she stomped through toward the side door in the kitchen. Here, she found the exit secured by a much simpler-looking slide lock that yielded to her first attempt. Clara gave a little *huff* of relief and tried the knob.

It wouldn't budge.

Yelping with pain and frustration, she tugged, she pushed, and she kicked—finally slamming her bruised hip against the door to try to jar it open.

Nothing worked. And there were no other doors to the outside world.

Panic set in. Clara ran from window to window, wrenching at the latches. They all appeared functional, and there was no sign that any of the windows had been painted shut, but all held fast and would not be forced open. In desperation she grabbed a heavy log from the stack by the fireplace and heaved it at one of the windows in the main room. She turned her face aside—eyes squeezed shut against the anticipated shards of flying glass. As the log bounced back, Clara cried out as she was sideswiped and nearly knocked off her feet by the ricocheting chunk of wood. She blinked down at the thing, then back up at the undamaged window. *It must have hit the stone casement.* She tried again, this time with her eyes open and taking extra-careful aim. The log hit the glass squarely in the centre hard enough to splinter the wood. Again it sprung back, as though the pane was made of rubber, and landed harmlessly at Clara's feet.

Clara stood exhausted with her strained arms hanging limply at her sides while she reviewed the impossible facts of her situation. The Old Hall would not let her out. There was no phone. Scott was not due back until Friday afternoon. The only other people she knew in the entire country—and who even knew exactly where she was—were Martin and Emma; and they were hours away, unreachable in Oxford. No one else would have any reason to stop in and check on the place.

Outside, the dog started barking again. It sounded closer than it had when it woke Clara up earlier that morning. Wiping away tears with her sleeve, Clara stepped up to the unrelenting window and pressed her face against the glass to peer outside. There was a Border collie frolicking around on the Old Hall's sunken lawn. It saw Clara and stopped, wagging its white-plumed tail as it barked a greeting. She heard a human voice and looked to see a boy about ten years old leaning over the stone wall running along the length of the property.

"Merlin!" he called. "Bad dog! C'mere!"

Merlin cast a baleful look over his shoulder at his young master before turning his attention back to the figure of Clara in the window. He began to bark furiously at her with his tail madly wagging high over his back.

"Good boy!" yelled Clara through the glass. "Stay! Make him come get you!"

If he came after the dog, he might come close enough for Clara to flag the kid's attention and send him for help. Her heart gave a joyful leap as the boy walked to the wooden gate and let himself into the sloping yard.

"C'mon, Merlin!"

He whistled and slapped his thigh, but the dog was fixated and ignored the command. The boy stared straight at the window where the dog's gaze was focused—but he didn't seem to notice Clara's wild gesticulations. Merlin whined loudly and continued to hold his ground on stiffened legs.

"Hey, kid! Help me! I'm locked in!"

Clara's shout sent Merlin into a renewed frenzy of barking.

"What's wrong with yer?" The boy whacked the dog on the hindquarters and pointed at the Old Hall. "There's nowt there, ye daft beast!"

He grabbed Merlin's collar and snapped his leash

back on, then wrestled the struggling animal back up toward the road.

"No! Wait! I need help!"

Clara pounded her fist on the window glass so sharply she felt sure she'd shatter it—until she remembered how the heavy log had failed to make any impact. The boy glanced back at the Old Hall as he turned to shut the gate. Clara leapt up and down, shrieking and waving both arms over her head. He seemed unable to either see or hear her, even though he had a clear view of the window from the road, and Clara was making enough racket to wake the dead in every churchyard from here to London. Yelping, Merlin strained at his leash, but the boy was stronger and soon they were both out of sight around the corner of the house next door. Clara gave up and stood nursing her bruised hand.

"Well, shit. That was hardly an episode of *Lassie*."

Behind her, the little clock cheerfully chimed noon. Clara was drained by her exertions and flopped down on the couch with her aching legs propped up on the coffee table. All appeared perfectly normal and cozy in the sunny room—except for the little fact that the Old Hall was keeping her captive. The anticipation of sunset and a new assortment of terrors gripped Clara by the guts. The rustic gent in the oil painting over the dining table held out his glass of beer toward her like a mocking toast, and she glared at his stupidly happy face.

"Yeah. Cheers, asshole."

Actually, that wasn't such a bad idea. Whatever fresh hell she might be confronted by later on, she had no desire to face it while sober. Clara heaved herself onto her feet and headed for the store of wine in the pantry to make a start on a long day's hard drinking. With any luck, she'd pass out before nightfall and be too far gone to dream.

* * *

Oxford.

Day two of the International Romantics Conference and by late afternoon, Scott was restless and wandering lonely as a cloud. The July day was dry and hot, and the streets and college quads were packed with tourists and conference-goers. Seemingly all were collected into happy couples or groups of cheerful young families in a conspiracy to remind Scott of his enforced solitude. Never had he seen so many couples at an academic conference. As Clara had pointed out, there was no rule dictating that one had to bring along their spouse. Much of the time no one did. Oxford was proving itself different: except for the ancient professors emeriti and a few stereotypical old maids, the Romantics seemed to have attracted a lot of lovers. Scott was miserable.

Weary with the effort of avoiding being run down by bicycles in the narrow lanes, and finding no peace by the Isis clogged with boats of shrieking punters, Scott ducked into Blackwell's bookshop. A few scholars milled about the aisles. Soothing Bach for solo violin played discreetly over the speakers. It was blissfully tranquil and cool in the shop—a perfect place to kill some time until Professor Wootton's much-anticipated Blake lecture.

Scott's head was giving him trouble again. Nothing seemed to take the edge off the stress headaches he'd been suffering since arriving in England. He massaged his temples to no avail. Perhaps he'd better go find a chemist's shop before hearing Wootton's paper, but he could always spare a few more minutes for the love of a good bookshop. Despite the explosion of e-books into the publishing world, Scott adored the solid heft of actual books with their beautiful covers and rustling pages. He squatted down on his haunches, head cocked to one side as he scanned the spines of the books. He wasn't looking for anything in particular—just taking in the titles as a kind of meditation.

A voice with a New York accent broke in on his reverie.

"Hello? Is that Professor Atkinson I see before me? Or below me, I should say. Ha!"

Scott glanced over to his left at a pair of knobby bare knees. He peered up past the touristy plaid walking shorts and the pale yellow polo shirt and recognized the smiling face of…

Oh hell—what's this guy's name again?

"Arthur Menzies," said the grinning man. "Princeton. We met at the 'Blake and His Followers' conference in New York City two years ago."

Scott stood and held out his hand. "Of course. Art. How are you?"

"Oh, still a bit jetlagged. Just got in yesterday morning. Janet is staying at home with our new son, so I'm here on my lonesome. He's too young to leave behind with my parents, and we didn't think that flying overseas with a four-month-old baby would be much fun."

"No, probably not. I haven't tried it myself."

"No kids yet?"

Scott shook his head and winced. The headache was really starting to pound.

"Well, I for one heartily recommend parenthood," said Art with his seemingly permanent grin. "I haven't had much sleep in months with all the night feedings and crying, but Benjamin is worth it. Janet is thrilled." He gave a sudden, startling snort of laughter. "I thought maybe I'd catch up on my rest here, but I missed them both too much last night to sleep! Funny, isn't it? It's hard to be away from the little fella, even just for a week. No wonder Janet couldn't bear to leave him. Of course, I have the male advantage of not being obliged to breastfeed."

He guffawed, spraying Scott with tiny droplets of saliva. Scott favoured Art with a thin-lipped smile and continued scanning book covers with intensified feigned interest.

"So, where's your lovely wife? Clara, isn't it?"

"Not here." Scott randomly picked out a volume of essays on the *Cantos of Ezra Pound* and made a show of closely scrutinizing the table of contents. He hated modern poetry.

"Too bad she couldn't make it. She's a lot of fun. Remember that dinner reception in New York? God! I had tears in my eyes, she had me laughing so hard—"

"Yes. Clara can be a real hoot." Scott squinted at his watch. "Oops... look at the time. I hate to abandon you so soon, Art, but I need to head out."

"Are you going to hear Matt Wootton's paper now? I'll join you."

Will I never be free of this jerk?

"No, I'm afraid I'll have to miss it. I've, uh... made an appointment to meet up with a colleague about a possible publication deal. It was the only time he could spare to see me."

"Too bad." Art clapped him on the shoulder. "Say, let's get together for a drink later on. I'll let you know what you missed, and we can catch up. We lonely husbands need to stick together, don't we?"

Scott disliked the unintentional homoerotic undertone. He needed to throw Art off his scent.

"Sure. How about the King's Arms? It's just up the way on Holywell Street. Seven o'clock."

After a quick and clammy handshake, Scott bolted for the door, leaving Art holding the Ezra Pound book. He hurried out onto Broad Street and screeched to a halt as he spotted Emma and Martin across the road. He'd been avoiding them since they arrived: Emma had asked too many prying questions from the backseat on the drive down.

"I couldn't help but notice that Clara seemed in base spirits, Scott," she'd said. "Is everything okay?"

"She's stressed out over her latest writing project—that's all," he'd said, burying his nose in a book and hoping she'd have the good grace to drop it.

"Well, if it is something more that that, Martin and I are here if you want to talk—"

"Thanks, Em."

"Sometimes it helps if—"

"Thank you, Em. Go back to sleep, Em."

The self-absorbed couple hadn't noticed him lurking in the shadows by the bookshop door. They were too busy taking photos and laughing at each other as they posed, imitating the goofily stern expressions of the carved Romanesque heads lining the walls outside the Sheldonian Library. Married two years longer than Clara and Scott, they still behaved like giddy teenagers in love. As he watched, Emma tenderly angled Martin's head down, giving him a lingering kiss. It was like a slap on the face to Scott.

(See? We're perfectly happy. What's wrong with you?)

"Thanks," came a familiar, loud American voice from just inside the bookshop. "Have a nice day."

Scott ducked down the side alleyway, flattened himself

against the wall and prayed for invisibility. Art strolled out with his new copy of Ezra Pound's *Cantos* and headed in the direction of the lecture venue at Trinity College. Emma and Martin were walking hand in hand the opposite way toward the hotel. It looked like Martin had a far more pleasant reason to miss Wootton's Blake paper than Scott had. He couldn't face it now.

I can't take this. Clara should be here supporting me when I give my paper... it's my right to have her by my side. It's her duty... I want Clara.

Scott's headache raged, but there was no time to lose in looking for a chemist's shop. If he didn't get out of town that instant, he felt sure he'd explode. He darted from his hiding place and wove through the tourists toward the train station, impatiently pushing through the slow-moving clumps of sightseers on the sidewalks. The trains would be packed at this time of day, and God only knew how long it would take to get where he had to be if he threw himself at the mercy of the British rail service.

Scott had a better idea. He raced up a side street, almost blinded by his headache. If he remembered correctly, he'd seen a sign for a car rental place not far from the station.

* * *

Mid-evening.

The shadows grew longer and deeper in Calverley Old Hall. Clara was drunk and jumpy, imagining swirls of movement and bloodstains in every corner. She holed up in the master bedroom with all of the lamps blazing to keep the room brightly lit and—she hoped—any ghouls at bay. Slipping in and out of alcohol-induced catnaps, she'd been tormented by the newest version of her recurring nightmare. Every time she drifted off, the Dream Woman's face would appear and speak the same words in her strangely accented, elegant voice:

"Hear me. Bear witness to our story."

The two sad little boys were always there just on the periphery: Clara felt their eyes silently imploring her to watch. Surely the raging man would come next—and with him, the violence. Clara jolted herself awake at that point. Whatever had happened to the family in the Old Hall, she did not wish to see it in detail.

Clara lost track of the amount of wine she'd drunk. Her symptoms suggested that she was at least as far-gone as she'd been on Sunday when Martin had done the pouring. The world was on a sickening tilt. Her motor skills were clumsy as she topped up her drink for a countless time, spilling half as much onto the surface of the bedside table as she poured into her glass. At least the alcohol dulled the pain of her contusions and strained muscles, for which she was truly grateful. Unfortunately, she seemed nowhere near her ultimate goal of the dreamless passing-out stage. The napping tendency had been an encouraging sign, but she never went deep and dark enough to be sure of complete escape. The visions kept her wakeful. Even her aim of a nightlong blackout might not guarantee she'd avoid the apparitions, but it would make them seem even more surreal—and much easier to explain away in the morning, when all other evils would be overshadowed by the ferocity of her hangover.

That such a slightly built woman could drink so very much and still be conscious didn't seem humanly possible, and yet…

Clara tilted her head back and drained her glass, spilling wine down both sides of her face. She grappled for the bottle and found it empty. *Another dead soldier.*

Better go to the kitchen for reinforcements now, she thought, while there's still enough light to check for blood on the staircase.

On the way to the foyer, Clara fixed her eyes on the front door of her prison while she plodded down the stairs. All day as she passed the front door on the way to the booze supply, she'd experimentally retried the locks and yanked on the door handles. There was never any change. She didn't have the heart to even attempt it this time. She tottered at the halfway point on the steps, lurching dangerously until her hands gripped the banister. There was no sensation left in her feet—a good indication that oblivion was within her grasp. The next bottle should be enough to do it.

A dog barked outside. Clara couldn't recognize if it

was Merlin or some other animal—her ears were ringing, distorting every sound into a weird hollow noise. The clock pinged the hours in the main room; sounding like it was deep inside a faraway tunnel. She didn't catch the time.

Car tires crunched and popped on the gravel drive out back. Listening, Clara paused on the stairs and decided it must be one of the neighbours getting home from work. The laneway behind the Old Hall seemed in common use for all the houses up and down the block. As the car's engine stopped and its door slammed, she perked up at the idea of trying to attract the driver's attention through the window. It was worth a shot.

Clara froze as she heard quick footsteps on the Old Hall's walk. The kitchen door banged open. *Someone's here! I'm saved!* Still reeling for balance on the stairs, she opened her mouth to call out to her rescuer.

"Phillipa?"

A male voice boomed from the side doorway. He sounded angry—and somehow familiar.

Clara clamped her mouth shut against her cry for help. The voice was accented like the Dream Woman's but with a harsher, more nasal edge.

"Phillipa! Show thyself!"

Slow, heavy boots stamped across the kitchen flagstones.

Clara's feet came unstuck and she launched herself

back up the stairs. Half-turning, she glimpsed a dark figure in the foyer, backlit from the overhead light she'd left on in the kitchen to ward off spirits. She miscalculated the top step and fell hard to her knees on the upstairs landing.

"Come down, whore!"

Clara scrabbled down the length of the hallway on her hands and knees. Remembering through her stupor that the lock on the bathroom door was broken, she knew the bedroom at the opposite end was her one chance at safety. It seemed miles away. She tried to get herself properly upright to run, but her legs were disobedient. Fear-weakened and uselessly drunk, she couldn't find her balance.

The man was stalking her, taking the stairs one slow step at a time. He seemed in no rush, as if sure that he had her cornered. His leather boots scuffled and slapped on the stone. Clara could make out a second sound—a harsh scrape of something metallic being dragged along.

Spurs? Or a knife blade…

Clara reached the bedroom and tumbled across the threshold. As she spun around to push the door shut, she saw the man's murky shadow just clearing the top stair. He turned and began to pace toward her, apparently savouring his leisurely progress as he lingered over each creak in the floorboards.

Her eyes flicked down, dismayed to discover that she'd been wrong. The bedroom had no lock. Clara heaved her weight against the wood, her sock feet finding no purchase on the polished floor. The door wouldn't close. Warped over the centuries, it no longer fit its frame.

The deliberate footsteps came to a stop just outside the bedroom.

"Dost thou defy me still?"

Clara could hear him breathing; could smell the blast of alcohol on his sour breath through the crack in the door. He sounded like a beast with his drawn-out, growling intake and his hissing release of air. Her own shallow breath—what little she could manage to get—was coming in quick, ragged pants. She could clearly see his black sleeve and dirty lace cuff through the two-inch gap as his fingers reached in and curved around the edge of the door.

"Stand aside, whore. I will not be prevented."

The sharp tang of his body's odour hit her nostrils. Instantly, her mind's eye was assailed by the recollection of the man from the other, lost night—the stranger on top and inside her, leering and triumphant. Clara gave a thin cry like a rabbit being murdered by a fox. Still struggling to brace the door shut, she cast about for something heavy she could drag over to use as a barricade. All the furniture was beyond her reach.

A low, mirthless chuckle came from the hallway. Both of the shadowy hands flew out and struck the door open with full force. Clara was thrown back. She rolled away into a protective ball, her eyes clamped shut, and her muscles tensed in anticipation of a blow.

"Clara?"

She jolted at the unexpected sound of her own name as though she'd been kicked. Peering out from beneath her arm, she gasped. There was no blood-spattered ghoul. It was only Scott, staring down at her from the doorway.

"Why the hell did you run away like that? Didn't you hear me calling you?"

Clara uncurled her body and rolled over onto her back, blinking up at her husband with a mixture of shock and confused relief. Her voice came out in a raspy whisper.

"Who's Phillipa?"

"Who?"

"I asked you first." Clara started to giggle in hysteria as she tried to explain the craziness. "I heard someone calling out for Phi… hill… ip-ha-ha-ha!"

Scott sneered.

"Christ! Look at you. You're pissed to the gills."

Clara snorted and heaved with waves of helpless laughter, her hands clasped over her streaming eyes. She parted her fingers playfully to take another look.

Peek-a-boo… yep. It's still just good ol' Scott.

"Boo!" she blurted, guffawing anew at his baffled expression. Scott's face and neck turned a blotchy red. He stepped over to his prostrate wife and prodded her in the ribs with his foot.

"Getting lots of quality work done here without me, I see?" he asked through gritted teeth. "Let me guess: you've got the play all done, and you're celebrating the glorious completion of your masterpiece by getting shit-faced."

Clara's breath hitched in her throat and her laughter stuttered to a halt. No point in telling the truth. He'd just think she was nuts. Maybe she was, but at least he was here now, and she could get out of the Old Hall. Her hands fell to her sides to fend off his prodding sneaker.

"Stop poking me. Whatcha doing back here? Issit Friday already?"

He stood back and crossed his arms over his chest.

"No. People have been asking after you, and it made me realize even more how ridiculous it is to be here in the same country and not put in an appearance, so I came to get you. I thought it might be fun to surprise everyone at breakfast tomorrow morning. Then you could be there to cheer me on in person when I deliver my paper. This is the turning point for my whole career, Clara. Why can't you see that?"

Clara's head lolled to the side and she peered beyond Scott into the empty hallway.

"Where're Martin and Em?"

"They're still in Oxford. They don't know I'm here. I rented a car and drove up late this afternoon. This is our little secret, Clara." His voice was flat and hard.

"Oh, thass good. Okay. Lessgo... I'm not getting much done here anyway." She loosely flailed her hand. "Help me up."

"No."

"Fine. Be that way. Gimmee a minute 'til I get my stuff together."

Clara flipped over and crawled up onto the bed, laboriously pulling herself into a sitting position amid the tangle of sheets and pillows. Her head wobbled on her neck as she furrowed her brow and looked around the room.

"D'you see my shoes anywhere?"

"Forget it, Clara. I have no intention of taking you back with me now, not in the state you're in." He smiled coolly. "You were bound and determined to be left on your own, so now you'll have it your way. You win this round, darling. Congratulations."

He turned and strode toward the bedroom door.

No! Not one of his moods! Not now!

Clara was hit by a surge of panic. The terror at being left alone in the Old Hall sobered her like a plunge into icy water.

"No! Please, Scott. Don't leave me here. I... I *want* to come with you."

He stopped, his back still turned against the dishevelled spectacle of his wife. He massaged the sides of his head with his fingertips as though he were trying to erase pain lodged in his temples.

"And I wanted you to come back with me, Clara. But not now. You're a disgrace."

Clara struggled for composure. She found her heavy-duty hiking boots buried in the mess of bedclothes alongside an empty wine bottle and began to undo a knot in the laces. She had to persuade Scott to hear her plea. Adopting a submissive and reasonable tone of voice, she fought hard not to slur her words.

"Wait… I'm sorry, Scott. You were right all along. I should have come with you in the first place. I wish I hadn't been so pig-headed, but I've been so stressed out… and now look at me. I guess I didn't handle it very well, did I?" She tried to laugh at herself, hoping he'd laugh back.

Scott wouldn't answer. He hadn't even turned around to face her again, but at least he was still in the room. Clara pushed on.

"I'll be okay by morning."

Scott finally glared over his shoulder at her, one eyebrow cynically raised in a high arch.

"Well, okay—maybe I won't make it to breakfast. But I'll come to hear your paper, and I'll be 100 percent by dinnertime. I can wear my black dress; the one you like from New Year's. I packed it, just in case. We can surprise Martin and Emma—exactly the way you wanted. All right?"

Scott appeared unmoved by her words. Clara's awkward

fingers had only woven the knot in her laces into an impossible snarl. She stopped the futile activity and adopted a new strategy to win over her husband. Flashing the drunken approximate of a seductive come-hither smile, she leaned back on the bed onto her elbows with her spread legs dangling over the edge.

"Or you could stay here and we'll drive back in the morning. You can remind me of what we did the other night."

Clara watched his knuckles whiten as Scott's hand tightened its grip on the doorjamb. He gave a sharp bark of bitter laughter.

"I am not the least bit tempted by your offer."

Clara's face flushed as she sat up and tried to think of a new ploy. Nothing came to her. She sagged, vanquished. A tear fell unchecked onto the bed. "Never mind."

Scott rolled his eyes and gave an impatient sigh.

"Look, let's forget all about it. We'll pretend I never came here tonight, and I'll drive back to Oxford on my own. I can't talk to you rationally until you're sober. Just do me a favour and try not to be drunk when I get back on Friday."

Clara sniffled and wiped her nose with the back of her hand.

"C'mon, Scott. Be fair. Stay, all right? I don't want to be here on my own. It's late, and I'm sick of arguing. We can drive down in the morning. I'll sleep it off in the car."

"Sorry, but that won't be possible. I have a lecture to give right after breakfast, remember?" Briskly, he glanced at his watch. "I have a long drive ahead. If I want to be back at my hotel and get any sleep, I'd better hit the road. Goodnight, Clara." He turned to leave.

Clara emitted a scream of frustration and hurled her boot at Scott's retreating back. It connected solidly between his shoulder blades. He froze, then whirled around to face her, his voice lowered into a chesty rumble.

"Don't try that shit with me or I'll kill you."

Clara was too gripped by hysteria to heed his threat. Crouching on her hands and knees like a madwoman in the centre of the bed, she spasmodically grabbed at clumps of the bedclothes in search of another missile to throw.

"Don't leave me here alone, you bastard! Take me with you!"

Scott stooped, picking up the boot from the floor. He reached the foot of the bed in two long strides. He wound up and delivered a stunning blow upside her head. The hard rubber slammed into her skull with a sickening thud, throwing Clara across the bed backwards to lie silenced and still.

* * *

"Mouse?"

Scott opened his hand and let the boot drop by his

feet, staring down at it with mild surprise. Clara made no move at the sound of it hitting the floor. Holding his breath, he took a few tentative steps toward her for a closer look. No blood, and her chest rose and fell as she breathed in a steady, normal rhythm. He perched on the side of the bed. The mattress sagged under his weight, but Clara did not stir.

"Oh dear. Out like a light, eh, Mouse?"

He spoke to her in a soft rational voice, stroking her hair from her face and arranging it on the pillow.

"I'm sorry it had to come to this, Clara. But you didn't give me a lot of choice, did you? You were hysterical."

He ran his fingers lightly over the reddening bump on the side of her head.

"Well—you're going to have quite the headache in the morning, but it doesn't seem too bad." He brushed a kiss on her forehead. "You're all I want, Clara. You've just been so distant, lately. I don't know what to do to get you back." He smiled. "It's funny. I'm actually glad you threw that boot at me. You really didn't want me to leave, did you? That makes me feel hopeful about us, in a way."

He cupped her limp hand between his own and chafed gently at the clammy flesh to warm her skin.

"I'll tell you what really hurts—Emma came to Oxford for no other reason than to be with Martin and show her support. He didn't even have to ask her, never mind having to beg or bargain. She looked so proud when he was up at the podium delivering his Shelley paper yesterday. And later… "

Scott rubbed furiously at the stubborn ache at his temples.

"Later in the night at the hotel, I heard them through the wall next door. I could tell she really *wants* him—and not just because she's drunk or trying to get her own way. We used to be like that, not too long ago. That's why I drove all the way back to get you. I don't know how we got off track, Clara, but I don't think it's impossible to turn things around."

Rising, he eased Clara onto her side in case she was sick in her sleep. After arranging her head into a more comfortable position, he untangled the bedclothes as much as possible without disturbing her and tucked the sheet up under her chin.

She'll be fine.

"The more you keep pushing against me and rejecting the life I want us to share, the worse it gets for us both. You have to live in the real world, Clara. You can't go back to being the theatre groupie you were in your twenties. It's time to grow up. Maybe start a family. I've been trying to tell you that, but you just don't seem to hear me. Maybe you're listening now, deep down. I hope so."

As he smoothed the covers one more time over his wife, Scott's fingers brushed up against something cold and hard buried in a fold of the sheet beside Clara's hip. He fumbled for the object and pulled out a bone-handled dagger. *Odd*. Turning it over in his hand, he felt the balance and heft of the weapon. The smooth handle was worn by use and felt comfortable—almost familiar—in his grip. It had some age to it like everything else about the Old Hall, but the blade itself was razor sharp and shiny with a lethal point. Not the sort of thing one leaves in bed for an unconscious person to potentially roll over onto. He carefully tucked it into his belt loop for safekeeping.

Clara hadn't moved. Scott opened the window a crack for some fresh air: it was stuffy inside the Old Hall. He stood over her for a few moments with his hands shoved deeply into his pockets.

"This trip isn't just about my career: it's *our* turning point too. Things aren't unfolding the way I would've ideally chosen, but maybe you needed something this extreme to shock you into facing the facts. Harsh lessons are sometimes the best. You need to dry out and consider what I've said. Things will be different for us from now on. Better than ever. I know it."

He leaned in and kissed her on the cheek.

"I'll be back by mid-afternoon on Friday, Mouse. Sleep well."

CHAPTER FIVE

Clara clawed her way back to the surface.

Too many of her days had been starting out this way. Her head was a searing mass of pain, and she was unable even to lift it from the pillow.

Hang on—this is no hangover.

Clara remembered. Not everything was clear, but she recalled enough to frighten her wide-awake. Scott's face changing. The snarl in his voice. The maniacal look in his eye—and the sharp crack to her skull. She lay helpless for a few moments, breathing deeply and gathering strength. It was close and hot, and the sheets were suffocating. The window was shut and it was difficult to get air.

It was daylight in the room. With great effort, she raised her wrist to her bleary eyes to check the time, but her watch had stopped. It seemed broken. *Must have got in the way last night.* The alarm clock was gone from the bedside. It probably got knocked down during all the hoopla, and she didn't feel up to conducting a search.

Clara's mouth was dry and her stomach was lurching in protest. It would feel so good to just give up and go back to sleep, but she knew enough about concussions to fight against the impulse. She eased herself to the side of the bed and sat up, her head roaring with a rush of blinding red as she cradled it in both hands. Her fingers discovered a sizeable lump over her left ear. She prodded at it gently, wincing at the fresh bolt of pain her touch produced. Her gaze fell on the hiking boot still lying in the middle of the floor. A sudden case of the shivers rocked her frame, and she hugged herself for comfort. It was a lucky thing she'd even come to.

The need to rise became urgent. Somehow, she got down to the end of the hallway to the bathroom in time. She knelt before the toilet, her elbows propping her up on the edge of the bowl with her hands clamped tightly on either side of her skull in a vain effort to contain the agony. Each heave of her guts was pure torture. Her head felt like it was going to split and fall off: she almost hoped that it would, and put her out of her misery.

The nausea subsided and she staggered to the sink to clean up.

"Well, you got your wish. You've spent the night out cold."

She lifted her hair out of the way and inspected her bump in the mirror. It looked nasty—lurid and purplish red. Her eyes welled up. Nothing mattered any more. Not the play… and certainly not rescuing her marriage. No chance of that happening. All she really wanted was to get to Leeds airport and fly home to her parents in Edmonton, but maybe getting on a plane right away with a concussion wasn't such a hot idea. A better immediate plan would be to go into the city and find a doctor.

Clara drifted downstairs to the living room and squinted at the Westminster clock. It wasn't ticking, its tiny golden hands frozen silently on nine-thirty. She wished she knew what time it was; she was curious to know how long she'd been blacked out. Looking on the bright side, at least she'd never have to hear that damned tinny chime again. She found her knapsack and checked to see if she had her passport. Let Scott worry about her heavy suitcase: the simple act of bending down to put on her sneakers was nearly enough to knock her back out.

In the kitchen, she sat at the table to breakfast on tap water and Tylenol, waiting for the wave of throbbing dizziness to ease up a little before she faced the outside world. The note for Scott was still sitting folded and unread on top of his book. The painkiller was starting to kick in, and her mind seemed to be clearing. Time to try to get out of the Old Hall.

Clara took up her pack and turned to confront the kitchen door.

"All right, you bastard—"

Gearing up for a fight, she held her breath and tried the knob. It turned easily with a click. The door swung open.

Clara gave a loud whoop of triumph—despite the jab of pain it caused—and stepped outside. She inhaled deeply. The air felt brisk and fresh in her lungs after being cooped up inside the Old Hall. Her arms were chilled even with her long sleeves, and she rubbed herself for warmth. The sky was clear and pink. It must have been barely dawn by the look of the quality of the light. There wasn't a sign of a soul about yet, not even the sound of early traffic on the nearby Bradford Road: just a few songbirds greeting the day. She wondered how early the bus service into Leeds started in the mornings. It could be a long wait, but Clara didn't want to risk going back inside now that the Old Hall had finally relented its hold and allowed her to walk out. She pulled the door shut behind her and set off without a backward glance, keeping her eyes fixed firmly on the ground to watch for potholes and uneven spots. If she tripped and fell down, she might not have the strength to get herself back up.

The back lane was terribly rutted and irregular, overgrown with clumps of weeds and long grass. Clara hadn't noticed it was this bad when they drove up the other day. Surely Martin's Fiat would've had trouble negotiating all of those humps and dips; a Land Rover would have been better suited to the task. It looked more like a cow path than a proper laneway. Clara struggled to keep her balance on her unsteady feet, slipping in the mud and splashing through the puddles left by a recent heavy rainfall. If it had rained in the night, she had no recollection of hearing it. Usually every little sound woke her. She must have really been out cold.

A blast of muddy water shot up inside the leg of her jeans.

"Damn it!"

Clara teetered on one leg and shook her foot in a hapless effort to dry off as her other sneaker foundered in the mud. She could have sworn the lane had been covered in gravel. Puzzled, Clara finally looked up at her surroundings.

The stone walls that ran alongside the laneway were gone. Where she'd remembered seeing a collection of cinderblock garages and tumbledown garden sheds, there was a low, half-timbered building with a sagging thatched roof. An unseen horse neighed from within the structure and was answered by a deeper whinny from the open field behind the stables. The tangy, rich scent of fresh manure was strong in the cool air.

Clara spun around. The tidy rows of nineteenth-century terraced houses and cottages were gone. In their place was a paddock of sheep staring at her curiously and a scanty-looking apple orchard. Pink and white blossoms lined the damp and twisted black branches. Petals blown by the constant breeze littered the ground at her feet and stuck to the wet mud on her sneakers. Why were the trees in flower at this time of year? It made no sense. None of this did.

"What the hell—?"

As her focus blurred, a fresh wave of painful nausea threatened. Dark spots swam before her eyes. Lights flashed and popped in the periphery of her vision. Groaning, she touched a shaky hand to the bump on her skull. *What has Scott done?* In this state, she couldn't even see the world properly anymore. Hallucinating was a very bad sign. The pain in her head throbbed in a frightening tandem with the rapid pounding of her heart. She had to find help—fast.

Clara jounced along as quickly as she could force herself down the hill in the direction of the main road. Every step jarred her aching limbs, but she gritted her teeth and pushed on even faster. She kept her eyes fixed on the path a few yards ahead, not caring to look up and see what else was there—or not there—along the route.

"Don't panic—it's not real," she coached herself

with flagging confidence. "Scott's really gone and done it with that boot to the head... but it's okay. I'll be fine, once I get to the main road."

There might not be time to wait for a bus if the concussion was as bad as it seemed. She decided to wave down the first vehicle that passed. Clara rounded the bend at the base of the slope and stopped dead at the corner where the pub should have been. The 'main road' was no more than a wide, glorified dirt path. There was no sign of the paved two-lane highway she had been driven along the other day. It was the right place for it to be, no question: the landmark of the old parish church of St. Wilfred's was across the way in plain view. Its simple square tower gleamed a clean grey-gold in the morning sun, the limestone unblemished by the as yet nonexistent black soot of Northern England's Industrial Age factory smokestacks. The adjacent cemetery had far fewer headstones than Clara recalled, and the orchard beside the grounds was vast and overgrown, its edges melting away into a wide expanse of impenetrable-looking hardwood forest stretching for miles down into the vale toward the river.

There would be no point in crossing over to wait for a bus. The dirt was deeply rutted with cartwheel tracks and the gouges left by hooves and human feet, but no motorized vehicle had ever been driven on this road. The air was so fresh and cool that it hurt her lungs to breathe, and it was horribly serene and quiet. The only sounds were the calls of birds and farm animals.

Clara was alone and impossibly lost out of her time.

Blinking through her tears, she turned and headed back in the direction of the Old Hall. At least it was a familiar point of reference, even if the thought of spending another moment within sight of the place was enough to make her scream. From there she hoped to regroup and get her bearings before she headed out to try her luck again.

This must be one hell of a concussion.

Clara rounded the final curve in the path up toward Calverley Old Hall. Light-headedness made her dizzy, and she paused to catch her breath. It felt like she'd run a marathon. She glanced up the hill to see how much farther she had to go before she reached the Old Hall. It stood isolated, a wide field separating it from the rest of the scattered village dwellings. The only closely neighbouring structures were the stables and a few wooden outbuildings. Since it was no longer mashed together cheek by jowl with ordinary terraced houses, the Old Hall looked imposing. Clara frowned. Something seemed different about its overall shape. Part of it was missing.

Clara gasped and dropped the backpack off her shoulder. The guesthouse wing was not there. She broke into a staggering run and halted in the grassy area between the Old Hall and the stables where the wing had been standing. Clara's bruised mind raced. Martin had told her that the 'new' addition hadn't been built until 1640, so that meant…

"Oh my God."

She roughly estimated the spot where the door to the kitchen should have been and planted her feet in place to wait. Whatever crazy shift had happened to pull her out of her own time, the crack between the centuries must have ruptured there. All she could do was hope that it would split open soon and draw her back into the time where she belonged. She squeezed her eyes shut and concentrated on the blobs and flashes dancing on the pulsing red field behind her eyelids. Struggling to calm her breathing, she drew a deep steady intake through her nose and emptied her lungs through her mouth with an audible *whoosh*.

Down the hill, the church bells began to toll.

Clara's heartbeat accelerated with every descending peal. The sudden additional sound of approaching footsteps redoubled her fear. Her legs were rooted in place, and even if she could have summoned up the strength, there was no safe place to run and hide. There was no choice but to stand her ground. Clara swivelled her body to face the side of the building as the steps drew closer. With a rustle of silk skirts, a figure appeared from around the corner of the Hall. Clara sucked in her breath.

It was the Woman from her dream.

The Dream Woman's eyes were fixed straight ahead.

She walked with a careful measured pace, the hem of her blue gown trailing behind her. Her feet seemed to instinctively know where to step, deftly avoiding the rocks and puddles with an easy familiarity born of a constant use of the path. She held her arms out from her body in an unnaturally stiff position—elbows bent, hands slightly to the front, fingertips not quite touching at her centre. It looked as though she could not bear to make even the most casual contact with her own body. In one hand, she carried a small, red leather-bound prayer book.

Clara gathered up courage as the Dream Woman slowly approached with her small, elegant steps. It didn't seem possible that she had not noticed Clara, but if she had, she gave no outward sign of surprise or acknowledgment.

"Excuse me—"

Clara's voice sounded sickly and mewling. Clearing her throat, she tried again to get the Woman's attention. Every other word cracked and was barely above a whisper.

"Could you please help me? I'm lost."

The Woman passed by so closely that Clara needed only raise her hand to touch her sleeve. A warm scent of rosewater and lavender poorly masked the aroma of stale perspiration in her wake. The Woman's soulful eyes never wavered from her destination farther down the path, as the church bells continued their intermittent summons to worship.

Clara unlocked her knees and lurched after her in a stumbling trot.

"Please wait. Don't ignore me… can't you see that I'm afraid?"

Still, the Dream Woman did not break her stride. Clara forced a burst of speed from her exhausted legs and rushed ahead of her by a few yards. Turning, she took a confrontational stance in the middle of the path. She tried to catch the Woman's eyes, but they were focused ever forward at a point beyond Clara's left shoulder, giving no indication that she could even see the madwoman blocking her way.

Clara would not allow herself to be avoided any further. Lifting her arms before her in a gesture of mute appeal, her face was streaked with tears.

Hear me.

Clara extended her hands in readiness to grab on to those strangely stiffened arms and force the Woman to stop. The Woman was four paces away, the damask gown swishing as she sidestepped the deep ruts in the earth. Three paces. Two. Clara's finger's darted out and grasped at her sleeve, making firm contact and sinking deeply into the silk material and the flesh beneath.

The Dream Woman did not waver. It was apparent that she couldn't see Clara and was unaffected by her touch. She pushed steadily onward and passed *through* Clara, the Woman's chest coming in full contact with

Clara's own, and the capacious skirts wrapping around and engulfing Clara's legs as the Woman continued walking steadily forward.

Clara felt her physical self slipping away… vanishing.

At first, there was a deafening roar like a sonic boom that threatened to burst her eardrums. A hot pressure within her skull mounted, and built to the point of splitting her open. She tried to scream. She tried to kick and push away the sensation to break herself free. No sound or movement was possible. Powerless to make it stop, the world itself gave way from under her feet. Clara felt her own solidity slip away and dissolve into nothingness.

At its zenith, the panic melted away. There was nothing to feel in this unearthly void but an emotionless state of containment. Clara's urge to fight calmed and her terror faded. Her body was gone—and with it, her pain. She was fully absorbed into the being of the Dream Woman.

Clara felt she was being taken along on an uncontrollable journey. Her consciousness passed through the blue-gowned body, and she drifted upwards to hover above the Woman—able to observe all from an objective point of view, like a film camera on a crane. All instinct to resist and struggle had vanished. There was no reaction she could summon to mourn for her utter and unaccountable loss of self. Clara did not question—she could not. Her will was gone.

Clara had become the dream instead of the dreamer—a phantom out of her own time. Bound to the scene by an invisible cord, she was able to swoop around and dive in from different viewpoints, to hear and see all. She realized that she had no control over what she would see, or any power to influence the events she would be shown. Omnipresent but ineffectual, there was nothing she could do but float insensate over the action and watch the pageant unfold.

Bear witness to our story.

PART TWO

'I see how ruin with a palsy hand
Begins to shake the ancient seat to dust—'

—*A Yorkshire Tragedy*

CHAPTER SIX

Sunday, 21st of April, 1605.

Lord in Thy mercy, hear me and grant me strength.

Each step along the dirt path—however careful she was in the placing of her feet—jolted Phillipa Calverley down to her bones. Along with the effort of walking, a great sense of unease quickened her breath. She knew that she ought to have stayed behind and waited for her husband, Sir Walter, so that they left the Hall together. After all, it was at his insistence that morning that the Calverleys would attend church services as a family. Phillipa did not know what to make of his sudden show of piety.

There had been no predicting her husband's humours of late.

He would catch her up soon enough. She wanted a few moments alone to practise her bearing before appearing publicly to the congregation at St. Wilfred's, and she was finding it a great challenge not to limp.

A sharp, sudden gust of wind blasted from the open fields and hit her with such force that she stumbled on an unseen stone. Phillipa gritted her teeth at the renewed waves of deep pain and paused to rest, allowing the pangs to subside. The discomfort was fierce: her body felt invaded, her very mind intruded upon by confusion and grievous affliction. She squeezed the prayer book in her hand.

Grant me strength, I pray—

Each drawn breath produced a burning sting in her lungs. *Perhaps some ribs are cracked,* she thought as she clasped a hand to her side. Dressing that morning had been pure torture. Her maidservant, Sarah, took extra care as she tightened the cage of whalebone stays around her torso but it had brought tears to Phillipa's eyes. The act of drawing breath with the added restriction was a challenge, but in the end she was glad of the stays' support of her bruised sides. They made it less taxing for her to uphold a properly dignified posture.

Phillipa cast a wary glance over her shoulder at the Hall. All was still. There was no sign yet of either her husband or of their four year-old son, William. The two-and-a-half-year-old baby, Walter, had been left behind in Sarah's care. Phillipa had pleaded the excuse that the child was not yet over last week's ague, and Calverley—in his constant state of growing distraction—had not chosen for once to view her decision as an act of defiance, much to her relief. The truth was that young Walter was quite well enough to be taken to church, if more than usually cranky with the residual symptoms of his illness. He was an impatient babe-in-arms when made to sit quietly, and she did not think that she could cope with his lively wriggling today. It would have been impossible for her to effectively hold or carry him with such sore arms. Her muscles had been badly strained during the most recent beating, and she ached deeply from shoulder to fingertip.

Lord, grant that no one takes notice of my bodily pains.

The audacity of the prayer made her flush. It reeked of womanly vanity to pray for a veil of goodly appearances to display before her neighbours, but she could not bear the humiliation of their pitying looks if they made the worst assumptions about her marital state: it was torment enough that they would be right.

Calverley had forbidden her in advance to converse with anyone. This enforced silence was a blessed deliverance. She could not trust herself to speak aloud and keep her misery from infecting the tone of her voice. At least he had not blackened her eyes. He had been most careful—even in the throes of his rage—not to do any damage to her face.

Phillipa sighed and gazed with longing at the upstairs windows of the Hall. She dearly wished to be hidden within nursing her wounds in bed, but Calverley's orders were not to be defied. Ever.

Lord, show him the True path.

Her husband's unprecedented vehemence to attend church was bewildering. Never a devout Christian, he had shown a progressive distaste of late for all religious matters. He mocked his wife's own sincere piety and was more often than not recalcitrant from services. Despite her dearest wishes, she knew that this sudden fervour was no sign of her riotous lord's repentance. Doubtless it was the proud show of a content man united in worship with his family that was important. Still, she clung to the hope that he would find some meaning in the sermon, and that she herself would find some peace. There was none to be found at home.

The bells would soon stop tolling and the service would be underway. Gathering herself, she gave her prayer book another little squeeze for courage and continued her slow progress down the pathway. Her back teeth ground together with each step as she avoided deep ruts and mud, but she took a kind of grim satisfaction in her own fortitude.

"Wait, Mama!"

Her eldest son, William, rounded the corner of

Calverley Hall and scampered to catch up. Bounding to her side, he grabbed on to her free hand. A fresh bolt of pain shot up the length of her arm, but Phillipa did not let on. She glanced past him and saw he was alone. The absence of his father was worrisome, but she assumed a cheerful attitude for the benefit of the child.

"Where is thy father?"

"Not yet done at breakfast."

I am surprised he has the stomach for food this morning.

"Does he know he is left behind?"

William hung his head, his eyes welling up.

"I tried to tell him we must hurry—but he shouted so, and frighted me."

Phillipa's heart lurched. Calverley's violence toward her had begun as mere shouting, too—and the boys had such tiny bones… She struggled to keep her tone light and steady as she soothed her son. It pained her throat to speak, and her normally melodious voice was raspy.

"Understand, my love; thy father is an important man much bound by duty. Most of this county's land belongs to him, and he needs must concern himself with the tenant farmers and their troubles. As with the seasons, some times are worse than others. We must bear his temper with patience. Remember: all that he owns and works for will one day be your inheritance."

If there is anything left to inherit.

The vast land holdings of the noble family had once

shone like a full moon around Calverley Hall and the surrounding village; but in the hands of her wild husband, the riches were waning and now barely showed as a quarter of their original splendour. Income from rents melted away as more and more property was sold off to pay Calverley's gambling debts. The cycle was insidious: the more he lost, the more he frantically wagered in the misguided hope he could win back his lost fortune. His love for the gaming tables had been there from the outset of their marriage six years before, but as time wore on, her husband had lost control. The real downward spiral had begun around the time his second son and namesake had been born. Since the birth of their third son, Henry, he'd given himself over to almost nightly games of dice. The boys were sorely neglected. He'd rarely even set eyes upon the infant, temporarily housed with a wet nurse at a nearby farm. On the rare occasion he did return to his marriage bed before dawn, he reeked of drink and whores.

Lord help us.

Nothing that Phillipa said or did had any good effect. The more understanding that she showed, and the more help she tried to offer, the worse the abuse inflicted. There could be no reasoning, she feared, with a man so... possessed.

"Hold up, there!"

Calverley's commanding voice boomed from the corner of the Hall. At the sight of her husband, Phillipa's breath caught in mingled fear and love. There was no outward sign in his fine appearance that betrayed him as a man out of his depths. His tall, lean frame was richly attired in his favourite doublet and sleeves; a black silk velvet shot through with delicate gold embroidery. His best lace ruff and cuffs clashed in a brilliant white contrast against the sable background. This was his London-tailored clothing: his pride in his noble station allowing only the boldest show of wealth to go on display at church. He had insisted that morning that Phillipa dress in her finest indigo silk gown—in truth, one of only two such garments still in her possession as their circumstances became ever more diminished—and together the couple cut such a striking pair that there was no denying that all eyes would be upon them as they took their place in the front pew.

Under the wide brim of his black hat, his face was set and impassive. His moustache and goatee appeared newly trimmed and shaped around the lines of his full-lipped mouth. Phillipa could read no displeasure in his expression; his dark eyes were focused stonily ahead. Calverley took little notice of either his wife or son as he caught up and quickly passed them by with his loping stride, leaving them in his wake as he marched down the slope toward church.

"Well?" he called back over his shoulder. "Do ye not hear the bells? It grows late."

Mother and son exchanged a look, then Will

dropped her hand and laughingly galloped off after his father. Just so long as the boy believed her reassurances and viewed his father's brusqueness as a kind of joke, Phillipa could cope. She pushed herself past her limits to keep a few long paces behind them on the uneven path.

Lord, grant me the strength to endure, and restore him to us.

Her gaze was fixed on her husband's back. She silently willed him to turn and see the pain he was inflicting. In the beginning, he had been an attentive and exuberant bridegroom, treating both her feelings and her body with a tender regard. Phillipa had at first counted herself as truly blessed in the match: she had seen many friends enter into their own arranged marriages with nothing but feelings of repulsion for their new husbands. Sir Walter had not yet been of the legal age of twenty-one, and was still under the control of the Court of Wards when their betrothal had taken place. Despite neither of them having any say in the choices made on their behalf, the two had been pleased by the intensity of their mutual attraction, and a deep initial bond had formed between the couple. The birth of the first of their three sons in 1601 had been the peak of their joy together.

She kept her reddened eyes on her husband in the vain wish that he would reach down and take his once-adored son's hand, as the boy gamboled at his side attempting to gain attention. The child's faith in his parents' love was strong. Will was laughing and making a great game of it, leaping up to grab at his father's sleeve and trying to swing from his elbow. Calverley impatiently snatched his arm out of the child's reach.

Phillipa's despair was great. If only Calverley could be made to understand the destructive effect his wild behaviour was having on his family and their future, then surely he would change. She would pray earnestly for such a blessing this morning—if her weakening legs would bear her the rest of the short distance to church.

Sweat ran freely from under her hooded hair and down the back of her neck as they approached St. Wilfred's yard. Her lungs felt on fire, and her breast heaved with effort as she reached the church porch and at last caught up with her family. The congregation was already within doors. Calverley waited to formally take her hand and support it on his arm, allowing her a brief moment to calm her laboured breathing. Almost as an afterthought, he reached down to take his son by the hand—much to William's delight—and the Calverleys made their final public entrance together as worshippers.

Phillipa's preoccupation with the beating two days before blocked out the words of the sermon. She struggled to focus; if not on the chosen text, then on the calming cadence of the ritualistic language, using the pure musicality of the speaker's tones to soothe her mind.

Phillipa felt sure that the whole of the congregation had their eyes upon her. Calverley's tenants surrounded them on all sides, and there had been a ripple of murmured comments accompanying their progress as they'd made their way to their seats. She held her gaze downward upon the open pages of her prayer book. Little comfort was to be found. It had been a wedding gift from the Brooke side of the family, and only served to remind her of how far she was from her beloved London childhood home and her friends. Her eyes watering, she traced a fingertip over the scrolled illuminations bordering the page—exploring for the thousandth time the colourful images of birds and animals intertwined with stylized flowering vines. There was a particular rabbit with comically bulging eyes that seemed poised to eat the largest red rose. Normally the sight of it made her smile, but not today. The text blurred on the vellum parchment, the sacred words rendered meaningless. She knew that few—if any—of the other parishioners at St. Wilfred's even possessed a prayer book, let alone one of such expense and beauty. It was yet another marker of her difference from them.

Lord, protect and keep me.

Phillipa had been the object of local curiosity since she had been brought north as a new bride from London. They had passed their first year of marriage in the familiar surroundings of Court, but Calverley had been uncomfortable and had grown anxious to return to his Yorkshire soil. His true home was amid the countryside folk; his rough manners and accent were not a standout in such humble company. Most in the village and parish of Calverley were farmers, or labourers in the manufacture of woollen cloth for which the region was famous. Their simple lives had a minutely localized focus; few had ever been farther a-field than the town square markets of Leeds. A handful had ventured as far as the cathedral city of York thirty miles to the northeast, but most were content to live out entire generations within a few miles' radius of home. For the majority, life was quiet and modestly prosperous.

Phillipa was the exotic bird in their midst. The silks of her gowns were lustrous, her every movement careful and refined. The few who had occasion to hear her speak reported her as possessing a musically accented voice bearing little resemblance to their own broadly nasal tones. To them, she could only ever be a foreigner: to be distantly admired rather than truly known and accepted. In a place so far removed from the social importance of her extended family and colourful London Court life, her world had sharply narrowed in scope. The influence of the Brookes' connections to the mighty Sir Robert Cecil had minimal import at such a distance. The great names of her relations invoked little reverence in a community concerned primarily with crops and the rearing of healthy sheep herds rather than the politics of London society at Court. No real protection remained for Phillipa in her family ties. She had immersed herself quite willingly in her roles as wife and mother at home. It would, she'd thought, be a happy—if quiet—new life.

But now? Oh Lord—

William's head slumped heavily against the side of her arm. A quick glance assured her that he'd been lulled into a doze by the long sermon. She sighed and let the boy sleep, knowing that he was likely to fidget and complain if she should rouse him and force him to stay awake. It would be hypocritical of her to insist that he pay attention to the lesson considering her own distracted mind. If someone were to ask her later that day what the subject had been, she would be unable to summon an answer.

On her other side sat Calverley. He took the aisle, hemming her in—his long legs barring any escape—guarding her jealously from contact with the other gentry sitting in the opposite pew. She felt herself under his constant scrutiny throughout the service. His eyes seemed to bore into the side of her face like hot steel, and she flushed with anxiety, scarcely daring to breathe. *Why had they come?* Tongues would wag either way, she supposed. Rumours of her husband's gambling debts had been freely circulating for a year. *Better to be at church than not,* she thought. Here there was a chance that he would repent his cruel ways. Or at least be seen to be pious. They had not been to a service in weeks.

As though cued by her very thoughts, Calverley's hand reached out, took hers and held it. There was no comfort meant by the gesture: he leaned his head close to hers and whispered poisonous words into her ear.

"Such a hot, damp hand indicates a wanton and lustful nature. I have long suspected thee for a whore, and here is my proof. Is your lover here in our midst? Ah... I see you blush to hear me speak of him. It needs must be true."

Smiling with false benevolence, Calverley cast his eyes about scanning the congregation in an apparent search for his wife's paramour. Phillipa tried to pull away and his grip tightened. He continued to spew wild allegations between his clenched teeth.

"I am sure he sits close by us, nodding his cursed head at the holy words... all the while laughing at how he hath made a cuckold of me."

He glared down at the sleeping child and his full lips stretched into a thin, bloodless line.

"No doubt these—'my' sons and heirs—are but his bastards. Think you this: is it not wondrous strange that 'twas only after we had settled here that you were suddenly able to bear me children, whilst your womb had proven barren in London?"

Falling silent, Calverley resumed his close scrutiny of her face. Phillipa fixed her blurry gaze upon her book and made no reply. *How could he think me so base a creature?* She had never given him cause. The workings of his mind were more and more a mystery: as the gambling worsened and the debts mounted, he seemed lately to find a perverse solace in this mad notion of her infidelity. He needed to blame someone for his misery, and she was the closest to hand. *Such shame… and all for naught.* All of her loving assurances fell on deaf ears. All the choice she had left was to sit and endure the insults. He no longer tolerated the tiniest of protests: she bore the bruises to prove that. Phillipa stirred uncomfortably, mortified that those sitting nearest to them must be straining to hear his hissing whispers.

"No, you cannot deny my words, for you know them to be true. Cunning wench—though the red of your cheeks confirms thee for a brazen whore, you clutch your prayer book and hide behind false piety. Think you not a careless glance will presently betray your lover to me? Doubt it not: I shall discover him."

Finished for the time, he turned his attention toward the front of the church.

Phillipa's hand was being crushed. Pure force of will prevented her crying out at the almost audible sensation of her knucklebones being ground together. Biting down hard on the inside flesh of her cheeks to suppress a sob, she tasted blood. She flexed her fingers to signal her husband to ease his vise grip, but her efforts were in vain as he ignored her struggles for freedom. Now—

when she most wanted to—she could not catch his eye. He stared ahead at the stained-glass window behind the altar. She followed his gaze to where it was locked—not on the crucified figure of Christ, but on his own family's coat of arms emblazoned above the cross. The six silver owls seemed to stare back down mockingly from their sable shield—a silent reminder of the wisdom that seemed so sorely lacking in this particular generation of Calverley blood. Below was a portrait of his ancestor Sir Robert, forever setting an example of devotion as he knelt flanked by a row of his sons at the feet of the dying Saviour.

With a low moan, Calverley released his hold on Phillipa and pitched forward onto his knees in an attitude of fervent prayer. She gasped and bowed her head in silent relief. Her freed hand sat on her lap like a lead weight, and she surreptitiously massaged it back to full sensation, her flesh throbbing and stinging as the blood began to flow back into her fingers.

What devil hath possessed him?

Panic seized her by the throat and she could scarcely draw a painful breath. More profound than the physical punishments was this groundless accusation of wantonness... and to name their three lovely sons as bastards bruised her very soul to the core.

Deliver us, Oh Lord...

Phillipa glanced at her husband's hunched shoulders, his strained and passionate expression, his hands clasped together so tightly that the colour was drained from his fingers. This sudden change was deeply affecting to witness. God had heard at last. Calverley appeared to be genuinely taken over by the act of prayer, and Phillipa felt a hopeful rush of relief at the sight. *Surely,* she thought, *this is a man in the throes of repentance for his cruelty.* God had touched his heart at last and he was taking the first steps to repent his wickedness. Tears of a happier sort wet her cheeks.

We are grateful for this, Thy blessing, Lord—

With great effort, Phillipa lowered herself to kneel in thanksgiving by her husband's side. She immediately regretted her mistake. The flow of mumbled words she overheard from her husband's lips were not prayers but a flood of blasphemy and curses.

• • •

At the conclusion of the service, Calverley helped Phillipa to her feet and steered her by the arm up the centre aisle and out of the church doors in a brisk manner that more suggested an arrest than a kindly escort. William had to dart around the other worshippers' legs to keep up. The family managed to get through the tight cluster of polite well-wishers with no more than quickly exchanged nods and bows. As ordered, Phillipa kept her eyes demurely turned toward the ground and spoke to no one. Calverley's gruff and haughty manner caused hesitation in any would-be conversationalists, and his tenant farmers and the few other families of rank kept their distance as he pushed through the loitering crowd of churchgoers with his missus and child in tow.

"William!"

At the sound of his name, William craned his neck over his shoulder. The Calverleys were well along the path through the gravestones and were almost at the gate to the road, but Will tugged free of his mother's hand and ran back toward St. Wilfred's and his young friend who had called to him.

"Edward!"

The Calverleys' nearest neighbours of rank were the Leventhorpe clan. Sir Thomas, like Sir Walter, was of minor nobility. His family's wealth in land holdings had for decades been second in the county to none but the Calverleys', but recently the gap between their fortunes had been narrowed by Sir Walter's heavy losses in the gaming circles. As Calverley sold off land to pay down debts and fund his revels, Leventhorpe had acquired much of his neighbour's property—and Phillipa had been saddened to see that this shift in balance had caused a strain in the two men's once-tight friendship. Leventhorpe's little son Edward was the same age as William. The boys had been devoted companions from their infancy.

Inadvertently, Phillipa's eyes caught and held those of Sir Thomas Leventhorpe as she drew near in slow pursuit of her wayward child. To her horror, she saw Leventhorpe's cordial smile of greeting fade as he beheld her stiff posture and her ill-concealed limp. He shot a glance at Calverley—waiting impatiently by the low stone wall at the edge of the churchyard—then took a step in her direction. He had a questioning expression on his face and seemed about to speak. Phillipa blanched and discreetly shook her head. Thankfully, he understood the subtle gesture and held himself back.

"William!" barked Calverley. "Come along! We are going home!"

William had inherited his paternal bloodline's trait of stubbornness. Feigning deafness, he held his ground, clinging to his playmate's arm and defiantly ignoring his father's command. Phillipa watched her husband's handsome face contort into a frightening mask—just as it had the other night before the first of the blows had fallen.

"*William!*"

The flow of conversation gave way to curious glances from the groups of chatting villagers. It was clear from the sharp tone of Calverley's voice that his son's willfulness would not be lightly tolerated. Phillipa held her breath as he began to stride toward them across the yard.

Elizabeth Leventhorpe blessedly intervened.

"Go to thy father, William," she said softly. "Edward shall visit with thee another day."

She bent down and took his small hand easily from her son's arm. Leventhorpe lifted Edward up onto his shoulders to prevent him from following as his wife led William back to his mother. Elizabeth's eyes flicked over the green and purple bruising on the back of Phillipa's outstretched hand. Phillipa kept her focus on her child as she gently admonished him for his disobedience, and refused to meet her neighbour's gaze. Elizabeth forced herself to smile and curtsy politely before returning to her own family.

Calverley appeared at her side and stared at the Leventhorpes with narrowing eyes. His neighbour bowed his head to him respectfully, but Calverley's only reply was to spin on his heel and march out of the yard toward the road. He dropped his carefully constructed pretense at family unity, leaving both wife and child behind in his wake to make their own way home unescorted.

The climb uphill was arduous for Phillipa; her steps made all the more painful by the thought of the wrath awaiting them as they drew nearer to the Hall. There was no sign of him ahead on the pathway. At her side, William walked silently and made no move to run or play, his usually ebullient manner subdued by the expectation of punishment.

Sarah came out to meet them in the yard holding young Walter on her hip. Phillipa caught her breath and called out to her servant.

"Where is my husband, Sarah? Is he already within?"
He must be avoided for the sake of the child.
"No, Madam. He straight way gave orders for John

to saddle his black mare, and has ridden for Leeds."

Phillipa felt exhausted. That her husband was not at home was both a blessing and a curse. By the time he returned, William would be asleep in bed—and with any luck, his earlier disobedient behaviour forgotten. But Calverley would no doubt be drunk and a few coins deeper in debt. Again.

"Very well. Come unpin me, Sarah. I needs must take to my bed."

Sarah kept the boys at her side as they climbed the stairs to the master bedchamber. Phillipa allowed the girl to strip her down to her cotton shift, past caring if she should see the bruises: just so long as the children did not. Sarah had deposited the boys out of sight in their chamber to play until their mother was under the coverlet.

"Shall I take the wee ones out for a walk, Madam? 'Tis fine weather today."

What a miracle the girl is. "Please do, Sarah. Leave me now. I must rest."

Sarah curtsied and closed the door, gently calling to the children from the next room. Phillipa listened as they chattered and thumped on the way downstairs and outside, their small voices fading into the distance as the three of them wandered off into the fields behind the Hall. She lay back in her lonely marriage bed and fell into a fitful slumber—spending the balance of the day slipping in and out of nightmares.

CHAPTER SEVEN

In the early hours, Phillipa was jolted awake by Calverley's yanking back the heavy crimson draperies from around the bed. It was the first night since the beating that he'd returned to their shared bedchamber. Lying motionless, she watched his moonlit figure through the slits of her half-closed eyes as he stripped down to his shirt. He was unsteady on his feet: fighting to keep his balance as he wrestled off his boots, he tottered over sideways and struck his head on one of the heavy oak bedposts. Staggering over to the dying fire, he returned to the bedside with a lit candle. He set the pewter candleholder down on a low stool with the exaggerated care of the very drunk.

Phillipa lay stock-still, her bruised body carefully propped up on the cushioned bolster. She shut her eyes and feigned sleep as the flicker of candlelight came near to her face. The mattress shifted under her husband's weight, and she could sense him leaning in close, as if watching her for signs of wakefulness. Her nose twitched involuntarily at the mingled stench of liquor and sex on his beard. He roughly pulled the covers from her body.

"Come now, Mistress. I know you are awake."

She opened her eyes and braced herself for whatever might happen next. There was no reading his expression as he perused her face at great length.

"Allow me to view the damage, dear Madam."

He gave her a drunken leer by way of a smile and pulled at the hem of her shift. Despite the chill of the air in the chamber, she could see that he was running with sweat. At his sharp-fingered promptings, Phillipa moved her body to accommodate him as he removed her thin cotton garment and dropped it over the side of the bed to the floor. She lay back naked and shivering before his eyes.

Calverley sat by her side and began to trail his fingertips slowly and lightly over her goose-fleshed arms, clucking his tongue in mock sympathy at the sight of the bruises he himself had so recently inflicted.

"Oh, see this—"

He pretended surprise to find her milky skin dotted

with dark finger marks and vibrant rashes from her recent struggles to escape his brutal grasp.

"—and look you here—"

His hands stroked their way downwards with an air of wonderment at every new discovery. Deep purple bruises showed in clusters on her thighs and shins; evidence of how his boots had kicked her legs out from under her in order to prevent her escape. Calverley stretched out his body on the bed alongside Phillipa's, his breath quickening and his hand drifting back upwards.

"Ah... and here is by far the worst—"

Her sides and stomach were the most sorely bruised areas. She tensed as Calverley traced the marks with a lover's feather-light touches, blowing his rank breath over the wounds in an airy caress. Phillipa dared not move. Her heart thumped furiously as he murmured nonsense, and passed a gentle exploring hand over each of the injuries. Calverley's roving came to rest over her pounding chest. He pressed down experimentally, as though asserting he could reach in and contain the pulsing organ within his grasp. One hard squeeze and he might forever still its beating. She half-hoped he would.

"I saw you," he intoned, cupping her breast.

Phillipa stared at him blankly.

"I saw you making eyes with Leventhorpe. *My friend.*"

He kept his voice light, his hands continuing in their gentle movements to trace circles over her flesh.

"The secret is revealed, Mistress." He gave her fear-hardened left nipple a pinch. "Hast thou no shame?"

He is mad. Possessed. What does he imagine he saw pass between us?

He seemed to be waiting for an answer. Phillipa was convulsed by shudders as she drew in a shaky breath and spoke in a halting voice.

"I encouraged not his approach. I must have appeared pale to him… I am in great pain—"

Calverley nodded, his lips pursed in empathy. He began to travel back down her body with his hands and mouth.

"Pray continue."

"He showed but neighbourly concern for my health, no more—"

"Ah," said Calverley, placing a delicate kiss on her bruised thigh. "So do you claim. But what I saw— *plainly*— was that you gave a signal to warn him away. What could you wish to conceal if his interest in you is guiltless?"

He trailed his goatee over a welt on her hip. Phillipa's breath hitched as her panic to prove herself innocent of the charges grew.

"'Twas your own command that caused me rebuke him! You ordered me to speak to no one. But William did not know—he is just a boy. He wanted his friend."

"Of course."

He gave another, wetter kiss and a lap of his tongue high up on her inner thigh. Phillipa gave in to her tears.

"I acted only as instructed... looked not to have dealings with the Leventhorpes, nor anyone else. I could plainly see your displeasure, but I am not to blame."

"Well, well. A loyal wife indeed! An excellent show of obedience. And you protect your bastard in the same breath. Commendable. But what I think—" He nipped at a bruise with his teeth, holding her hands down on the bed as she jerked in pain. "—and what I could 'plainly see' was you brazenly cautioning your lover to keep his distance. 'Tis not seemly to flirt at the porch of a church on a Sunday, even for a sly London whore."

He bit her again more roughly. Phillipa cried out.

"No!"

"'No,' strumpet? Go on with your pleas of innocence then, I beg you. A pity your sex is banned from the stage. Women would make the best actors—so convincing are they in the telling of their lies, they could fool all the world."

He squeezed a handful of her flesh as if to force the words to burst from her mouth. Tears flooded her face as she made a renewed attempt to defend herself from the groundless accusations.

"The man is naught to me but our neighbour, and your own good friend! Why do you name me as a wanton? As God is my witness, I am none. What can I say to please you? The more truth I speak, the less you hear—"

Calverley continued as though she had not spoken.

"I know not why it took me thus long to discover

your lover's name. It could be none other but Leventhorpe." He crushed her breasts hard in his hands. "With your high-bred tastes for all that is fine, you would hardly spread your legs to lowly sheep farmers. You would want your sons to have a noble bloodline—though they be bastards."

He grinned at her stricken expression. Phillipa's voice caught in her throat, and she could only shake her head violently in wordless protest. He talked to her like he was admonishing a small child.

"How could you think to hide the secret from me? I am your lord and husband. I will always find you out."

He pulled his shirt off and crouched over her body.

"Did you sully this very bed with him, whore? No matter. He has had his last fill of you—that I can promise."

Calverley pulled her thighs apart and thrust himself inside with a rough cry of triumph. He pinned her aching, unresisting arms over her head and bit a new mark into her shoulder alongside a fading bruise. Phillipa turned her head aside and concentrated her gaze upon a carved face on the bedpost. The image of the grimacing bearded man danced in the light of the guttering candle, and she imagined that she could almost hear its obscene laugh of approval at the coarse scene being played out before its wooden eyes. A thankfully brief period of time passed before Calverley bellowed his pleasure. Having proven himself her master, he rolled off to one side and fell immediately into a deep sleep. Phillipa pulled the coverlet back over her abused body and curled herself into a tight ball as far away from her husband as the confines of the bed would allow. Sleep for her was impossible.

Bad turned to worse. Lord, how could it be so?

A crushing pang of defeat sat on Phillipa's chest like a lead weight. All around her the family was falling into ruin. Her dowry had long since vanished, and her jewellery had been taken piece by piece from her silver casket to be sold. She was never informed: her hand would reach for a particular brooch or ring and find it gone. All she had left was her wedding ring and her garnet cross—a relic of her grandmother's that never left the chain around her neck. As time went on, the silver casket itself went missing. It was much the same story below stairs. The best wedding silver—a prized pair of engraved goblets and a charger—was nowhere to be found. Saying nothing, Phillipa instead drank her wine from pewter goblets. One day, even those had been replaced at table by horn cups—and she dared not pass comment as the increasingly meagre meals were served on simple wooden trenchers fit for peasants.

Lord knows I would begrudge him nothing, if it meant the debts were answered. But they grow, and with them his madness to keep his sins alive.

That past fall, she'd been returning home from a visit with the newborn Henry when she was greeted by the strange sight of three large wagons parked hard by the Great Hall entrance door. She'd paused unseen on the slope to watch. Calverley stood by as sweating labourers emerged from the Hall hauling out the heavy oak ancestral furniture and loading it onto the backs of the wagons. The colourful tapestries were rolled and sitting in the smallest wagon on top of the benches and chairs. Even the great long dining table—one that had for two centuries dominated the Calverley family's grandest room—was broken down to be taken away. She rushed to her husband's side but stopped in her tracks as he turned to regard her coldly.

"I looked not for you to return so early, Madam."

He bowed to her curtly then turned his back, dismissing her. Phillipa had not the heart to return to the Great Hall since that day. She did not care to witness how barren the room must have become.

The household was diminished in spirit and bodies alike: of the half-dozen house servants they'd once employed, only her Sarah remained. The poor girl was not above seventeen and of slight build. She'd struggled valiantly to adjust, taking on the combined chores of housekeeper, nanny, cook and lady's maid all without complaint. Phillipa loved her for such selfless loyalty. She shared the duties as best she could, but her privileged upbringing had left her woefully ill equipped to be of much use. Phillipa was a deft hand at needlework and well trained in music, but these were not skills that contributed to keeping a manor house in order. Between them, they could just manage. Phillipa lived in constant worry that one day she would wake to find her sole female comfort gone: she could hardly be blamed if she did leave such an endlessly demanding and melancholy household.

Lord, bless and preserve my Sarah.

Calverley held back a single manservant for his own use. John was a brawny, ruddy-faced lad of eighteen, originally hired to see to the stables and grounds keeping. He now bore the added duty of acting as a kind of steward to his master; a job he handled with an earnest clumsiness. A shy youth, he seemed happiest when doing manual labour around the Hall's grounds, and preferred the company of horses and dogs to people. He had been run to rags in the past months trying to cover the duties of three men. Unlike the mistress of the house, Calverley was not kindly disposed to share in the work burden. Sarah was often seen at John's side in the kitchen garden, her slender back bent to the task as she hoed and dug with as much vigour as John himself displayed. Sarah had blushingly confessed to Phillipa that the two of them had made a pledge: to stay at the Hall as long as they were able for the sake of their Mistress and her bairns—and for the growing love they had for each other.

But in the end, despite such devoted protestations, they were only servants. The time would come when Calverley would send them away rather than pay their wages, and she would have no power to stop him. Phillipa would be alone.

Lord, what will become of us? All will away, if my hus-

band does not cease in his riot to consume both his credit and his house...

Calverley was snoring loudly at her side. She could bear lying in his bed no longer. Rising, she pulled on her shift and a woollen shawl and descended to sit quietly with her thoughts in the stillness of the Solar wing's main chamber. She set a few small logs on the weak orange embers in the fireplace to encourage a blaze and drew a low stool close to the heat within easy reach to use the poker if the flames threatened to die out. Dawn was hours away. To pass the time, Phillipa once again combed over her marriage's history—searching for a clue to this state of dissolution. If she could find the root, perhaps she could discover a way to turn it right again.

How have we become so lost?

The isolation she felt was unbearable. The extended Calverley family was a large one, and most lived close by in neighbouring ridings; but none of these could be counted as Phillipa's friends. Her husband would have no contact with his brothers and sisters, except for his next youngest brother, William, away at Oxford studying to join the clergy. For all their proximity, the rest of his family might well be dead as far as he was concerned: he'd had little to do with them since his father died, leaving Sir Walter a minor of seventeen and a ward of the Courts.

And a pawn to the social ambitions of his widowed mother, Katherine.

The Court of Wards and Liveries placed young Walter under the legal guardianship of a local wealthy family until he reached the age of twenty-one—and a bargain was made to secure the substantial income of the Calverley estate for the local Gargrave family by arranging a betrothal between their ward and their daughter, Mary. A dowry of fifteen hundred pounds was agreed upon. Permission to marry was sought from the Master of the Court of Wards in London: Phillipa's cousin, Sir Robert Cecil.

On paper, young Calverley appeared to be a most eligible bachelor. Cecil had brought him to the attention of Phillipa's mother, Lady Anne Brooke, and a new deal was struck to make a bid for the young man and his attendant wealth of Yorkshire landholdings. Sir Walter was summoned to London and offered Phillipa with her lesser dowry of a thousand pounds. Social ambition won the day. Katherine pressed her son to accept the new deal and bring the glamour and influence of the London Court to the family name. The guardianship was transferred to the Brookes, and his previous attachments with the Gargraves were hastily severed. Heartbroken, Mary Gargrave had never married. Her well-connected family had met the Calverleys' eventual return North with coldness and—between their hostility and her husband's lack of warmth for his own family—the couple had found little social intercourse with any of the country's gentry, except the Leventhorpes.

Perhaps the jilted girl Mary hath turned to witchcraft

and cursed our house.

Phillipa crossed herself and prayed forgiveness for such a wicked and uncharitable thought. Poor Mary could hardly be to blame for their troubles. If anything, they were being punished for Calverley's cruelty in turning her aside.

The demons of revelry had begun circling Calverley early in their marriage. He'd been lonely in London society—viewed as a lost country bumpkin. The great city's Royal Court was quite literally the centre of the world, swirling with noisy distractions and temptations he'd never encountered in the quiet countryside of West Yorkshire. Phillipa truly loved her new husband: it pained her to see him so at odds among the elegant, courtly crowd. He was a standout with his rough manners and his unstylish mode of dress. He'd confessed to her one night in bed that his Northern accent jangled harshly even to his own ears, and that he knew nothing of the politics and fashions of the London scene.

He once used to tell me his troubles. Now all is but silence… or worse.

Sir Walter's social 'salvation' came in the form of the high-stakes gambling and gaming so wildly popular with the young men of the Court. Only in these circles did Calverley find anything approaching acceptance with his haughty peers, and he threw himself in wholeheartedly. Inexperience and a weak will proved to be a most dangerous combination.

Debts had soon begun to mount, and rumours of

Calverley's reckless behaviour started to circulate. The Brookes' disgraced Northern son-in-law was an unwelcome embarrassment in London. Lady Brooke pressed him to place still more of the Calverley estate under her family's trust, and Sir Walter in his humiliation had retreated with his new bride to the familiarity of his Yorkshire homestead. He blamed his manipulative mother for forcing upon him the choice that had left him in his troubled state. For her part, Katherine had been informed of her son's wild habits. Sir Walter had outrun his course of usefulness, and she refused to pass any further wealth to her eldest son. He'd been played as a bargaining chip to secure mutually beneficial ties between their two wealthy families. Now he found himself distrusted and scorned on both sides.

Calverley's reaction to the betrayal had been swift and decisive. He immediately cut all communication and referred to his mother as 'the toothless bitch' and his nearby brothers and sisters as 'her litter of whelps.' Even his brother William—whose letters from Oxford he had once taken delight in reading to her aloud—was no longer accessible to Phillipa. If any missives arrived, Calverley now kept them to himself.

Neither of them had a friend left in the world. Her husband seemed to have run out of scapegoats as well—and now Phillipa unfairly found she was blamed as the sole cause and centre of all his misfortunes.

I should have seen that one who can despise his own family would soon hate me too. He calls me a whore.

Drawing her shawl tightly around her shoulders, Phillipa pulled her stool closer to the fireside. Nothing seemed to ease her chill, just as no answer could be found to ease her base spirits. Only a few days before as she sat sewing by that same fireplace, a letter from London had arrived at the Hall. The news within had presented what seemed to her to be a perfect solution to their desperate state. Fresh tears sprang to her eyes at the pity of it being so brutally rejected by her husband. He had turned his back on the one last hope for himself and his sons, and had taken Phillipa down to a more wretched level than she could have thought possible.

• • •

A few weeks before, Calverley approached her with a plan.

"Come, my lady. We have a letter to write."

His tone was gentle. He'd not addressed her so kindly in ages—in fact, he had barely spoken to her at all—so Phillipa was more than willing to comply. He led her to the table in the Solar wing and sat her down before setting out a quill and a fresh page of parchment.

"Think you: may we depend upon your family's enduring affection?"

"To be sure, my mother's letters speak of naught but love."

In truth? Her too-infrequent letters I needs must burn, lest my husband read of her contempt for what he has become...

"Very good." Standing behind her, Calverley placed

his hands upon her shoulders. "Then we shall put her to the test, and see if she has charity in her purse as well as her heart. I am loath to make any direct request of your family of vipers—it is meet to come from the pen of a beloved daughter rather than such a *'wayward'* son-in-law."

As he dictated, Phillipa added her own touches and composed a carefully worded cry for assistance.

"Hast thou done yet? Read it me."

"'I know not where to turn, but to you, my dearest Mother. I should be happy with the three lovely boys that I have been Blessed withal, but they have no Wordly Prospects but Beggary and Misery if their loving Grandmother and good Cousin Sir Robert does not show them Christian Charity.

"'My Husband continues to dote upon me as ever, and is an excellent and loving Father to his sons. Indeed, he is faultless but for the missteps he hath taken in the waywardness and inexperience of Youth. Ill-advised financial moves have brought our household to the brink of Ruin, and no solution can be found.'"

(I shall make no mention of his gambling, whoring or cruel neglect. That cannot win my cause.)

"'My dearest Husband is so sick with worry that he nightly paces the floors and will not sleep. I fear a melancholy Ague may settle upon him and claim his very Life, leaving myself and our poor children Destitute.

"'He is too proud to ask for your Help. I make this Petition on his behalf, and for the sake of our boys. He knows nothing of this Plea. I pray to God that you may find it in your Heart to assist us in this our Darkest time.'"

Calverley grunted in approval.

"Good, good... I like it well. It has about it an air of conspiracy that should greatly appeal to one such as your mother. No doubt but she shall fly to your worthy cousin Cecil and secure us the funds."

He squeezed her shoulders hard enough to leave an imprint of his fingers.

"This must not fail, or all is indeed lost."

She sealed the letter with candle-wax dripped by an unsteady hand.

Phillipa had spent the weeks waiting for her mother's reply in earnest prayer. Calverley Hall boasted a private chapel from its Catholic past, and she'd knelt in the cool white-washed room for hours on end, her eyes fixed on the plain Reform cross set into a nook in the wall, and begged God to send a solution to their miseries.

It had been more than a month when a courier finally arrived at the Hall on the previous Thursday afternoon, bearing the news from London. Calverley had not been at home. Phillipa had set the sealed letter on the table in the Solar. Pacing up and down the length of the room, she'd chewed her fingernails to the quick in her impatience for her husband's return so that she might learn its contents. It had grown too much to bear and she'd given in to her restlessness, justifying to herself that as she had no guarantee that Calverley would even come home that night, she had no other choice.

She sat. She broke the seal. She read her mother's words.

Late into the night of the letter's arrival, Phillipa kept a light burning upstairs in their bedchamber, waiting her husband's return from the gaming tables. Despite the unaccustomed hour, she was far too excited to sleep. She knelt in the centre of the bed and greeted him with a smile when he at last entered the room.

Calverley stood in the doorway for a long moment and regarded her in silence. Happiness and hope radiated in her beauty: her hair hung loose in mahogany waves down her back, her cotton shift had slipped off one shoulder, and her skin—which had of late grown sallow with worry—glowed rosily in the candlelight and the flames from the fire. He slowly returned her smile.

"So, my lady—I see we have had our reply. Welcome news?"

Phillipa nodded, holding out her arms, and Calverley stepped into her embrace. He lifted her from the bed and swung her about like a girl, laughing as she squealed and tightened her arms about his neck. He set her down and held her at arm's length, closely examining her happy upturned face—her eyes half-closed and expectant of a rewarding kiss. Though she could smell wine on his breath, she was glad to see that his gaze was alert and sharply focused.

"Well?" He chucked her under the chin and looked around the room. "Where's the money? How much did they send? Let me see it. Have you already locked it away?"

He dropped her hands and went to the oak cabinet by the front window. Fumbling with the key, he opened the leather box that sat on top and squinted in at the contents with a furrowed brow. He hefted the box's weight and gave it a shake. The coins jangling inside were pitifully few in number.

"Why, there is no more here than I had this morning. Where hast thou hidden it?"

He strode to the large carved chest at the foot of the bed. Phillipa raced to sit on its lid, preventing his opening it. The effort of containing her imminent announcement caused her to wriggle like an excited young child.

"There is no money to be found within either, my lord."

"Where, then? Do not toy with me, woman. Have I not waited long enough?"

"There is no new money—not anywhere in the whole house."

Calverley's face darkened.

"Then what devil doth possess thee to smile and greet me thus when the news is not good?"

"Bear me out in patience and hear me speak, sir. My news is good indeed, dear husband."

"I pray you speak it, for I am most curious to learn

how any news other than a heavy bag full of sovereigns can be named by you as *'good.'*"

Phillipa smiled up at his frowning countenance. Sliding from her seat to the floor, she padded barefoot to the cabinet and retrieved her cousin Sir Robert Cecil's precious letter. Calverley took her place on the high chest with his arms crossed. As he restively swung one leg, the back of his booted foot steadily drummed against the wood. Phillipa stood bravely in the face of his impatience and presented her news.

"As thou shalt hear presently, this reply bears far more value than a mere bag of coins."

Thuk… thuk… thuk… pounded Calverley's heel on the side of the chest. Phillipa cleared her throat and continued.

"My mother and cousin believed my report of thy mild kindness to me—"

Thuk… thuk…

"—They have taken pity on us for our debts, and would not see our children suffer. Though I made no mention, they did rightly guess that thou hadst fallen back into your gambling ways—"

The drumming increased in urgency.

"—and as Cousin Cecil owns a share in thy financial interests, he is kept informed of the steady increase in land sales and new mortgages. Indeed, he knows far better than I of the true state of affairs."

Calverley glowered at her with unblinking eyes, the boot still beating out an ominous tattoo. Phillipa's anxiety grew and she hurried to finish her explanation, forced near to shouting to be heard above the racket.

"He writes that to pour more coins into our laps would in the end solve nothing, and so—"

She paused to draw a deep, shaky breath and delivered the heart of the matter.

"—he hath instead provided for thee a place at Court."

The drumming abruptly ceased. Phillipa laughed at her husband's surprised visage and held out the letter containing the further details for him to read. He made no move to take the papers from her hand.

"'Tis a goodly position of great worth and credit, which will see us on solid footing. We shall be provided with fine London lodgings and a handsome steady income. The boys shall have the best tutors when it comes time for their schooling. Oh, my love—is it not joyous news indeed? We are saved!"

Phillipa climbed onto her husband's lap and hugged him hard around the neck.

Calverley leapt to his feet and sent her tumbling to the floor. He towered over her as she lay in a confused heap, her hand still proffering the letter to him.

"Didst not hear? A goodly place at Court—"

Calverley's boot shot out and kicked her squarely in the ribs one—two—three times. He rolled her over onto her back with the tip of his toe like she was no more to him than an unsavoury mound of garbage. Too winded and shocked to cry out, Phillipa lay stock-still and gulped for air.

"Stupid whore!"

He landed another vicious kick then pressed his dirty boot on the base of her bare throat. Phillipa's hands flew up to prevent her windpipe from being crushed. Her eyes bulged as she struggled for breath. Calverley shouted down at her with a shower of spittle, punctuating each of his points with a downward thrust of his foot on her neck.

"Hear me, you base slut—I will *not* be dragged back to London to be made a Court fool! I will *not* have my pleasures stolen from me, and be forced into servitude for a pack of the King's fops and dusty old councilors! And I will *never* again be displaced from these my father's lands!"

Phillipa could not breathe. At last, he jerked his foot from her throat and she drew in a ragged sob of air.

"But the offer is but kindly meant! It is to help—"

"Yes, I see only too well how this vile offer would 'help.' It would help *thee* back into the company of thy fancy courtiers to play freely amid a circle of lovers—whilst I, cap in hand, would be made to bow and scrape before the very men who make me a cuckold! Look you not forget: they are the self-same cheating bastards who tricked my fortune from me with their crooked gambling—all the while pretending friendship as they sent me willy-nilly toward my ruin."

Phillipa cowered and curled her arms over her head to cushion her skull from any further kicks. Further speech was pointless. Nothing she could say would persuade him to see reason, and would only provoke his wrath. Calverley reached down and grabbed her by the wrists. Wrenching her to her feet, he marched her backwards across the room and trapped her up against the wall.

"I have done with playing the pawn, mistress. I would see us all dead of hunger and buried in good Yorkshire soil before I am made to lick shit from the boots of your precious London lords and dukes."

Calverley lashed out again with his heavy feet and kicked her legs out from under her body. Wailing, Phillipa sunk to the floorboards and closed her eyes so that she need not watch the final, killing blow.

Nothing further happened. She heard him step back, panting hard. Apparently satisfied with having driven home his point, he stormed from the chamber and left the Hall.

Sir Walter had not been seen within the walls again until that Sunday morning, when he'd returned at dawn and ordered his wife and son to church.

* * *

The embers of the fire grew cold toward dawn. Phillipa's recollections had once again borne no fruit—not a glimmer of hope for salvation came to ease her mind. Exhausted, she had no will to stoke the flames again, and let the poker slip from her grasp to the floor. It was nearly time to summon Sarah and get dressed. Outside, early birds greeted the first light, signalling the approach of a new day.

God only knew what fresh grief was held in store.

That which some women call great misery would show but little here, would scarce be seen among my miseries. I may compare for wretched fortunes with all wives that are. Nothing will please him until all be nothing. He calls it slavery to be preferred—a place of credit, a base servitude.

What will become of us?

CHAPTER EIGHT

Phillipa kept the boys in their bedchamber that morning to breakfast with Sarah. She could hear her husband pacing the floors of the Solar wing where they usually dined, and the sound of his boots on the flagstones made her shudder. No doubt he would leave the Hall before long to run riot. Though she regretted no longer taking meals as a family, at least he could not upset the children by flying into a rage before them at the table. Calverley did not seem to eat at all of late, preferring only a cup of ale or wine at midmorning.

William left his stool to lean against his mother's

knee.

"May we visit with Henry today?"

Phillipa's heart lurched at the mention of her infant's name. She had not been able to make the short journey to visit her youngest at the wet nurse's home since last week's beating. Jane and her husband, Stephen Carver, were a happy couple with a large cluster of small, rambunctious children: all noisily crammed together cheek by jowl in their modest cottage, they seemed content enough. Phillipa would almost be sorry to see Henry weaned. The excuse of visiting him had provided her with her only real escape from the melancholy of life at the Hall, and William and Walt loved tagging along to play with the other wee ones. Once the ties there were broken—as soon they must be—the children would lose their only playmates.

Poor Will shall be so lonesome. 'Tis unlikely he shall continue friends with young Edward—not after the mad accusations levelled against his father.

Phillipa banished the unhappy thoughts to the back of her mind and smiled down into the face of her eldest son.

"Splendid idea, my love. We shall leave after we have breakfasted."

Will's eyes lit up.

"Shall my Papa come too?"

"No, Will. Your father is too burdened by duty to take the time."

Will sagged against her knee with a whine of disappointment.

"Father *never* comes to see Henry."

"Perhaps another day. Look thee not so sad! Sarah shall join us, and little Walter. Walt has been sorry to have been ill and miss out on his visits. Right, my sweeting?"

She tickled Walt's feet, and he laughed and gave a little sneeze. Sarah rushed to wipe his nose.

Outside came the sounds of a swiftly approaching horseman toward the front of the Hall. Young William and Walter hurried to the window, standing on tiptoe and peering out through the smudged diamond-shaped panes of glass. Phillipa rose stiffly and stood watching behind them as Calverley came out to meet the visitor. She did not recognize the man or his mount. The figure on horseback was so mud-splattered that it was impossible to determine what colour his garments might truly have been. The black steed hung its head and gave a weary snort. A great distance must have been covered. The stranger did not dismount: he exchanged a few words with her husband, produced a letter from the leather bag at his side and handed it down to Calverley. Curtly, he nodded his thanks as he accepted a coin for his trouble but was apparently offered no rest or refreshment. The messenger rode off, turning south at the stone gateposts of the Hall. Calverley watched him go, staring down at the letter in his hand for a long moment before he turned and slowly returned to the Hall.

"Who was that man, Mama?"

"I know not, Will. I shall go to thy father and discover what news has been delivered."

The morning's earlier chill returned in a rush and bit down to Phillipa's bones. It seemed of late that all letters brought nothing but further miseries; even the most glad of tidings were soured and twisted by her husband's dark mind. Her cracked ribs throbbed under her own embrace. Touching the soft curls on the heads of her darlings, she found enough strength to venture downstairs and attempt to unearth the nature of the message. She left Sarah to dress the boys and descended to the Solar wing.

Calverley stood before the fire, turning the letter over and over in his hand. The seal was still unbroken. From across the room, Phillipa recognized the looping script as the handwriting of her brother-in-law William and felt a hopeful wave of cheer.

She scuffled her feet deliberately on the flagstones to announce her entry into the chamber. Wearing a grey pallor on his cheeks, Calverley spun around at the noise and regarded her with a blank expression, returning her formal curtsy to him with a stiff half-bow. His eyes were half-closed as he touched a hand to his temple, seeking to soothe the headache that was certainly plaguing him as it did every other morning of late. Nothing in his manner suggested that he recalled the events of the previous night, and she felt it safe to approach. It was too early for the beasts of drink and cruelty to have taken firm hold of him just yet.

"What news, my lord?"

Her voice was steady and she held herself back cautiously beyond his arm's length. Calverley locked his unreadable gaze upon her face but made no reply. She took a small step closer and indicated the letter with a gesture.

"This writ is from our brother William, is it not? How doth he fare? I pray thee, sir, I have sorely missed hearing his gossip of Oxford, and it hath been too long since you have read his words aloud to me."

Phillipa took her accustomed place on the stool beside Calverley's armchair and touched the seat to invite her husband over.

Calverley held eye contact with her as he flicked his wrist and mutely tossed the unopened letter onto the fire. Gasping, Phillipa instinctively put out a hand as if she might prevent the destruction, but she sat too far from the fireplace to reach the letter. She watched as the edges curled and blackened, the melting wax seal hissing as the words were engulfed by the flames.

Her husband's mouth twitched into a smirk. He made a low, courtly bow with an exaggerated flourish of his hand and strolled past her through the heavy oak door into the Great Hall. He was well ensured of his solitude. Phillipa would not follow, and no other members of the household cared to venture there. Murky shadows in the corners and the imposing height of the hammer-beamed ceilings looming twenty feet above filled the boys with fear. The servants, too, had no need to enter: now that the days of entertainment at the Hall were over, they were not required to clean or heat the space. The huge chamber had been abandoned to dust and darkness.

Calverley haunted the place. It seemed to be the only room in the Hall fit to contain his rages and his hours of obsessive pacing.

Phillipa sighed and took up the smock she was embroidering for little Walt from the sewing basket by her stool. Black fragments of the burned letter fluttered upwards, disturbed by her restless movements and the air stirred up by her husband slamming the door in his wake. She willed her mind to go blank as she bowed her head over her work and tried to concentrate on the stitches. It was not enough to distract her from morbid thoughts. Tears welled up as she clumsily gouged her finger with her needle, spotting the child's garment with blood and spoiling her hours of tedious labour. She let it fall from her hands to the floor and kicked in into a heap with her toe. It seemed such a meaningless task while her life was in disarray.

A tentative knock on the outside door brought Phillipa back to herself. Wiping the tears away on her sleeve, she bid entry to John. He gave an awkward bow and addressed her in his deep, mumbling voice.

"Beggin' yer pardon, Mistress, but there is a gentleman from the university at Oxford come to speak with the Master. Is he not with ye? I'd just left him here after I built up the fire."

He looked about the room as if Calverley would magically appear from behind the furniture. Phillipa rose.

"The university?" She frowned at the ashes left by the letter, now more curious than before to know the contents. "Show the gentleman in to the fireside, John. He must be weary after such a journey."

John bobbed his head and vanished back outside. Phillipa sucked the blood from her fingertip.

Strange. I did not hear his approach—It needs must be William, who else? A tall stranger in a black riding cloak entered and gave an elegant bow to Phillipa. She returned a polite curtsy, fighting to hold back her confusion at the sight of the man. This could not be her unmet brother-in-law: his beard was grey. He was old enough to be her husband's father.

"Sir Charles Richardson, Madam. Master of Jesus College at Oxford."

"You are welcome, sir."

The rich Southern tones of his accent were a familiar music to her ears, but Phillipa was chilled by his unaccountable presence in her home. She turned to John, who hovered uncertainly in the doorway.

"Take our guest's hat and cloak and see if you might remove some of the mud. Then fetch Sir Walter from the Great Hall."

Favouring the stranger with a tense smile, she indicated her husband's armchair with a quavering hand.

"Please you to sit, sir."

Richardson sat and ran his fingers through his thick, greying hair. He returned her smile tersely and addressed her formally in the resonant voice of a practised lecturer.

"I fear I am come on most urgent business, Madam. I must speak with your husband on grave matters concerning the welfare of his brother."

"Is William unwell?"

"He is well enough in body, be assured." His voice grew stern. "But I warrant that his future is every bit in doubt as that of a man upon his deathbed… as I am sure you can well imagine, given the circumstance."

"Oh—?"

Phillipa lowered herself with a wince onto her stool. The Master raised his heavy eyebrows in question.

"You seem greatly puzzled, Madam, at my being here: and yet both your brother William and myself have written more than once of my intent to visit."

"There have been messages, yes… one even just this morning. But—"

"We have been barred in our attempts to resolve the

matter at a distance. Your husband's obstinate refusal to favour me with a response to repeated appeals has left me little choice but to make this journey, and seek satisfaction face-to-face for his brother."

"My husband is a private man, sir. He keeps his troubles locked within."

Richardson gave a mirthless chuckle.

"His brother, too, is *'locked within'* by these self-same troubles: he lies imprisoned."

"Imprisoned? Why?"

"He hath stood himself in bond for your husband's debts. As the money is lacking to answer the creditors, William Calverley now pays for his brother's neglect with his very freedom."

Phillipa reeled in her seat. The Master put out his hands, preventing her falling to the floor, and she clutched hard at his wrists to steady herself.

"I knew not of this! How could I? My husband hath concealed his brother's letters—or else burnt them before my face. I am told nothing."

Richardson stood, his face reddened in anger. Knotting his hands into fists behind his back, he paced the length of the room.

"He is a fool to be the cause of such misery—both to such a loyal wife and his own pious brother. William Calverley is one of the true hopes of our university. He needs be cut free of these bonds or his excellence for the greater good is lost."

Phillipa fixed her eyes downward on her lap. John rapped once on the door and entered, too flustered to remember to bow.

"I am dreadful sorry, Mistress, but I canna find the Master anywhere. I searched in the Great Hall as ye bid, and in all th'out-buildin's. His horse is still in the stable, so he must not have gone far. Do ye want me to go through the village and search him out?"

Where could he be gone to at this hour? Sure 'tis far too early for the tavern or the dicing tables. Unless—

Phillipa recalled his drunken promise on the previous night of his intention to 'deal' with Leventhorpe. The idea that he had gone to confront their innocent neighbour with charges of adultery crept upon her like an icy hand on the back of her neck.

"No, John. I have a sense of where he may be found. I shall go myself. Instruct Sarah that she is to take the children to see their brother—without me."

Rising, she turned to Richardson.

"Please forgive the sorry lack of welcome, but you must believe me when I say that I was not forewarned of your visit. John shall fetch you some cheese and ale. I hope not to tarry long, sir."

Her mind too unsettled to heed any of her bodily pains, she snatched her cloak down from its hook by the door and hurried from the Hall.

* * *

Lord, let it not be too late.

Phillipa stood at the crossroads at the bottom of the hill and fruitlessly cast her eyes about for any sign of her husband. There was no time to lose by staying on the road, so she stepped gingerly through the ditch by the churchyard and took a short cut to the Leventhorpe's estate through the fields along a narrow path at the edge of Calverley Wood. The grey stone Leventhorpe Hall—smaller by half than Calverley Hall—was clearly visible high on the ridge of the next hill. Ignoring the distress in her aching legs, Phillipa willed herself to move as quickly as possible.

Would that I could fly…

A rustling sound a few yards up the path gave Phillipa pause. She cocked her head, listening, but the sound had ceased. Thinking it must have been a fox in the underbrush, she continued on. A twig snapped. *No animal is that clumsy.* Phillipa peered into the shadows to see what at first glance appeared to be a bundle of clothing lying in the shade of the hedgerow. The bundle was moving. Sounds now came more clearly to her ears. Voices: a woman's raised in laughing protest at a man's playful commands. Their half-clothed bodies were moving in a rhythmic tandem.

Mortified, Phillipa stopped. She glanced back over her shoulder, but it was much too far to return to the main road and go around the long way. Treading quietly, she attempted to enter the woods in order to slip undetected around the entwined lovers—but she could find no readily accessible break in the hedgerow, and the forest was too dense to easily negotiate off the path: it would take her twice as long to reach Leventhorpe Hall if she tried to go through the trees. God alone knew what could happen between her husband and Sir Thomas in the meantime. Taking a deep breath, she tugged her skirts free from a thorny tangle of bushes. There was no choice but to pass close by the bawdy couple.

Phillipa stepped from the path farther out into the field. The way was too muddy and full of deep water-filled ruts from the recent heavy rain and she could not get her footing by that route. Try as she might, she'd not be able to avoid walking virtually on top of the sweethearts. She modestly averted her eyes as she drew near. Her own foot snapped a twig with a loud *crack*, and the woman gave a cry of surprise.

"Oh! Someone approaches. Please, sir, let me hide myself!"

"Lie still! I care not. I have not yet done with thee, lass."

Phillipa froze in place at the sound of the familiar voice. Slowly, she turned her gaze toward the jumble of half-naked flesh. The woman twisted her face aside in a vain attempt to conceal her identity as she struggled to extricate herself from underneath her insistent lover. Phillipa could see enough to recognize Sir Walter's jilted former betrothed, Mary Gargrave.

Calverley made no pause in his enjoyable labour and panted heavily as he continued to pound between her splayed thighs. He threw back his head to shoot a defiant look of challenge at the interloper. Surprised, he stopped in mid-thrust and locked gazes with Phillipa. He smiled—then resumed his coupling at double the pace, laughing at both Phillipa's shock and Mary's throaty exclamations of mingled shame and delight.

Phillipa stood her ground and waited until her husband shouted his pleasure and pulled out of the redfaced woman. He landed a jaunty slap on Mary's thigh as she tugged her skirts down and scrambled to hide in the shadows of the trees. Rising, Sir Walter shamelessly tucked himself away without bothering to turn his back. He scooped up his muddied cloak from the ground where it had served as a makeshift bed and ambled over to his wife, stretching out his arms in a theatrical gesture of contentment.

"Well, Madam? Why dost not fly at me in a fit of jealous rage? Dost thou not love me enough to upbraid me for my brazen wanderings?"

Phillipa's face was a stone mask. Calverley lay a hand over his breast in a mock show of remorse. Rolling his eyes upward, he addressed the heavens.

"Ah, Lord! Her silence speaks as loud as thunder: she loves me not."

He dropped the playful edge from his voice.

"Thou art are wise not to pass judgment, Mistress.

Though I lack thy subtlety in my trysts, I merely act as thou hast done with my esteemed neighbour." He nodded in the direction of Leventhorpe Hall. "Is that your destination, my lady?"

"Is it not yours, sir?"

"I freely confess, 'twas my intent to pay a call upon my dear friend Tom 'til I had the fortune to be set upon by this delightful creature. She still dotes upon me, poor wench, and oft times wanders the fields in sad distraction."

He smiled over at Mary, who had reassembled her dress and was vanishing hurriedly into the woods through a small break in the underbrush, heedless of the scratching twigs and brambles. Calverley turned back to Phillipa and regarded her coldly through narrowed eyes.

"I should have insisted on keeping my original bargain with Mary rather than bending to the will of other influences. I am well punished for my mistake."

Spitting on the ground at Phillipa's feet, he started in the direction of Leventhorpe Hall.

"Will you not accompany me, Madam? No doubt but this meeting shall have much to hold your interest."

Casually, Sir Walter touched a gloved hand to his left hip. Phillipa followed the motion with her eyes and saw that he wore a long, bone-handled dagger in his hilt. She gave shudder and struggled to speak in a steady voice.

"Sir, I came merely in search of you. There is a Master of Jesus College but newly arrived at the Hall. He awaits within, bearing most urgent news of your brother at Oxford."

Clutching his dagger's hilt, Calverley turned back, sneering at the solemn expression on her face.

"Speakest thou the truth? I warn thee: do not hope to divert me from my revenge with lies."

"I swear by God in Heaven that I speak true."

His eyes blazed into hers, but Phillipa did not allow herself to falter. Blanching, he released his grip on his dagger and let his hand fall limply by his side. All former bravado fled as he addressed the turf.

"So. It hath come to this."

Calverley covered his face with both hands, his fingers digging deeply into his flesh. He stood still for a moment gathering himself, then straightened up to his full height and returned to Phillipa's side, taking her firmly by the arm and steering her down the sloping field back toward the village and Calverley Hall.

"Let us go to our guest, Madam. We shall visit your lover together another time."

* * *

Calverley strode into the Solar wing with Phillipa in tow, and found the sombre College Master seated by the fire. Richardson rose as the couple entered the chamber. Released from her husband's vise grip, Phillipa slipped into the shadows by the door and listened intently as the men began their business.

"Sir! You are most heartily welcome!"

Unmoved, Richardson's pale blue eyes flicked down at Calverley's proffered handshake. His own hands remained tightly clasped before him as he gave his host a slight, barely civil bow of his head.

"You must pardon me, sir, if I mistrust your words."

Calverley's smile faded in the face of Richardson's glare.

"No matter, sir. I am not come to be made welcome but to speak with you of urgent affairs concerning my student and your brother, William Calverley."

Richardson raked his sharp eyes over Calverley's dishevelled state. Noting the dirt and grass stains on the knees of his breeches he raised an eyebrow, and then paused as he noticed Phillipa huddled silently in the doorway. Calverley followed his gaze and waved a dismissive hand in his wife's direction.

"Thank you, Madam. You may leave us."

Phillipa curtsied in keeping with the formal tone and retreated out of sight to the halfway point of the stairwell. From there, she could plainly hear the men's voices as they conversed in the chamber below. Richardson spoke first.

"To the purpose: I have given ample warning—as has your brother—of the danger inherent in the lamentable circumstances now fast upon him. William hath shown admirable fealty by his willingness to stand in bond in surety for the repayment of your debts, but his loyalty is answered only by cruel neglect. As was forewarned, the creditors have called in the bond and your brother is now confined to gaol. He cannot hope to repay the sum of one thousand pounds."

"Marry, 'tis considerable—"

Phillipa could hear Calverley's boots scuffle as he paced the chamber. She leaned her head heavily against the wall and squeezed her eyelids shut.

"Agreed. And now he waits imprisoned, all pleas for your assistance ignored. I stand here before you as his representative shadow to make his case. What is your answer? Is your dear brother's hopes for a future in the Church to be snuffed out in the cold cell of a debtors' gaol?"

Calverley cleared his throat, but made no reply.

"I implore that you think not only upon his life, but of the countless eternal souls he might deliver to redemption—if only he can be freed to follow his vocation."

"Ah! Lord—"

Richardson raised his voice a level.

"Come, sir! How shall I answer for you? Will you restore hope, or heap misery upon your most valiant brother? Your long silence hath been barbarous. He daily awaits a reply with unshakable faith, and I will not see him suffer further torments. So valued is he at Jesus College that I myself have undertaken this journey in order to see him rest satisfied. I shall not return 'til you have supplied me with the means to secure his release."

"Alas, my poor brother—"

Phillipa turned and silently crept up the few remaining stone stairs, her hands supporting her heavy progress. She could not bear to stay and hear her husband's answer.

How indeed might William be satisfied? Lord help us all.

There was no money. That could only mean prison for one or the other. Quite possibly both brothers could be locked away—and with them, all of the family's waning hopes. The only option would be the sale of whatever holdings Calverley still had in his possession, and she feared he no longer owned anything but the very Hall in which they lived. There would be nothing left.

We are ruined.

Phillipa's breath came in ragged sobs as she reached the top of the stairs. Thankful that her boys were not at home to witness her despair, she stepped through the door leading from her chamber to the upper level of the private chapel and sank to her knees. She pressed her forehead hard against the carved wooden screen and peered down through the slats at the cross on the far wall below. Her lips moved, but no words came forth. There were no prayers that she had not already repeated a thousand times over, and all to no good effect.

She had nothing more to say to God.

• • •

The children returned with Sarah in late afternoon to a house filled with whispers. Calverley was still in discussion with the College Master, and paused only briefly as the boys were ushered in and hurried upstairs to their chamber, out of the way of the men's important business.

Phillipa heard their high voices approaching and rose from her devotions to await them in their room. She held her arms out to them, and the boys rushed to kiss her damp cheeks. William stepped back and regarded her seriously.

"Why dost thou weep, Mama?"

"I miss Henry, and was sorry not to visit. How fares my littlest one?"

"Henry is very well and bonny. He grows strong. He pinched Walt on the arm and made him cry!"

"Did he now? And how doth Mistress Carver and the rest?"

"We played games with a ball, and Mistress Carver told us a tale of a great monster called the Dark Beast. It hath a thousand teeth and sleeps in shadows."

"My, what a fine day you have spent!" Phillipa turned to Sarah. "Have the children eaten?"

"Yes, Madam. We have all supped together."

Thank God for that, at least. There is little enough to be found in our larder.

"I think it best they be put to bed at once."

"Mama! 'Tis far too early for sleep!"

"No matter, Will. 'Tis been a busy day, and thou hast dined well. Besides, your father entertains an important guest below stairs, and we needs must keep quiet and let the men have their peace. Look, you! Little Walt doth agree with me—see how he yawns!"

Phillipa stroked the curls of her younger son out of his eyes as he sleepily leaned his head onto her lap. *How did his hair grow thus long so quickly?* She had been too distracted to notice it needed to be trimmed. Both lads were looking a bit tattered.

William scowled and stamped his foot.

"But I am not yet tired!"

"Then tell your brother stories until he sleeps. Pray do not disobey. Your father must not be disturbed, and I needs must rest."

Sarah lifted Walt and carried him to the children's bed. William dragged his feet as he followed behind.

"Father never wishes to have us within sight. He *hates* us."

Phillipa caught her maid's eye over the bowed head of her eldest son.

"No, Will—never think such dread thoughts. Your father loves us, and must be left to solve his troubles for the good of us all."

Will continued sulking, but voiced no more complaints as Sarah undressed the boys and put them into their nightgowns and caps to say their prayers. The two women kissed the children and withdrew to the doorway to watch as Will propped himself up on the bolster and began to tell faerie stories to Walt in a dramatic whisper. The child took his storytelling very seriously. He became so engrossed in relating the tale of the Dark Beast and a magic prince that he did not notice that little Walt was no longer paying the least attention and had nodded off with a snuffling snore. Sarah smiled at her pale mistress and whispered what little comfort she could offer.

"The lad's cold is all but gone today, Madam. And wee Henry is as bonny as ever. Marry, how he thrives!"

"God be thanked."

Phillipa's voice was dull and heavy. The women fell silent. The men's voices could be heard below and, though they could not make out any individual words, there could be no mistaking the gravity of their tones. Phillipa reached for her maid's hand.

"I am glad the boys are fed. I've no stomach for food tonight. All is most grievous, Sarah—"

"Ma'am."

The girl gave her mistress's fingers a gentle squeeze. There was not much else to be said.

"The Lord have pity upon my poor children. My pretty beggars—"

Phillipa's voice cracked. She withdrew her hand and went to her own chamber.

"Listen for the gentlemen in case they should want

serving."

"Shall I attend you presently, Madam? Once Will falls asleep, I can help with your stays."

"No, no—'tis not very like that I shall take to my bed this night, Sarah. Please just leave me be."

"Good night, Ma'am. And God bless."

Phillipa turned back in the darkness of the windowless corridor. She could just make out the silhouette of her maid and only friend, backlit by the fire from the children's room.

"Amen. My only hope indeed is that He shall bless us, Sarah. Good night."

CHAPTER NINE

It was past dusk when Richardson finally raised his hand to cut off Calverley's ceaseless flow of empty pleas and promises. Rubbing his eyes, the Master rose from his seat.

"Nothing further is to be said, Calverley. Words lead us nowhere. I grow weary with listening, and yet you offer me no sound answer."

"As I have said, I must have but a little time—"

"There is no more time."

"Grant me but a few days—"

"No. I shall return tomorrow at midday, and I trust

then to find satisfaction to ease your brother's plight. And so I leave you. I have lodgings with a former student some four miles hence and wish to travel while there is still some light."

The Master strode through the door with Calverley trailing in his wake. John was loitering just outside, and Calverley barked at him to fetch Richardson's mount from the stable. The two gentlemen stood in awkward silence as they waited. Richardson had evidently done with words, and Calverley's throat was sore and dry from bargaining. John returned with the horse after what seemed an eternity. Calverley snatched the reins from his servant's hand and dismissed him, holding the mare steady as his guest hauled himself onto her back. He looked the Master firmly in the eye.

"Good sir, your sobering words hath awakened a new sense in me. I am humbled by the damage my revels hath wrought upon my poor brother and—though the revelations sting and burn me to my very heart—I am grateful to find myself awakened to my duties. I humbly swear to you, by morning's end I will have furnished you with what is needed."

Richardson returned his gaze with a grim expression.

"I can only hope that to be true. Good night."

"Your servant, sir."

Calverley bowed deeply and released his hold on the mare. With a snap of the reins, the Master gently clucked his tongue at his mount and started at a modest pace out of the gates and down the hill. He never once looked back.

A hot sensation of panic prickled over Calverley's scalp.

How must I answer? There is nothing can be done by tomorrow at midday—or any other day!

A sharp laugh jolted from his chest, catching him off guard. A few hours or a few days: it made no difference. There was nothing left to give. As the lure of the dice possessed both himself and his property more and more, Calverley had further stretched his limits by squandering his diminished resources on the provision of whores and drink for his shady circle of 'friends.' He'd hoped to pacify his fellow gamblers into forgiving his obligations—or to at least be more tolerant of his increasing slackness in paying what he owed. He could no longer afford such generosity. His purse was empty.

Calverley's fingers itched. It was an easy walk for him to find a ready gathering of men, coins and dice. He thrust his hat on his head and began the short trek to the Leopard Inn. The back room was notorious for its nightlong gaming sessions. When the wind was right, he could almost hear the shouts and laughter from his own gates. He stopped in his tracks.

No. I cannot.

There—so close to home—he was too well known to risk it. His neighbours knew intimately of his troubles, and may have noted the arrival of the College

Master to the Hall and rightly deduced that the visit was evidence of further miseries. He would not be made welcome. No man that he owed money to could be counted as a true friend, and Calverley had not been blind to the coldness in the eyes of those around at the inn the other night. It had been the last game of many for him that evening: he had been unable to resist the lit door of the tavern on the way back from his latest orgy of loss farther a-field in Leeds. His luck had been no better closer to home, and the patience of the other gamblers had worn thin. Payment—he'd been warned—would be exacted at any cost. He half-remembered the words so recently breathed into his face by his slightly less drunken neighbour:

"Blood or coin—it matters not to me, Calverley. Be ye well prepared to shed one or t'other when next ye cross this threshold."

He could not chance it. In York, he had once seen a wretch run from a tavern and chased down like a dog on the streets by his knife-wielding 'companions'. They'd slashed open his midsection, spilling his entrails and leaving him to bleed to death alone in the shadows of Skeldergate Bridge on the banks of the River Ouse. Better to try his luck farther away in Pudsey—or even Halifax, where he was not yet well known. He would need to take his horse. Turning back from his gates, he walked around the east wing toward the stable block and made it only as far as the Great Hall entrance before his steps grew heavy.

It would be too simple to vanish into the dark back room of a tavern and scratch a rough circle in the dirt floor with his knife blade. With a shout and a palsied shake of the hand, he might easily take up the three dice and roll away the very last of his fortune.

Or I might as easily win it all back ten-thousand-fold. Surely, 'tis my due—

Fool.

The more rational inner voice won the day. Calverley felt the will drain out of him and he leaned up against the outside wall of his ancestral home. There was no use. News of his ruin preceded him as far away as York and Wakefield. No man would play him—not out of any pity for his fallen affluence, but because it was pointless to win from him what he no longer possessed. Besides, there was not enough remaining in his purse even to buy his place in the gaming circle. He would have to find another diversion to take his mind from the troubles.

A woman would serve to take the edge from my want.

Not his whore wife waiting upstairs. He could not stomach her affected tears and sighing—knowing all the while that she laughed inwardly at making him a cuckold with Leventhorpe.

They shall yet be made to pay…

His meagre resources did not stretch to hire one of his usual harlots. They, too, were weary of being owed for their services. He'd been hard-pressed of late to get anywhere near a girl before her pimp would appear between them and demand his payment in advance. That left only the foolishly smitten Mary Gargrave to open her legs from her misguided age-old devotion to him.

But no. Even as he thought of it, the urge fled. He did not want to bother sniffing her out only to have his power fail: it had been a new problem of late, and that was a further humiliation he did not care to face.

Idly, Calverley tried the outside door of the Great Hall. The latch gave way, and he swung the heavy door open.

A curse on John—he knows this door is to be kept bolted.

But he could not blame the lad for having forgotten: the Great Hall was long unused, and there was nothing inside worth the taking. Besides, it would save him from having to enter through the main part of the house and attract the attention of his wife. Despite his increased discipline of Phillipa, she had grown ever bolder in pestering him about the state of the household. The hussy would not be taught her place. He could not bear the idea of being further molested by her stream of questions—and no doubt but she would have many, following the appearance of the Southern visitor.

The rusty hinges squealed as he closed the door behind him and slid the bolt. Blinking, Calverley's eyes adjusted to the dimness of the light, and he took in the gloomy surroundings. It was an enormous space and had always been his favourite part of his family's manor. He squinted upward, barely able to make out the details of the projecting hammer-beams high overhead. He could trace out their features in his memory and easily pictured in his mind's eye the richly carved decorative scrolls and circles that added such magnificence to the high, vaulted ceiling. It had once been the envy of the county. The grand stone fireplace in the north wall was itself the size of a small room, large enough for a man to stand upright. Calverley had fond memories of huge blazes roasting whole beasts on a spit as his father held his regular nights of extravagant entertainment. The echoes of laughter and music rang about the ceiling to cascade down upon the dazzled young heir to the family seat. What pride in his name he had once known! He could scarcely wait for the day when he'd take his father's place at the head of the long oak banquet table to be cheered and loved as the best of all hosts. Indeed, in his first years as master of Calverley Hall, he had put even his father's lavish efforts to shame.

Those happy days were over. His riot had reduced the pride of West Yorkshire to an empty, dust-filled cavern. The beautiful table now graced another, lesser man's home. Gone were the sideboards and the oak settles and benches, his father's best armchairs, the tapestries of dancing nymphs that had flashed red and gold in the firelight—all sold long ago to pay off debts.

So many debts... I cannot keep track even if I so choose. What would be the purpose?

The only piece of furniture was a single, rough-hewn bench left by the cold hearthside. Calverley circled around it, stooped and stepped inside the fireplace. He kicked aside a stack of musty straw to reveal his stashed bottles of strong wine. He smiled grimly: here was one indulgence still within his grasp tonight.

The Great Hall grew black. Throughout the endless night, he paced and drank, fumbling for a second bottle after he had drained his first... and a third to drown the second. Without the hangings to muffle the harsh sound of boots upon the flagstones, his footsteps reverberated off of the bare walls with hollow echoes. His legs grew numb beneath him as the effects of the drink took hold.

He felt something clutched in his closed fist. Puzzled at what he might discover, he paused where the moonlight shone the brightest from the largest window and unclenched his hand.

Dice.

Calverley had not even been aware of pulling them out from the depths of his leather purse. They were his first set, owned from the outset of his gambling 'career' born in the Royal Court of London. He carried them at all times as faithfully as a Papist would carry their rosary beads, continually worrying the ivory cubes together until he had ground the square edges into a dull, rounded smoothness. In that state, they were no longer of practical use: they had become mere talismans to remind him of his folly.

"Bastards!"

Calverley hurled the cursed objects into the farthest corner where they struck against the wall with a satisfying *clack*. His chest heaved with painful breaths. He felt urgently possessed to hunt down and smash all that caused him torment. Tossing his head back, he drained the bottle in his hand, feeling the wine spill over from his lips and down either side of his neck. The sudden draught made his mind reel. With a shriek, he pitched the empty bottle into the gaping maw of the fireplace where it exploded, sending shards of glass flying out into the room. Calverley's boots crunched in the debris as he resumed his pacing with the crazed momentum of a caged beast.

"No way out… "

His foot caught the first abandoned empty bottle and sent it rolling. He followed the sound of glass bouncing across the stone, scrabbling after it until his fingers closed around the neck. As he bent to seize his quarry, Calverley felt the world lurch under his feet, and he lost balance. He fell down hard, skinning his hand and driving some glass fragments deep into his palm. Sitting like a child with his legs splayed out before him, he heaved the second bottle into the corner. The muted smash was less gratifying—it must have landed partly on some straw. He cast his unblinking eyes about in the darkness, straining to find something else he could destroy. He needed to tear something to shreds.

"All is gone... nothing left."

Calverley scrambled onto his hands and knees and felt the sharp bite as he drove the broken glass still further home. He jerked back in pain and felt a dull jab in his ribs. Fumbling with his bleeding hand, his fist closed on the hilt of his dagger. He squeezed the bone handle tightly.

"Would that I had made it as far as Leventhorpe Hall this morning!"

He shut his eyes and replayed his favourite fantasy of revenge. He could picture the scenario with wondrous clarity...

After walking the unwitting fool out from the safety of his Hall into the depths of Calverley Wood, I would knock Leventhorpe off his feet. I'd have him pinned and helpless before he could catch his breath. How I would revel in tearing open the miscreant's breeches, and running my blade up the inside of Leventhorpe's thigh in a sick parody of my wife's amorous touch. I want to hear him beg for mercy before I grab him by the balls and castrate him, allowing the full force of his agonies to drive him half-mad before I slit his throat. I'd leave the corpse for the dogs and crows to feed upon—then return home to my whorish wife and calmly deposit her sometime plaything into her lap...

His face burned with delight at the delicious thoughts; but as the daydream waned, his self-hatred redoubled. It was too late for such acts of vengeance. The Calverley name had been stripped of all honour by his wild behaviour—there was nothing left of the family's reputation to defend.

The knife could be put to better and more immediate use.

A sickly, pale light was hinting around the window casements. The long night was nearly over, and there was no time to waste. Calverley knelt on the cold dusty floor, tearing open his doublet and shirt. He unsheathed his dagger and kissed the cross formed by the junction where the hilt met the blade. A single, well-placed thrust would release him from all his worldly miseries. Bracing himself, he held the lethal point out before his bared chest… and paused.

How best to strike?

He must be sure of his success. If he managed only to maim himself, his troubles would only be compounded. His wife would become his nurse as he lingered helpless in his bed—at the mercy of her tears and meaningless prayers while the last of his inheritance collapsed around their heads.

"God guide my hand to strike true—I cannot fail."

Calverley's grip faltered.

God? What God? He and God had long since abandoned each other. And even if his dagger did strike home, his debts would not die with him. His wife would be left a widow with three small children. They would eat up whatever little was left, while his brother William languished forgotten in debtors' prison. Tears of self-pity stung his eyes.

"If even one of her bastards is indeed my own flesh, then the legacy of their father would be a cowardly abandonment by self-slaughter. I have left them prepared for naught but thievery or beggary."

He gave a hollow moan at the thought. The boys would become wards of the Court as he himself had upon his father's death—never allowed control of their own destinies, and without even the security of a fine inheritance to win them decent marriages.

"'Tis bootless. All of us are damned."

The dagger slid from his sweaty grasp and clattered to the floor. In a fit of despair, Calverley's head dropped forward and his hands flew up to clutch his skull, pressing hard to contain the deafening roar of confusion. His eyes bulged unseeing in their sockets. He felt he could burst his own head like a melon—if only he could summon up the strength. His teeth ground together until his jawbone threatened to snap. He tore at his hair, pulling out clumps by the roots and drawing blood from his scalp.

"Is there no escape from this Hell?"

"Sir?"

Calverley choked back his cries. Peering over his

shoulder, he saw John standing at the interior door. The lad stared back at him with wide eyes and cleared his throat.

"Are ye all right, sir? I thought I heard a shout."

John hung on tightly to the latch and seemed unwilling to venture any farther into the Great Hall.

Rein yourself in, Calverley.

"'Tis only me, John. Praying for guidance. There is a great deal on my mind of late, as you cannot help but know."

Calverley inwardly cursed the womanish quaver in his own voice. He drew himself slowly to his feet, trying to appear casual and taking pains to conceal his dagger as he rose. Luck was kind; his back was turned to the interior doorway where John hovered like a nervous maiden on her wedding night. Certain that the lad had not seen the drawn weapon, Calverley turned to face him.

"So!"

His voice rang out loudly with forced jollity and caused John to start.

"'Twas a rough night for our household, but now a new day is before us. I have resolved a way to put all of our troubles at an end."

"I am heartily glad to hear it, sir."

Calverley wagged his finger at his servant as he made his way toward him across the Great Hall, his feet crunching on broken glass.

"Ah—but now comes the real work, John. There is much to be done on this day... much to be seen to before I may rest."

As Calverley drew nearer to the lad, he noted John's gaze on his torn clothes and the dried streaks of blood on his hand.

"Are ye hurt, sir?"

"'Tis nothing of consequence. Fetch me some water to wash, and a clean doublet and shirt."

Briskly, Calverley began stripping to his waist. His sense of purpose was strong and his focus was sharp. He knew what had to be done.

"Right away, sir."

"Then get you to the Carvers' farmstead and bring wee Henry home to me. On such a day as this, our entire family must be gathered together under one roof. At last, the Calverleys shall stand as one and give the rough world its answer."

He held a bloodied finger up to his lips.

"But mind you—say nothing. I wish to surprise my wife."

John lingered on in the doorway, shuffling his feet.

"Are ye deaf, sirrah? Get on with it!"

Calverley's tone left no room for further delay and John hurried away to carry out his orders.

CHAPTER TEN

The swirling darkness between the children's bed and the chamber wall harbours a black horror...

Will has kicked off the coverlet in the night, and his foot dangles over the edge of the mattress perilously close to the gaping, thousand-fanged maw of the Dark Beast.

The demon has haunted his dreams for as long as he has memory. At last, it has been given a name—and being named, it wields more power. The Dark Beast lies in wait, coiled around itself in a pool of its own slime. It hisses rank breath as its craggy jaws creak open to engulf whatever limb has carelessly ventured within its reach. Now, its pointed green tongue slavers vile ooze as it stretches out to taste the sweetmeat of Will's toes… and the Dark Beast's deep gullet emits a raspy growl of delight. At the last instant, Will snatches his foot from the shadows and the thwarted creature's yellow fangs snap shut onto empty air. Will's shrieks are drowned out by the Beast's frustrated howls as it is again denied its coveted meal of boy's flesh—

Waking with a jolt, Will leapt—still moaning and half-dreaming—across the body of his startled little brother. Walt's face screwed up in confusion at his big brother's terror, sending up a thin wail as Will's flailing hand clipped him in the ear. Will blinked at the sound and caught hold of himself. His skin felt electrified with residual fear, and he could still feel the imagined slime on his toes where the Dark Beast's tongue had brushed. He wiped away at the mucky sensation with a handful of the coverlet. Gesturing his fussing brother to be silent, Will eased back across the mattress on his stomach, held his breath and peered over the edge into the depths of the shadows. He could swear the tip of a snaky tail withdrew under the bed, hiding from the growing daylight in the bedchamber. There was still a deep pool of darkness between the bed and the wall. It would not be safe until the morning sun filled the room with daylight and burned away all such dread creatures of the shadows.

"Come, Walt—we must not tarry here."

Grabbing his brother's hand, he helped Walt down

to the floor and they padded barefoot across the hallway into their parents' bedchamber.

"The Dark Beast cannot follow us. It greatly fears all mothers—for the very softness of a mother's voice banishes the creature back into the pits of Hell."

Walt nodded in understanding. For him, there were unerring rules to Will's dream world and the faerie tales he spun, and Walt accepted them without question. Both boys possessed a solemn faith in the absolute power of the Otherworld and its myriad inhabitants.

Will pushed open the door, and the children stood uncertainly at the threshold, gazing inside. Their mother lay propped up against her bolster cushions. Though sound asleep, she was still fully dressed from the day before. Walt started toward the bed, but Will grabbed his arm.

"No, I think that Mama wants to rest. We must go back."

Walt's eyes widened at the suggestion.

"Beast!"

"Shush! I know—it waits for us. But if we find Sarah, she shall help us keep the Dark Beast at bay until Mama wakes and the sun shines full."

He pulled the door quietly shut and the two of them went back on tiptoe to find Sarah in their chamber, kneeling before the oak trunk in search of their clothing for the day. The boys snuck up behind her and tapped her between her bowed shoulders.

"Oh!" she cried in mock surprise. "There ye be! I came in to see an empty bed and feared that the goblins must have carried ye both off into the woods!"

Will met her jesting with a serious visage.

"The Dark Beast did try, but we escaped."

"Did you now? What doughty lads! Come and give me a proper 'good morning.'"

Sarah held out her arms and the brothers launched themselves into her embrace, nearly knocking her over and smacking kisses on both of her cheeks.

"Have ye seen yer mother yet this morning, Will?"

"Mama fell asleep in her day clothes."

Sarah's face clouded.

"Indeed? She must be weary indeed, and we shall leave her to rest. I myself slept but a little."

"I, too! That is when the Dark Beast came after us!"

"Oh, Will—leave dark thoughts to the grown folk. The two of ye need to sleep at night."

"Me?" chirped Walt. "I sleep!" Sarah giggled.

"Yes, my sweeting—*you* could sleep sound through the very end of the world itself! And now I suppose ye'll be wanting some breakfast?"

The boys nodded their heads.

"Very well, then I'll tell ye what we shall do: first, I shall dress this bonny wee master—" Sarah tickled Walt's round tummy "—then you, my young sir—" she said, chucking Will gently under the chin "—and then the three of us shall fix oat porridge."

Will sat on a low, three-legged stool by the fire to wait his turn. Walt squirmed with the vigour of a riotous drunkard fighting off an arrest, kicking and pinching Sarah's arms as she struggled to get him into his day-gown.

"Ow! Peace, boy! What has gotten into ye? Have the imps taken ye over in the night? Be still, ye changeling!"

"Where is my Papa?" asked Will. "I want Papa to take breakfast with us!"

"Pa-*pa*… Pa-*pa*… Pa-*pa* !" chimed Walt, slapping at Sarah's hands in time to his chant.

"Cease yer prattle, Walt!" Sarah forced one arm into his day gown. "Be thou patient 'til I dress ye both, Will. We shall all go together and search out yer papa."

I only pray that the Devil has carried the cursed man off to Hell while we slept, she thought. *But I fear we shall never be blessed with such good fortune… God forgive me!*

Will jumped to his feet.

"I shall find him now and bring him to table!"

Ducking easily from Sarah's reach, he scampered out the chamber door.

"William! Get back here! Yer not yet dressed!"

Walt caught a handful of Sarah's loosened braid and gave it a mighty yank.

"Argh! Heaven help me—ye're both nowt but a pair of beasties!"

Heedless to her pleas for his return, Will was already down the stairs.

"Papa? Where are you?"

Will peered around the corner of the door into the Solar wing. Maybe his father was playing a game of hide-and-go-seek. Keeping to the centre of the room—well clear of the Dark Beast's brethren lurking in the shadows—he paced the length of the large main chamber to the kitchen, peeking in any possible hiding places behind doors or beneath the furniture. All was still but for a black iron pot of oats simmering over the fire. Will swallowed hard; sore afraid he may have to continue his search in the Great Hall with all of its looming shadows and cobwebs… He'd try the friendlier, more homey parts of the Hall for just a little longer while he worked up his nerve. The stone floors were chilly this morning, and they were making his bare toes ache with cold. He wanted to rush upstairs and let Sarah dress him in warm stockings, but it was too late to turn back. His Calverley pride would not allow him to return to the others without having first found his father. Hugging his arms about himself, he soldiered on.

"Papa—?"

* * *

"Papa—? 'Tis me—Will! Come to breakfast, Papa!"

In the Great Hall, Calverley could easily hear the high-pitched cries of his son calling from the Solar wing. He felt no need to answer. The boy would find him soon enough without his guidance.

After cleaning his master of dust and blood and furnishing him with fresh attire, John had departed on his errand to fetch the baby from the wet nurse. Calverley perched on his bench beside the empty Great Hall fireplace. There was a jug of wine at his elbow, and he'd already drained two full tumblers before becoming aware of Will's approaching cries. He topped up his wine with a strangely steady hand and took a deep draught.

How much have I drunk? I know not—and yet for the first time, I see the path I needs must take. 'Tis clear and meet. I am resolved.

"Papa? Are you within?"

The boy's voice came from the other side of the Great Hall's interior door. He was almost found. Calverley downed his wine and set aside the tumbler.

And so now I must begin.

Calverley held his breath and waited as the heavy door swung slowly open. At first, Will started at the sight of his father, then confronted him with his feet braced apart and his hands on his hips.

"Papa! Why did you not answer? Didst not hear my calls?"

Calverley smiled.

"I knew that I would be discovered, soon enough. Thou art a cunning lad."

The child did not return his father's smile.

"I would have found you all the sooner if you had but called back to me!"

"All's well." He extended a hand out to the boy. "Here I am at last."

His small feet slapping on the flagstones, Will stomped across the room to slide his hand into his father's large palm. Calverley closed his hand around his son's with a firm grip. Will began a one-sided game of tug-of-war to try to pull him to his feet.

"Come, Papa! Rise! I have outrun the Dark Beast himself and shall not be defied by any mortal!"

Calverley had no idea what the child was prattling on about. The little boy was hopelessly outweighed, but he bravely put his back into the task and strained until he nearly toppled over. By some small miracle, his bare feet had managed to avoid the shards of broken glass on the floor. Calverley observed his son's efforts with a feeling of detachment.

Bastard or not, he is a staunch and fearless boy. 'Tis pity.

"Come on, Papa—stand up! We are going to take breakfast now."

Calverley locked eyes with Will and shook his head.

"No, lad."

The boy ceased battling to haul his father from the bench. Meeting his unblinking gaze with furrowed brows, Will shifted his slight weight uncomfortably from side to side.

"Why do you stare so, Papa?"

He made no reply and released his grip on the

child's wrist.

"Shall we not have breakfast?"

"No, we shall not—not today, or any other day. There can be no more mornings for us."

"Why not?"

Like a striking viper, Calverley shot out his hand out and grabbed his son hard by the shoulder. He brought out his hidden dagger and plunged it into the boy's abdomen. They held each other's startled gazes as the blade came to rest. Writhing to pull free, Will's hands grasped at his father's wrist, but he only succeeded in driving the weapon in still deeper.

Calverley gave a twist and jerked the blade out, tearing the child's muscles apart. The knife no longer there to hold him upright, Will collapsed forward with a breathless cry. Blood sprayed onto his father's clean shirt with a garish splatter. Calverley hugged the boy spasmodically against his breast and rocked him as though soothing him to sleep, crooning with a singsong voice.

"Bleed, bleed, rather than beg, beg. I will not see thee live a pauper. This is but charity I show."

At this, Will redoubled his struggles, gasping as he flailed his weakening hands at his murderer's face. Calverley was disappointed. He had hoped to deliver the lad an instant death. The blow seemed mortal enough, but the end was peevish and slow in coming. He could not in good conscience leave him here. Time was short.

It would not be long before John returned—and the College Master was due for his reckoning.

"Thou shalt not stay behind to die alone. Come, view thy second brother."

Calverley stood and awkwardly heaved up the squirming child in his arms. Blood coursed freely from the gaping wound, making the boy slippery and difficult to hold. Managing a solid grip around his son, he ran to the other wing in search of the rest of his family.

There is no way but this.

* * *

Sarah had finally outfitted the unruly little Walt into his day clothes and set him to play with his doll in the corner of the room farthest from the hearthside.

"That's you set, my lad. Now- where be thy brother?"

She'd not heard Will calling for some minutes now and listened for his voice. A muffled sound came from downstairs. *Soft—could that be him?* Leaving Will's clothing laid out on the bed, she stepped forth and peered down the dark staircase. Someone was scuffling about at the bottom of the stairs and there were moving shadows at the foot of the steps leading up from the Solar wing. Sarah called out softly, not wishing to wake her Mistress. It was a miracle she was not roused already with all the racket Will had sent up in search of his father.

"Will?"

There was laboured breathing, but no reply. Sarah felt the flesh on her arms crawl.

Hesitating, she cast her gaze back over her shoulder at Walt. She did not dare leave the wee one alone in the chamber with the fire burning: more than once he'd nearly burned himself, even with Sarah in the same room. Only last week, he'd clambered onto a tottery stool reaching for a toy on the mantel, his gown flirting with the licking flames. Today, he seemed more interested in his doll than the fire. Sarah approached the top of the stairwell. Uneven footsteps were slowly ascending.

"William?"

As Sarah's eyes adjusted to the gloom, she saw a dark, hunched figure lumbering up the stairs. It was her Master, Sir Walter.

Clutching his son's limp body to his chest.

"Will? Oh, laddie!"

An answer to her shrill cry, the boy found his voice and gave a wordless, liquid sob. Tears flooded Sarah's eyes and blurred her vision as the Master came closer. Father and son were both panting heavily: Calverley half-choked in frenzied humour, and the boy straining with the effort to stay alive. As Calverley's glassy eyes met hers, Sarah froze under his reptilian expression.

"Oh, sir… how came he hurt so grievously?"

"Take him."

Brusquely, Calverley thrust Will into her outstretched

arms as he pushed her aside and strode into the chamber. His cold gaze searched until it landed upon Walt in the far corner. Intent on tearing the arm from his stuffed poppet, the child was oblivious to his father's entrance.

Sarah moaned at the horrible spectacle cradled in her arms. Will was pale and heavy with oncoming death, his nightgown slashed and mottled with gore. He struggled to raise his head, and his tear-stained face twisted into a rictus of agony. She instinctively rocked him gently to quiet him, unable to stop herself though the motion caused him to wince in pain.

"Oh Lord Jesus! What's happened to ye, my poor darling?"

Gasping, Will lifted a hand and pointed.

"Papa—"

Sarah's legs buckled and she sank to the floor. She lay Will down as delicately as she could, stroking his brow and shushing him as his body jerked at the soft impact. Blinking back tears, she spun to confront Calverley as he loomed over the second boy and raised a long blade in his hand.

Still on her hands and knees, Sarah scrambled to reach little Walt, who stared mesmerized at the bright blood splashed on his father's shirtfront. Sarah's foot accidentally caught the lad in the chest as she threw herself between him and the assailant, and Walt dropped his mangled toy and sent up a keening wail. Sarah grasped her Master hard about his legs.

"No, sir! What will ye do?"

Calverley stared blankly down into her face.

He yanked back his left knee, brought it up sharply against the underside of Sarah's chin and sent her sprawling. Having cleared his way of the obstacle, he crouched down to reach for his second born as the screaming boy crept away to hide behind the settle.

Sarah shook off her daze, launched herself at Calverley's back and clawed at his face from behind. In a single lightning movement, he regained his feet, threw her off his back and spun to grasp her by the windpipe, pointing his bloodied dagger at her eye. He thrust her out at arm's-length and backed her across the room in three quick paces.

"Leave off with your clamour or I'll break your neck!"

He tossed her backwards toward the doorway with a brutal shove to her throat. The half-throttled Sarah staggered and lost her footing as she stumbled out into the stairwell, slipping in a streak of Will's blood. She had no breath to cry out as she crashed down the stairs.

Calverley stood, listening. There was only silence.

Good.

He stepped back into the bedchamber over the gasping William and again knelt down before his small namesake. Walt—unable to squeeze his body into the narrow space between the wooden settle and the wall—had crammed himself into a ball in the farthest corner of the room beside his ruined doll. He shrieked and flailed as Calverley reached out and grasped him by the shoulders.

"Beast!"

"Walter—?"

Calverley turned at the sound of his name. His wife stood in the door.

Phillipa disbelieved her own eyes. Dreamlike, she moved into the chamber and bent over Will as he lay in a widening pool of blood.

"Do I yet sleep and dream? This vision cannot be true. Will?"

"Mama—"

Will's voice was barely a whisper. As she held his cold, limp hand in hers, the touch made it all too real.

Tearing herself away from her dying son, Phillipa flew across the room and thrust her crouching husband off balance with her hip. As she scooped up her hysterical baby, little Walt lashed about violently in her arms before he saw who she was and buried his face into her shoulder. Phillipa spun around as her husband rose to his feet and keeping herself positioned as a barrier between Calverley and Will. Her husband's breast heaved as he gulped in air. Sweat poured from his brow in a steady torrent, mingling with his son's blood to drip from his face and spread into a sickening pink stain across the front of his shirt. Calverley's eyes were flinty, bright and unblinking. He bared his teeth at her in a parody of a smile.

"Give me the boy."

"Prithee, what would you do then?"

The question rang with absurdity: the answer lay all about her in splashes of gore.

Calverley took a step toward her, and she sidestepped Will, trying to get back to the door. Walt had fallen silent but for a shocky panting, and she held him more tightly. His breath was hot against her neck.

"Harlot… give me the child."

"What have you done to us?"

Calverley danced with her in an eerie imitation of a courtly pavane. Both took looping, carefully controlled steps as they spun a wide and strangely elegant circle about the chamber. Their eyes were locked. He held his bone-handled dagger at a ready angle and kept his voice even and rational.

"There are no means to keep the bastard brats."

"I pray thee, no—not my children!"

"I'll see us all bleed before we fall into beggary."

"But your own sweet boys—"

Phillipa was forced back against the wall farthest from the door.

"There are too many beggars in this vile world."

"Good my husband—"

There can be no bargaining where the Devil holds sway.

Phillipa bolted. Calverley pounced and caught her arm in a vise grip as he raised the dagger to strike the child. Twisting sharply, Phillipa met the blow with the side of her own body. White-hot pain sent her reeling, but she kept her feet and held fast to her son. Calverley dragged her and shoved her back against the oak-panelled walls by the fireplace. The door to the staircase seemed miles away and was fading from her dimming sight like some unobtainable and vital thing in a nightmare—the one thing that might save you.

"Now then, Mistress: I will not be prevented."

Calverley feinted with his dagger. His wife lurched aside to shield her child, but he'd fooled her. Diving in with a quick thrust under her raised arm, he ran the blade through to the boy's heart. Walt gave a single writhing heave as he arched backwards—making no sound as his eyes rolled in surprise. Hot blood gushed through the front of Phillipa's blue damask gown and stained it black. This time, his aim had been true. He had delivered instant death to his son.

Calverley's arms dropped to his sides as he released the hold on his wife. He stood back and stared at her as deep animal cries tore from her chest. Her face became a contorted mask, coated in tears and blood. Saliva poured freely over her chin from her gaping mouth. She did not flinch as he once again raised his steaming knife. It was as if her eyes no longer wished to register sight.

Calverley impassively brought the weapon down into his wife's shoulder, making a curious chopping sound at impact. Phillipa sank from the blade as it was retracted, and fell senseless to rest half overtop of her murdered son. He prodded them with his boot. Both lay still.

Calverley swayed on his feet in exhaustion from his efforts. His own wheezing was the only sound in the chamber as he surveyed the scene. Blood splattered the fine oak wall panels and lay in puddles on the floorboards. Turning, his boot heel slid in one of his own smeary footprints as he saw that—

How is it possible?

—the first boy was gone.

He staggered and cast his eyes about for his son. From the coagulating pool where he had been, there was a wide streak trailing through the doorway. He followed Will's path out of the chamber to the hallway at the head of the stairs. In the dim light, he could only just make out the form of the child lying up against the huddled body of the nursemaid at the base of the stairwell. Evidently, he had dragged himself in search of some final comfort.

A brave and hearty lad. Rest well, now.

Calverley glanced over his shoulder into the boys' bedchamber for one last look. Phillipa remained motionless, her face pressed into the floor. The baby's eyes stared back at him from underneath the crook of her arm.

Calverley picked his way carefully down the stone steps. Even with his hands guiding his balance against the narrow walls, he had to fight to keep from tumbling headlong in the slick blood. Stepping over the heap at the bottom of the stairs, he walked out the front door and navigated the length of the grounds on stiffened legs to stand vigil by the gates. There was no sign on the road yet of anyone approaching the Hall from either direction.

I want but one small part to make up the sum, and then my poor brother shall rest satisfied. There will be enough to buy his release when there are no heirs left to feed.

He leaned against the stone wall to calm his breathing and willed John to hurry home with the third and final bastard.

CHAPTER ELEVEN

John had disobeyed his master.

He lingered on the pathway between the open fields of Calverley Hall and the Carvers' farmstead, unsure what to do. He could not bear to face the punishment he'd earn by returning without small Henry, nor could he bring himself to walk as far as the Carvers' and raise their suspicions. Calverley had always sworn him to silence when it came to the situation at the Hall, and John had always been careful not to give anything away. His master would not take kindly now to any neighbourly intrusions.

But this felt different… and dangerous.

I wish my Sarah were here. She'd know best what course to take.

John spent the better part of an hour tearing at leaves from a prickly hedgerow growth until his hands oozed blood from a dozen tiny cuts. The sound of an approaching horse and rider roused him from his thoughts.

"John?"

He started guiltily at the sound of his name and turned to face the wrath. Instead of his dreaded master, he found himself facing the kindly Sir Thomas Leventhorpe, who sat astride a grey mount regarding him with a curious tilt of his head.

"Are you quite all right, John? You seem melancholy."

Despite his loyal promise of silence, John could not stop his mouth.

"Oh sir! There came a visitor from the university yesterday morn—"

"Yes, I've heard of a College Master but lately arrived. He is lodged with my neighbour Marlowe to the west of my orchards. What is his purpose to come hither from Oxford?"

"I know not sir, but sure 'tis a matter most grave. He shut himself up with my Master within doors—and there they stayed all the long day into the evenin'. Both were in choleric humours at their parting. The Oxford visitor is to return this noon and see his wishes satisfied."

"What was said? Know you anything, lad?"

"Somethin' touchin' upon his brother, and that he would have the money to… to 'furnish what is needed.' The Master has since been possessed by a fit of brooding the like I have never before witnessed."

"Oh?"

Leventhorpe's apparent agitation at the news made John still more anxious, and he spoke more and more quickly, spilling out what little more he knew of his master's secrets.

"Sir, he passed the night alone in the Great Hall. He slept not one wink, I am sure—but drank I know not how much, for there were broken bottles scattered about the four corners of the room. I came upon him at dawn, kneelin' upon the flagstones and near to howlin' like a beast at the Fates."

"'Tis wondrous strange. I like not that."

"Indeed, sir—'twas a most discomfortin' sight to behold; his clothes all streaked with blood from cutting his hand on the glass. But when I approached to help, he affected good spirits. He spoke bravely, and ordered me fetch the wee lad Henry home from his wet-nurse. 'Faith, sir, he was most firm that I bring the babe directly, but he has never before shown a moment's interest in the poor bairn and—"

"And hast done as you were bid?"

Leventhorpe's face was grave. John's voice cracked

and tears began to flow unchecked down his ruddy cheeks.

"N-no, sir. I am sore afraid to go back—with or without the infant!"

"Thou hast acted well, John. Here is what must be done: go you to the Hall and report to your master that his son is ill and could not leave his nurse. I'll to Marlowe's house where the College Master stays, and we shall all three join you presently. To wait until noon may be too great a risk. I fear Sir Walter should not long be left unwatched."

The gentleman's grim manner struck deep with John.

"Pray do make haste, sir, I beg ye. I have tarried from the Hall above an hour as it stands!"

Leventhorpe's jaw tightened at this news, but he recovered himself to favour young John with a thin-lipped smile.

"Take heart, lad," he said as he spurred his horse. "I'll be with you shortly!"

John felt little reassurance. He dabbed away his tears with his dirty sleeve and hurried off in the opposite direction toward Calverley Hall.

* * *

John kept his swollen eyes fixed upon the ground as he made his final approach home up the hill. Halfway across the yard, he was sent flying off his feet by a running tackle from behind. Winded, John snapped his head around to confront what looked like a blood-soaked demon hurling wild punches at his face. He screamed and threw his elbow up to catch it squarely in the chest. Spitting curses, the hellish fiend sprawled away and scrambled to its feet to ready for a new attack.

"Wretch! Damn thee for thy insolence!"

"Oh Lord... *sir?*"

John barely had the time to raise his hands and ward off his master before the snarling Calverley was again fast upon him, kicking away his arms and clutching his throat in his bloody grasp. John struggled to pry him loose. His fingers clawed for purchase in the slick mess of sweat and gore.

"Where is the boy? Why hast thou not fetched me the brat?"

Calverley's hands were crushing his windpipe. John's eyes rolled wildly in his head until his gaze fell upon the dagger lying in the grass a few feet away. He managed to draw enough breath to choke out an answer.

"Heaven help him had I brought him home to such a villain!"

Calverley banged John's head back hard against the ground, narrowly missing a jagged rock. He glared down into his face.

"The Devil take thee! I'll to the Carvers' myself, and there cut the bastard's throat!"

With a final shove, Calverley leapt to his feet and strode off toward the stables. As he stooped to pick up his dagger, John scrambled after, knocking him to the ground. He straddled his master and blindly rained punches about his face and head.

"What have ye done? Are all the family dead? And what of Sarah? Ye'll need to kill me too before I let ye reach Henry!"

Calverley arched his back and heaved them both over. His hand scrabbled at the turf as they rolled, and he grabbed for the bone handle of his dagger. John's body was racked by sobs as landed blow after blow to little effect: his aim impeded by the flood of tears. Every attempted strike was parried by the steel of Calverley's weapon. Blood covered John's knuckles. Though no stranger to a brawl, he'd never before encountered such a foe as this—the man seemed possessed. A split-second's hesitation gave his master the chance for a clear swipe at John's face. He felt the blade connect just under his right eye, tearing a long gash across his cheek. Screaming, he lurched away from Calverley on his hands and knees, grasping at the streaming wound. His master feinted again with the dagger. Swinging blindly, John knocked the knife from Calverley's grasp. Calverley lashed out and landed a kick to John's throat. Gasping bloody spittle, John struggled to rise and give chase. Calverley didn't give him the chance; he stomped down hard on the lad's groin with his heel. John groaned as he curled his body in upon itself and lay still. He couldn't move. The searing pain was unbearable. He could only watch helplessly as Calverley hurried around the corner of the Hall toward the stable, then darkness took hold and he passed out.

* * *

True to his word, Leventhorpe soon arrived at Calverley Hall—along with Richardson, his host Marlowe and his young son, Tobias, and a pair of able-bodied manservants.

They were greeted by the sight of a body lying out front.

Before his mount came to a full stop, Leventhorpe leapt from his skittish horse and ran to the battered form of John. He felt a rush of guilt thinking his instructions for the lad to return to the Hall had cost him his life. To his great relief, John's head turned at the sound of Leventhorpe's approach. "Hurry, good sir— the Master has ridden away to destroy his infant son." The lad struggled to raise himself from the turf. "I fear he's killed the others... all dead—" He fell back, exhausted.

Already, Leventhorpe was back in his saddle and spurring his horse to a full gallop, gesturing for the two servants to follow. They raced down the hill to cut through the fields to the Carvers' farm. Leventhorpe's stomach was in knots.

Pray God we are not too late.

* * *

Left behind, Richardson, Marlowe and Tobias went to the aid of the wounded man. Richardson knelt down to comfort the poor soul and gently examined the damage. The servant's eyes were purple with bruises and swollen shut, tears seeping out into the angry-looking gash on his cheek. Marlowe sucked in his breath at the sight of the blood.

"'Tis monstrous!"

The beaten servant groaned.

"Good sirs, I bleed but am not killed. I prithee—look to the women and children within—"

Racked by a fit of fresh sobbing, John was unable to continue.

Richardson glanced up at his host, and both men turned to stare at the windows of the eerily silent Hall. He stood and wiped his hands on his cloak. Marlowe—a thin and nervous man—looked pale enough to faint. They knew there was no other choice but to enter. Marlowe laid a shaking hand on his son's shoulder.

"Ride and fetch the parish surgeon, Tobias. Quick as you can."

The gangly lad seemed thankful to be spared from viewing any further horrors. Mounting his pony, Tobias sped away. Richardson glanced back to the servant. Mercifully, he'd passed out from the pain; though his wounds were grievous, they did not appear fatal. Marlowe spread his cloak over the young man, then the two friends slowly made their way toward the front door of Calverley Hall.

• • •

From the outset of his murderous quest, Calverley had struggled to control his anxious black mare. The beast danced and reared its way along the road as if reluctant to bear its rider.

I'll ne'er get to the brat at this rate!

Digging in his spurs and yanking at the horse's head until its flanks and mouth ran with bloody foam, Calverley forced the animal from the main road and onto a footpath cutting through the fields. The Carvers' farm cottage was in plain sight halfway down the vale. The horse balked and pranced about in a tight circle, refusing to go any farther.

"The spavin take thee!"

Calverley landed a vicious kick into an open sore on the horse's side. Letting out a screaming bellow that echoed around the bowl of the valley, it reared and bucked, throwing its master to the turf. The animal lowered its head and seemed to glare hatred at Calverley. Its reins trailed tantalizingly close by on the ground. As he scrambled for them, the horse snorted and tossed its head, jerking the reins out of his reach. The mare landed a final sharp kick as it trotted past Calverley, sending him sprawling and cursing before it broke into a canter toward the main road into the village.

"Damn thee for a Devil! Come back!"

Calverley leapt to his feet to give chase and his right leg collapsed out from under him. He rose again, this time more gingerly. It was no use. Whenever he put the slightest weight on his injured leg, pain bolted from his ankle to his groin and doubled him over. There was a mere half-mile left between him and his final goal. He could almost taste it…

Dispatch the little beggar and all's done!

He cast his eyes about for a stick he might use for a crutch, and his gaze fell upon a sturdy fallen branch jutting from beneath a bush in the hedgerow.

Gritting his teeth against the jolts of pain, Calverley slowly half-hopped, half-hobbled across the path.

• • •

As they turned the corner by the woods, Leventhorpe and his men heard the high-pitched neighs of a horse. Breaking through a gap in the hedgerow, Calverley's riderless mount snorted to them as it crossed over the ditch and shied near to the small posse. The mare rolled its eyes and snapped its head away as one of the men tried to grasp the dangling reins.

An unmistakable stream of curses reached their ears.

"Leave it! Calverley must be yonder in the field! Follow! Follow!"

Leventhorpe held his breath and urged his steed to leap the ditch, with the others fast at his horse's heels. They crashed through the break in the hedges and Calverley whirled around at bay, waving his knife and shrieking blasphemous oaths.

"Fie upon the treacherous nag! Damn God for trying to stop my hand! But I am not yet prevented. Is it Leventhorpe I see before me? Damn your eyes! Come! Have at you!"

The three men circled the madman cautiously on horseback. Unwilling to lay hands on a man so possessed and wary of his wildly slashing blade, the two servants shot glances at their leader. Leventhorpe reined in his mount. Steeling himself, he slid from his mount and approached Calverley with slow, careful steps—one hand ready upon the handle of his sword. As if closing in upon a fear-maddened hound, he spoke gently in a low voice to calm the beast.

"No more, Calverley... Walter. Dost hear? 'Tis finished. Put up thy blade."

Calverley threw back his head and barked out a crazed, exhausted laugh.

"Finished, quotha? Alas, 'tis not so." He waved his dagger in the direction of the distant farmer's cottage and made a weak stabbing motion in the air with his dagger. "Oh, that I could here reach the infant's heart! Then all would indeed be finished!"

Calverley's shoulders slumped as he heaved with sick mirth, tears streaking through the filth on his face. He tottered off-balance and sagged down to one knee, his head dropped forward in defeat. A mix of bloody pink sweat and tears dripped from his nose and chin to the ground.

Leventhorpe stepped in and took away his knife. Calverley made no move to prevent him.

. . .

Inside Calverley Hall, Richardson and Marlowe happened upon what they at first took to be the corpse of the maidservant at the base of the stairs. Marlowe recoiled in horror as Richardson leaned down to gingerly turn her over, and the girl stirred at his touch.

"Thanks be to God! She yet lives."

His relief was banished by the pitiful sight of the motionless boy huddled against the skirts of his nurse. The child was horribly pale and bloodied, and did not respond to the contact of Richardson's hand. His breath was stilled. Richardson hurried to pull the girl away from the dead child and out into the room—unwilling to yet reveal the ghastly discovery to his uneasy companion.

"Help me, Marlowe."

Together, they lifted the maid to the settle by the fire. Marlowe sat by her and murmured soothingly as he felt her wrists and ankles for signs of breakage. The semiconscious girl twisted and moaned as the pain roused her slowly back toward waking. Marlowe called over his shoulder to his former teacher, who had withdrawn back to the staircase.

"The Lord be praised—she has no broken bones, though she's been sorely beaten."

Richardson made no reply. He stood and came back into the chamber carrying something wrapped in his cloak. Laying the bundle out on a long, low bench by the hearth, he bowed his head and choked out a brief prayer before turning to face Marlowe.

"It is a child. Dead."

Marlowe's hand flew to his mouth and stifled a cry. Richardson reached out and took his friend by the shoulders.

"Steady on, man. We must now go upstairs."

They made their way on leaden feet, taking great care to avoid treading in the streaks of blood on the narrow stone steps. Richardson went before and strained to listen for any signs of life from the rooms above. All was deathly silent. Drawing a shaky breath, he noted dark footprints leading from a chamber to the right at the top of the stairs. He turned to grasp Marlowe by the hand.

"Ready?"

Marlowe squeezed back.

"No."

They stepped into a scene straight from a butcher's shambles.

Blood spattered the walls. The furniture seemed like it had been tossed about by a windstorm, and an earthenware jug of water had shattered—adding to the mess by spreading the congealing blood in ever-widening pools across the floorboards. Marlowe fell to his knees and retched.

At first, Richardson's eyes could only register the massive amounts of blood. He focused with great effort and took in the sight of the victims. Mistress Calverley lay face down in a heap against the far wall, her fine blue silk gown cruelly torn and stained black with gore. Richardson raised his handkerchief to his nose and breathed in shallowly through his mouth—the sharp, coppery stench in the room made his stomach heave. He forced himself across the chamber and gently turned the woman over onto her back. Acid bile flooded his throat. A small boy was clutched in a bloody bundle to her chest, his tiny fists still gripping handfuls of his mother's hair.

"Is this how he means to satisfy his brother?"

At the sound of Richardson's cry, Phillipa Calverley roused.

"Come, sir. The woman lives!"

Marlowe wiped the vomit from his lips with his sleeve and joined Richardson by her side, averting his gaze from the glassy stare of the dead babe. Though elated to see that the mother was breathing, they only prayed that she'd keep her eyes shut until they could pry the child's body from her arms and remove her from this horrible room.

Normally stoic, Richardson could not prevent himself as he tenderly pulled her fingers open to release her grasp. Phillipa groaned and thrashed her head. Shushing her, he held her still, trying haplessly to clean her face with his handkerchief. Marlowe—with an extreme effort of will—lifted the small corpse free of its mother's hold. Richardson better examined her wounds. A gaping slash to her shoulder bled profusely, and he tore a strip of material from her underskirt to staunch the flow. The farther cut located on the lower left of her torso should have proved fatal. The bodice of her gown was raggedly torn along one side, revealing the boning of her corset. By a miracle, the killing blow had only glanced off her body—the whalebone ribs of her stays had deflected the blade.

"See here, Marlowe? 'Tis God's own mercy."

Phillipa's eyelids fluttered open. Her vision flooded with tears as she beheld Marlowe cradling her baby. Reaching out, she took his small, limp hand and whispered to Richardson.

"What mercy is this, to half-live and see my child bleed before my eyes?"

How must such a question be answered? I am not God.

"Come, Madam. You must not stay in this dread chamber. A surgeon is sent for, and will presently see to your wounds."

"Rather let me die—"

Her body slumped back in Richardson's arms. Marlowe let out a wail.

"Oh Lord! She too is dead!"

"No, Marlowe, she does but swoon. "I'll carry her to another chamber. Go you and lay the child by his brother's side."

CHAPTER TWELVE

Leventhorpe brought Sir Walter Calverley to the home of the local magistrate, Sir John Savile. The captive stood impassively with his hands bound before him, his face blank. He listlessly shifted his weight onto his good leg for support.

The elderly magistrate paced the chamber with his hands clasped into fists behind his stocky body, regarding Calverley with an expression of open contempt. Savile enjoyed presiding over his quiet jurisdiction. He was accustomed to settling minor land disputes and petty squabbles among neighbours: murder was something quite new in his experience. His deep baritone voice wavered as he struggled to maintain control.

"I have long known thee for a man of loose morals and poor judgment, Calverley… but *this*? How must I comment? I am sickened past all speech! Nothing is to be gained by my ranting at a ruthless killer of women and babes—"

Savile choked on the last word. He cleared his throat and planted himself directly before the prisoner.

"Why, Calverley? I command you to speak—though what possible excuse under Heaven you could make is beyond all ken."

Calverley uttered no reply. He stared ahead at the far wall past the

magistrate's left shoulder.

"Well? For God's sake, man! If you cannot repent, will you not at least admit to your deeds?"

Again, there was no answer. Savile made a loud sound of disgust through pursed lips.

"Puh! No matter—I need no further evidence than you wear on your clothes. Your family's blood speaks condemns thee of these crimes."

Savile turned to Leventhorpe and the two manservants waiting by the door.

"There is yet the threat of Plague rampant in the streets of York, and I would not see the creature taken by disease before he can meet the executioner's justice. In the morning, he shall be taken to the new gaol at Wakefield to wait out the pestilence. I pray that York may be clean enough to see this devil there tried in the next Assizes. I'll not waste any more breath."

Exiting, Savile spun back once more to confront the impassive Calverley.

"Have you no human quality? A wild beast would not perform so savagely upon its own offspring! Yet there thou stand—unmoved neither by thy deeds nor the promise of death. How can I reason with such a base spirit?"

As the booming voice echoed around the large hall, Leventhorpe and his two companions flinched. Calverley did not. He gave no indication that he'd even heard the outburst, much less been affected by what was said. Savile snorted and spat a gobbet at the captive's feet. He barked out a final, general command.

"Someone clean the bastard off. The very sight of him poisons the eye."

Savile marched from the chamber as the small cluster of men bowed to the back of his departing figure. Leventhorpe's men glanced at Calverley, then exchanged an anxious glance. Neither seemed willing to make a move to follow the magistrate's orders. Leventhorpe sighed.

"Fetch me water and fresh clothing, and some rags to bind his ankle. I shall clean him up myself."

Brightening, the two men hurried off to retrieve the supplies. One paused at the door.

"Thank you, sir. I could not bear to touch the devil."

The door banged shut and the bolt was fastened from the outside. Approaching with caution, Leventhorpe warily took Calverley by his elbow.

"You must sit—that ankle will not bear your weight."

Calverley submitted, allowing Leventhorpe to lead him to a rough-hewn bench against the far chamber wall. The bolt on the lock slid back and the door opened halfway. The servants hurriedly set a jug of water, rags and a change of clothing upon the flagstones just inside the chamber, then the two men instantly retreated and left Leventhorpe alone to tend to Calverley.

Leventhorpe encountered no resistance as he stripped his neighbour of his muddy, blood-soaked clothing and began the task of wiping him clean. Calverley's manner made him as soft and pliant as an obedient child, and he allowed his naked limbs to be manipulated with not a sound of complaint. As he scrubbed the gore from his face, Leventhorpe uncovered not a beast but the kindly expression of an old friend. Nothing remained of the recent animosity or the mask of mad rage he'd worn at his capture. As Leventhorpe tore long strips of cloth and tightly bound his sprained ankle, Calverley helpfully held out his leg. The glassy expression had fled, leaving the murderer's eyes clear and focused. As Leventhorpe performed his nursing tasks, he felt himself being regarded with interest.

In a quiet, even tone of voice, Calverley broke his

silence.

"I had consumed all. 'Twas the most merciful deed I could do, to cozen beggary and knock my house on the head."

Leventhorpe sat back on his haunches to hear the confession, his eyes fixed on Calverley's pensive countenance.

"I meant to die as well once the others were dispatched. Only then might I leave my brother William the means to buy his freedom. 'Tis naught but a shadow of the fortune I once possessed, but with no more bastards to feed and clothe, it would suffice."

Leventhorpe was struck dumb. Leaning forward on the bench, Calverley grasped him by the hand.

"All my life I've been under the control of others. My father oversaw my youth, and after his death the Court of Wards dictated my path. My mother chose my wife. Another man fathered my heirs."

He shot Leventhorpe an ironic smile and patted his hand with an air of forgiveness. "'Tis no great matter, sir. Bad hath turned to worse: I've been made Fortune's fool by a miserable pair of dice, and creditors have picked the bones. In the end, the Crown shall kill me for my cruel charity. They are most heartily welcome to my life: they can have no more of me but my skin, and that wants but flaying."

Calverley's smile broadened.

"You see, silence ensures that the bloodhounds cannot lay hands on what few coins remain. Dost thou know the law, Tom? If I refuse to plea—speak narry a word protesting guilt or innocence—the Crown has no power to seize my estate. I cannot prevent their killing me. Marry, I deserve no better. But I *can* control this, my final wager: dear brother William shall inherit all. At the last, I may rest assured that I alone commanded my outcome."

Calverley winked and, with a final squeeze of Leventhorpe's hand, he let go. He leaned back against the wall and closed his eyes in contentment. Leventhorpe stared at the killer's face as the silence again descended. Finally, he found his voice.

"Hast thou no apology to offer? No word of remorse?"

Calverley did not open his eyes. A slight sneer twisted his lips as he spoke, his voice coming thick and heavy.

"Apologize? For ridding the world of your strumpet and bastards? 'Tis meet *thou* shouldst seek forgiveness of *me*! But it matters not: I have done, and I leave thee alive to suffer. From this day forth I'll speak no more."

"Why make you these base accusations, Calverley? Thy wife was a goodly woman of virtuous honour. Her sons were thine! They bore the clear stamp of their sire for all the world to see—"

He trailed off, exhausted. Calverley did not seem to hear. His breath deepened and he snored gently, like a simple labourer at rest after a long day's hard work. He looked so peaceful in his repose.

Leventhorpe felt sick. Rising, he carried the bowl of rags and filthy brownish-red water to the fireplace and emptied it into the ashes. He wiped his hands on a clean rag and set the bundle of fresh clothes on the bench at Calverley's side, leaving him to dress himself when he awoke from his nap. *To look upon him thus you would not think 'tis a man possessed by a mad devil.*

Leventhorpe went to the door and knocked loudly. As he stood waiting to be let out, he turned back and addressed the oblivious sleeper in a flat voice.

"I shall return to Calverley Hall and clear up your mess. In the morning, I'll accompany thee from hence to the gaol at Wakefield."

Leventhorpe left Calverley snoring and naked on the bench. No food or light was ordered for him. Indicating the dark heap of bloody clothes to the guard, Leventhorpe requested that they be gathered up and kept as evidence.

* * *

Near silence engulfed Calverley Hall as sombre tasks were undertaken. Leventhorpe dispatched the College Master and Marlowe from further duty and saw them off, embracing Richardson. He envied not the man's long journey back to Oxford to deliver the terrible news to Calverley's brother. Leventhorpe busied himself supervising the activity in the Hall. Standing in the doorway of the murder room, he watched the fruitless efforts of the brigade of cleaners as the oak panels of the children's bedchamber refused to yield their testimonial stains. The old woman in charge of the scrubbing turned to see him and paused in her labour, wiping the sweat from her brow with the back of her hand.

"There is nowt to be done, sir. Murder hath took this chamber full in its hands, and I fear the marks will never come out."

In the years to come, the old woman's words would prove to be prophetic: dark blemishes remained visible in the wood grain for as long as the panels stood in place.

Leventhorpe drifted from room to room, silently overseeing a team of stony-faced cleaning servants he'd brought from his own estate. The diminished household staff of Calverley Hall could hardly be expected to scour the bloody floorboards and steps. Sarah and John were at rest after being seen to by the local surgeon. By some miracle, Sarah was only badly bruised, and John's wounds looked far worse than they actually were. In time their bodies would heal, but Leventhorpe feared both of the young people were forever shattered in spirit. They remained sequestered together in Sarah's chamber behind the kitchen to find whatever solace they could in each other's company.

"Poor lass," the old woman confided to Leventhorpe. "She offered to help me clean the wee boys, but just fetching their best clothes was more than she could bear. Once she saw their faces, she fell to such fits of weeping that she had to be carried off to her bed."

Sir Thomas could not imagine how stricken the girl must be. He could not bring himself to view the boys, cleaned and laid out side by side in the Solar's main chamber. Leventhorpe was racked by the notion that, if only he'd acted in more haste, the children might yet live. His guilt was unbearable. William and Walter were to be buried the next morning with neither parent in attendance. Sir Thomas would at least be there to bid them to eternal slumber: he couldn't fathom how a man might make martyrs of his own children. Edward was his soul's joy. The very idea of killing his own dear son... *no devil could force my hand.* Though he dearly wished to hold his child to his heart—to feel the boy warm and breathing in his arms—Leventhorpe could not face going home.

How must I tell my wee Edward such dread news?

The enormity of the servants' labour was overwhelming. No sooner was one part of the Hall rendered clean than another gory mess was discovered elsewhere. All of the window casements were flung wide open to admit the fresh spring breeze, and bunches of dried marjoram and lavender were brought from the stillroom and scattered in corners in the sad hope their scents would rid the air of the acrid stench of death.

Once Leventhorpe was confident his staff was doing as well as could be expected, he slid into the master bedchamber and stood in the doorway watching the surgeon tend to Phillipa Calverley. His heart bled for the woman. He'd been amazed to find her alive when he returned to the Hall after delivering Calverley to the magistrate and was moved to offer up a prayer of thanks in the private chapel.

Phillipa was not yet out of danger. Her eyes were clenched shut, and her damp hair lay in an unruly tangle on the bolsters. The generally rosy countenance of her cheek was as pale as the bed linens. Her ragged breathing filled Leventhorpe with alarm.

"Is she in grave peril?"

Wiping his hands on a clean rag, the surgeon turned at the sound of his whisper and favoured him with a weary smile.

"Mistress Calverley has shed much blood and is very weak, but with God's will she should recover in time."

Leventhorpe stepped up to the bedside and took her hand. He felt a brotherly urge to protect the woman; her family and friends were so far away in London, and she looked so small and alone.

"'Tis indeed a miracle that she yet draws breath."

Phillipa was not asleep as he'd thought. Her cracked lips gaped and formed a husky reply:

"What manner of life is it? To see my children murdered, and my husband lost to me? My life is done."

"Courage, Madam. Thy husband was captured before he could reach the door of the wet nurse's cottage. The infant Henry is safe and well: there art thou happy."

Phillipa's eyes fluttered open and she struggled to lift her head from the bolsters.

"What? He yet lives?"

"Yes. Young Henry is sound, God be thanked."

Phillipa's dark eyes glimmered with a strange light.

"I speak of my *husband*... he is still alive?"

As she gazed quizzically at the doctor, Leventhorpe's smile faltered. He turned to the surgeon, who flushed a bright red and hissed a flustered explanation.

"I had told the lady that he was dead. I'd thought it for the best."

"Then it is not true?"

"No, Madam. He lives."

"Then God be thanked indeed!"

The men were speechless—*Such mad charity! Sure the woman is made distract by grief!*

Phillipa sighed. Sinking back onto the bed, she closed her swollen eyes. Her breathing became more even and calm and she drifted into a deep slumber.

* * *

The following morning, Leventhorpe returned to the magistrate's hall to collect his charge. He was admitted alone into the captive's room, finding Calverley fully dressed and waiting on the rough bench. Leventhorpe stood expectantly over him to no effect: Calverley's eyes were again clouded over and he did not acknowledge his neighbour's presence. To quell his urge to strike out, Sir Thomas squeezed his leather riding gloves tightly in his fist. He'd spent the past twenty-four hours battling for control over alternating waves of unspeakable grief and a murderous rage. It was all he could do to contain his emotions.

"A most melancholy day for thee, Calverley: henceforth, thou shalt never see your namesake village more. But the villagers will not mourn your loss. Only this morning at St. Wilfred's, they wept with one voice for your two murdered sons. A piteous sight to behold their small corpses sealed into the crypt with neither sire nor dam present to see them out of this world."

Calverley did not respond. Blank of expression, he stared at Leventhorpe's chest. Sir Thomas struck his leather gloves hard against his own palm with a report that exploded and echoed about the chamber like a gunshot. Calverley did not so much as blink.

"No! I forget myself—their father *did* see them both from this world, by virtue of his dagger. *Their own father!*"

Slowly, Calverley's gaze travelled upward and met Leventhorpe's cold eyes.

"I can tell thee, there was many a man who'd have joyfully torn you to sheds at the altar, had thy black soul been allowed to corrupt the house of God! Not one of your siblings or cousins dared show their faces—so ashamed are they to bear the Calverley name. And their poor mother is yet too weak, both in body and spirit, to undertake even such a short journey to church."

At this, Calverley's dark eyes widened into focus. He gave a strange moan in the back of his throat.

"She yet lives?"

Leventhorpe favoured him with a slow, sickly smile.

"I see thou art moved at last, Calverley. 'Tis true. The blade failed to find its mark, and God has seen fit to preserve her life. Thy youngest son still has the comfort of a mother to ensure that he does not grow up friendless."

By nature, Sir Thomas was not a hard-hearted man. He could not maintain his cruel smile as Calverley's face crumpled. He watched in horror as Sir Walter's body shuddered and heaved, pitching forward off the bench as though jerked from it by a rope. Huddled on his knees, Calverley reached out a trembling hand and grasped the hem of Leventhorpe's cloak. His dry voice broke with raspy sobs.

"She is truly a good woman, if God hath saved her life! Her proven innocence is my torment. I beg you, Thomas—have pity on me… please. I must be allowed to see my wife. I want no more but a few last words."

"Such a base creature as thou deserves no such pity. None was shown her in thy foul deeds."

"Please! God have mercy—"

Calverley's speech failed. He raised a fistful of Leventhorpe's riding cloak to his quivering lips and kissed the hem, pleading wordlessly with his streaming eyes. Leventhorpe prised his clutching fingers open and yanked free his garment, taking a quick step backward out of the range of any further such pitiful gestures. He waited until the weeping tapered off before giving his considered answer.

"I make no promises, Calverley: should thy wife agree to such a meeting, I shall see it is permitted."

"Bless you, Thomas."

Calverley snuffled like a child and wiped the stream of mucous from under his nose with the back of his hand.

"Do not thank me for what is not to be. I warrant 'twill not be her wish to again clap eyes upon thy cursed face."

Leventhorpe strode to the heavy oak door and signalled to the waiting guards outside with a sharp rap of his knuckles. The two burly men were less squeamish than their predecessors of the day before: they entered without hesitation and chained Calverley's wrists together before half-dragging their hobbling prisoner out into the foreyard.

Leventhorpe sent a messenger boy ahead to Calverley Hall. If they were to make the stop, he wanted to give the inhabitants due warning of the former master's arrival.

"Go you to Mistress Calverley, and inform her that we shall pass the Hall's main gates on the way to the gaol at Wakefield. Her husband begs admission to her presence."

The boy shifted his weight from foot to foot as the two guardsmen placed the captive murderer into the saddle of a docile mount. As the mare was tethered to the lead horse, the boy stared hard at Calverley.

"Is this sad man the Beast? He hath not a devil's horns."

Leventhorpe laid a gentle hand on the lad's shoulder to regain his full attention.

"Mark me carefully: if the lady agrees to hear him, stand by the Hall's front doors and we shall know at our approach that she wishes us to enter. If she does not—which is most like—then stay you close by the front gates to signal her refusal. I will not allow the killer to set foot in the foreyard if the mistress is unwilling and her household not forewarned. Get thee gone. We shall follow presently."

As he passed Calverley, the boy lagged in his steps before crossing himself and spitting on the ground by the hooves of Calverley's mount. The messenger scrambled up onto the back of his pony and galloped through the gates and out of sight around a bend in the road.

Sir John Savile hung back and watched the proceedings from the front entrance of his Hall, taking regular pulls of strong wine from an ornately embossed silver goblet. Ensuring that Calverley was safely subdued in his saddle, Leventhorpe approached the magistrate to take his leave. Savile made a signal with a sharp wave of his free hand. Leventhorpe paused—unsure if he should proceed—then realized the gesture was directed at one of the household servants. The thin steward met Sir Thomas at the door with a smaller, slightly less ostentatious cup of wine. Gratefully, he took a swallow and felt an immediate rush of heat through his veins. He was exhausted by the ordeals of the past day and sleepless night and leaned heavily against the massive doorframe.

The older man held out his goblet to be refilled by a second servant standing at the ready with a silver ewer on a tray. Savile raised his brimming cup, admiring its surface in the glinting sun.

"How like you my drinking vessels, Leventhorpe? The finest silversmith in all of London crafted these."

"Indeed, my lord? They are most handsome."

"Have you not seen their like before?"

The magistrate's eyes gleamed with amusement. Leventhorpe was puzzled by the frivolous topic of conversation, given the circumstances. He squinted at the cup in his hand and wrinkled his brow.

"Marry, sir… now that you mention it, they do seem somehow familiar."

Savile turned his goblet and indicated with a touch of his beringed forefinger a coat of arms embossed upon its side.

Six owls on a shield: the Calverley family emblem.

Leventhorpe half-choked on his wine as Savile threw back his head and laughed at his friend's expression.

"Worry not, good Sir Thomas! These came to my hands as an honest bargain last year when Calverley sold off so many of his fine goods. I thought it fitting to see him off to gaol with a toast from his own wedding silver."

Turning, Savile turned and raised his arm at the captive in a mocking salute.

"God damn you, sir!"

Leaning ahead in his saddle, Calverley fixed his glassy eyes upon the bend in the road leading toward his Hall and was heedless to the jibe. Savile's merry face grew solemn. He faced Leventhorpe and made him an earnest salute.

"God speed thy journey, Thomas. I envy thee not having to further endure the devil's fellowship. Thou hast borne too much already. Let the guardsman take him; you need not take this duty on."

"Nay, sir, but I must. I need to see it is well done."

"Thou art a godly man, Thomas. Farewell."

Despite his queasiness, Leventhorpe drained his cup before joining his restless entourage.

* * *

The village was empty as the men rode through. No one seemed to be about on any regular daily business, and they met no merchants on the road to Leeds, though it was a market day. The steady clumping of their horses' hooves reverberated from of the walls of the close-set cottages and outbuildings. Through the corners of his eyes, Leventhorpe could glimpse pale faces peering through windows or peeking around doorways. All seemed to want a look at the devil incarnate as he passed—but none seemed willing to risk being seen by him in return.

At last, Calverley Hall was in sight. Leventhorpe glanced back at Calverley, straining forward in his saddle as if willing his horse to break its stately pace and gallop him up to his front doors. Leventhorpe gripped the lead tether more tightly in his hand in case he tried to bolt.

Leventhorpe's heart sank as they neared the gates: the messenger boy was nowhere to be seen, even though he'd had ample time to deliver his message and take up his position. Leventhorpe flicked his gaze up to the Hall. There by the front doors, the boy stood and raised his hand in a joyless greeting. Leventhorpe brought his horse to a stop outside the gates, mumbling under his breath.

"This cannot be right—"

He gestured to the boy and pointed to the grey stone walls flanking the drive with a shout.

"Do you not mean to be standing here?"

The boy shook his head and pointed to the ground at his feet. Leventhorpe twisted around to look at his charge. The tendons in Calverley's neck stood out in sharp relief and his breath was coming in an audible hiss. He met Leventhorpe's glance with a fiery eye and raised one eyebrow.

Well?

Leventhorpe called to the guardsmen.

"Come. Help him dismount, and then await my signal to bring him into the Hall. I shall go before."

They rode single file into the yard. Numbed by exhaustion, Leventhorpe slid from horseback, not feeling the ground beneath his feet as he approached the front entrance. The whole thing seemed like a nightmare from which he could be roused. The boy was near tears as he bravely held Leventhorpe's gaze. The lad opened his mouth to speak, but could only shake his head in misery.

"It's all right, boy. Get you home."

The snivelling boy ran down the sloping foreyard to collect his pony and rode off, giving Calverley as wide a berth as possible.

Leventhorpe entered the Hall and found himself unmet. This was no surprise. He suspected the two young servants were closed up behind doors to wait out their former lord's visit. Venturing upstairs to the master bedchamber, Sir Thomas found his way barred by the surgeon. The man's ruddy face was twisted in fury as he planted himself with outspread arms, blocking the doorway.

"I know why thou art come, though I could scarce believe the boy when he told me. I can well see the damnable creature standing out front. How *dare* you bring him here?"

He jerked his head toward the windows. Calverley stared up at their very casement. Undaunted, Leventhorpe tried to push past into the room and was surprised by the old man's strength as he held fast to his arm.

"'Tis madness! Mean you to kill the lady?"

Leventhorpe heaved a sigh.

"Please you, may I speak with her?"

The surgeon locked eyes with him for a long moment. Shaking his head, he eased his grip and stood aside, allowing Sir Thomas free passage.

"'Twill do no good, especially now that she knows he waits below. She will not be made to see sense. The poor woman is much distract by her grief and knows not right from wrong."

Halfway out of bed, Phillipa's legs were wound up in the coverlets as she struggled to reach the window. Leventhorpe rushed to her side and gently pressed her back against the bolsters, smoothing the covers around her legs and gently stroking her hands to calm her agitation.

"No, good Madam. You must not tire yourself."

"But he is *here.*"

"And you need not speak with him. 'Twas cruel and

unnatural to bring him so near to thee—I shall take him away."

Leventhorpe rose from her bedside, but she clutched at his arm and held him back.

"My husband wishes to speak to me. That was the message."

"You owe him nothing, Mistress."

"It is his desire, and so I will obey. I will deny him nothing."

"Dear Madam, I beseech thee—"

"I *will* see him."

Leventhorpe shot a look at the surgeon over his shoulder. Dismissively, he flapped his hand at Sir Thomas.

"Bah! 'Tis neither here nor there. 'Twill upset her mightily if he is permitted entrance—and yet if he is dragged from hence, the lady's rest will have been greatly disturbed for naught. Either way, the damage is done. Do what you will; I can no more!"

Stepping before the windows, Leventhorpe signalled the guards to bring in their prisoner. The silence of their anticipation was broken by the uneven scrape of Calverley's boots approaching on the stairs. Sitting up tall, Phillipa hurriedly smoothed the front of her nightgown and combed through her matted hair with her fingers. Leventhorpe stood by with his hand gripping the bedpost so tightly that the carved vinery imprinted into the flesh of his palm. There was a shuffle at the door as the guards hung back to position themselves outside in the hallway, barring any attempted escape.

Calverley stepped into the chamber unescorted. Fixing his gaze upon the figure in the bed, he ignored both Leventhorpe and the surgeon.

Phillipa regarded him with unreadable eyes as her pale hands tossed back the coverlet. Swinging her bare legs out of the bed, she rose and stood shakily, her hand digging into the mattress for support—waving away both the doctor and Leventhorpe as they sprang forward to her aid. Gasping with feverish effort, she hobbled forward to face her attacker, her gown clinging to her sweaty form.

Calverley stood waiting, his hands still held helplessly shackled. Phillipa held her arms out stiffly at her sides to keep her balance. Her legs quaked with exertion, but her determination did not falter as she came to stand directly before her husband. Leventhorpe kept watch, ready to intervene. As she slowly raised her open hand, Phillipa took in a deep breath. Calverley closed his eyes to accept the anticipated blow.

The hand descended.

The touch landed lightly on his cheek and stroked the length of his face with a loving caress. Calverley's eyes flew open, his head jerking back as though her fingers burned his skin. Phillipa's other hand came to rest on his opposite cheek, cupping his face and tilting it down toward her own.

Phillipa smiled.

Calverley's eyes welled up and overflowed. He sank his head forward onto his wife's bandaged shoulder and shook them both with the force of his sobbing. Phillipa shushed him and grasped his bound hands, raising them to her lips. Calverley's voice was choked.

"What? Can you kiss the hand that hath murdered thy sons... that would have murdered thee?"

"Many times have I kissed this hand that has proved long cruel to me. Unkindness cuts a deeper wound than steel."

"Demons have been my undoing—blinding me from the true path. The Devil himself wielded that knife, not I."

"In faith, I do believe thy words."

Tears flowed unchecked down both their faces. Blinking fast, Calverley gave his head a violent shake.

"I feel the demon fly from me, depart my joints, heave up my nails. His hellish games at an end, he doth abandon his earthly puppet. And yet thou dost not, though I have wronged thee to the quick. My dearest soul!"

Calverley raised her hands in his chained grasp and pressed them to his mouth.

"I have been too cruel for too long. Now I shall die for it."

"Thou shalt not, for I forgive all."

Calverley collapsed against her and Phillipa staggered

backwards under her husband's weight. As Leventhorpe stepped in to prevent her from falling, she turned to him with shining eyes.

"My thanks, sir. You may leave us."

"Madam, you know that cannot be."

"But he is my husband. I forgive him!"

"The law, alas, does not. Come—make your last farewells."

Leventhorpe gestured to the men in the hallway. His own eyes blurred with unshed tears of pity for Phillipa as he gently pried her fingers loose and eased her away from her husband, holding her back as Calverley was pulled from her embrace by the guardsmen. Phillipa's legs went out from under her and he could not keep her from sinking to her knees.

"Stay… you shall not leave me."

Calverley was dragged backwards to the chamber door.

"You see it must be so. Farewell."

The guards gave his arm a final, wrenching tug and Calverley made his final exit from his marriage chamber.

Phillipa let out a keening wail and stretched the length of her body along the floor, her arms reaching out toward the now-empty doorway. Leventhorpe knelt at her side.

"Mistress, thou must take to thy bed. Do not you waste your little strength on him—think of thy little boy Henry at nurse. Take joy in his life."

"Dearer than all is my poor husband's life!"

The surgeon appeared to take her other arm.

"You cannot mean that! Please, Madam—be sensible."

Phillipa lashed out at both of the men and battered away their touch. They pulled back in surprise as she struggled into a kneeling position at their feet and held her clasped hands before her in supplication.

"I beg thee, sir… pardon him as I do! Didst not hear his repentant words? Thou must restore him to me!"

"Madam, I cannot."

Phillipa's hands dropped to her sides and her head fell forward as one condemned to the block. Sir Thomas bowed deeply to her.

"God be with you."

Swallowing back tears and a rush of nausea, Leventhorpe left the chamber and followed out after the men to the front of the Hall.

"Milady?"

Phillipa felt the surgeon's hands reaching out to assist her.

"Do not touch me!"

She half-crawled, half-dragged herself over to the window and hauled herself up onto the windowsill. Leaning her forehead against the glass, she watched as her husband was helped to remount.

Calverley hung his head, obscuring his face from

Phillipa's sight. Leventhorpe swung himself up onto his horse and waved the guardsmen on with his hand. The horses filed through the gates and turned left down the hill toward the road to Wakefield. Not once did Calverley raise his head to look back at the Hall: he did not see the pale face in the upstairs window watching as the last horse rounded the bend and disappeared from view.

Calverley was gone. She would never see him again.

"No—"

Phillipa felt a searing heat smash into the back of her skull. The sensation forced her face hard up against the glass, her back arching as the spasm of pain raced down her spine. Her limbs jerked out of control. She was dimly aware of the surgeon as he rushed forward to steady her convulsions, but he was too slow in preventing her head from cracking hard against the window frame. Phillipa slumped to the floor, her hand still clutching the windowsill. Her entire being felt as though it was detached and sliding away, floating high above where she could feel no more pain. No further grief. Just blank nothingness.

Lord, I pray that I may never again wake.

PART THREE

'Now glides the devil from me,
Departs at every joint, heaves up my nails… '

—*A Yorkshire Tragedy,*
Act I, Scene viii

CHAPTER THIRTEEN

Drowned—

It feels like I have drowned. But at least I feel something—so I must still be alive.

Clara heard herself as if from a great distance as she gasped in a halting breath. A violent cough racked her form, jolting her consciousness a little closer toward the murky surface. Guttural moans sounded from deep in her chest as she willed herself to kick free of the sensation of being held under, until at last the depthless black behind her eyelids began to glow red around the edges. Small bursts of white light flashed and popped with each cough. The luminous patterns formed and faded as her breath strengthened and began to come more easily. Air again flowed freely in her arid throat.

Next, the feeling slowly returned to her limbs. Blood tingled and rushed through her veins—prickling like a thousand razor-sharp needles.

It hurt. A lot.

Clara's lips twitched into a weak smile of gratitude: the pain was proof that she was really back in her own body. Her eyes opened into slits as she tried to regain her lost bearings. She found herself on her back, looking up at the ceiling of the Old Hall's master bedroom from underneath the front window, where she lay slumped on the floor.

One arm was extended upward with her fingers clutching the windowsill. Blinking hard to focus, she verified that the hand was indeed her own by the familiar gold wedding band on her third finger. She gave a clumsy tug, and her arm fell back across her torso like a dead thing. The weight of it seemed genuine, and that was a source of some comfort: it confirmed that she was once again composed of solid matter.

Clara rolled her throbbing head to one side as gently as possible to look around the room. There was the unmade guest bed, an open suitcase spilling out clothing, her backpack ready by the door.

One of her hiking boots lay in the middle of the room with its black tongue lolling out. Her memory flooded back.

It was too much to process all at once. Overwhelmed, she couldn't decide whether she was delusional or truly had been out of her body and time to bear witness to another life. Either way, she was in deep trouble. Satisfied that at least she seemed to be back in her own era, Clara heaved herself into a sitting position against the wall, gritting her teeth at the high-pitched whine ringing in between her ears.

How long have I been lying here?

Twitching her wrist over in her lap, she glanced down and saw that the LED display on her watch was again functional.

'2:48 P.M.,' it flashed. 'FRI.'

Friday. The Oxford Romantics conference had wrapped up: that meant Scott could be back at the Old Hall any moment now.

* * *

In Oxford, the rest of the conference week had not gone smoothly for Scott.

He'd returned from the impromptu Yorkshire visit early in the wee hours, dropped the rental car off in the car park near the train station and walked the short distance to his hotel through the deserted streets. Scott deeply inhaled the cool night air. His mind buzzed with feelings of regret and a vague, nagging guilt. Severe headaches were a constant torment that seemed to fog his very memory: he had only the most fleeting recollections about his conversation with Clara. One thing was clear: they must have quarrelled, or else he wouldn't be back here in Oxford on his own.

The next morning, Scott was feeling woozy and under-slept as he ascended the podium of the Divinity School lecture hall.

The big moment had arrived.

He took his time, casually setting out papers on the stand in front of him. He wouldn't need them: with his steel-trap memory, he never needed notes. The papers were really just his scribbling of unconnected thoughts—they were only there for show.

The careful whisper campaign he had waged through Twittering and blogging over the past months to create advance buzz had borne remarkable results: the audience of his peers filled the benches and chairs of the august, ancient lecture hall to capacity, with a number of people standing against the back wall. Despite the soaring fan-vaulted ceilings, the air in the room was stuffy and the sun beamed hotly through the leaded Gothic windows to add to the general discomfort. There was a distracting level of murmuring and reconfiguring of bodies as some latecomers tried haplessly to find seats. Many fanned themselves with programs in an effort to keep cool. The white flashes of fluttering papers made Scott's aching temples throb anew.

It was time to start. He coughed sharply, and the chatter died down. All eyes were on him with expectations running high. Scott's gift for self-promotion was matched only by his keen ambition. Word of mouth was that his paper on Keats promised to be a particularly illuminating one. After this imminent triumph, the subsequent planned book on his findings was destined to become required reading on university reading lists worldwide The full house was proof positive that the hype was about to bear him an orchard brimming with fruit. As Scott pushed his glasses up on the sweaty bridge of his nose, he noted that a couple of the big academic publishers' representatives were seated at the front of the audience—notebooks and pens in hand—eager to hear his revelations.

This could start a bidding war for the manuscript.

"My honoured colleagues—allow me to begin by expressing just how gratifying it is to see so many of you here in this magnificent room this morning for my talk on the life and work of the greatest of all the English Romantic poets—John Keats."

The last of the restless whispering had faded away. They were all his.

"Keats, the greatest? Many of you must be thinking me in error. 'What about Lord Byron?' you may ask. 'Or Blake? And what of the divine William Wordsworth?' Keats has long dwelt unfairly in the shadows of these momentous figures, but what I propose to reveal to you today will—I know—bring the 'bright star' of a relatively neglected genius to take his proper place in literary history at long last."

Look at them, said the smug voice in his head. *They're hooked.*

Clara— answered a smaller, more sinister voice from the depths. *She should be here to witness your triumph.*

Scott's throat suddenly went bone dry. He grappled on the small table to the side of the podium for a glass of water, but the organizers had forgotten to fill the jug.

"*Ahem*. In my defense, let me first outline what my research has done to convince me that this overlooked genius was the pinnacle of the English Romantic style, and the truest voice of all his poetic movement. As Keats himself once said in a letter to Shelley: 'A man has not—"

Someone chose that moment to switch on an ancient electric fan in the back corner of the room. A rhythm of squeaky, rattling bangs—like the sounds of a rickety World War One biplane attempting take-off—shattered what remained of Scott's tenuous concentration.

He blanked.

"Uh… "

No words came. Frozen, he stared out stupidly at the expectant faces. Sweat soaked the back of his shirt under his navy blazer. A few people exchanged glances with their neighbours as the tense silence lengthened. Some faces registered sympathetic pity—others seemed cruelly amused by the humiliation being played out before their eyes. Scott thought he heard a snicker from the cluster of undergrads standing at the back of the hall and shot a dirty look in their direction.

"He said that… um… One moment, please. I have the quote here somewhere… He said—"

Scott rifled through his useless 'notes' in a desperate search for his thesis statement. He was hoist on his own petard. The notes were hopelessly incomplete because of his egotistical overconfidence that he would never stoop to refer to them. He'd been over this lecture in his head a hundred times. It had practically written itself after Scott's groundbreaking discovery in the private library of a Wiltshire stately home following the funeral for one of his well-connected father's political friends. Scott alone knew the value of his find, and made a lowball bid to the Peer's widow who happily accepted—glad to be shot of the clutter of musty, foxed papers. The obscure collection of unpublished letters and journal entries was illuminating and shocking in scope, outlining unwritten works in progress by Keats and his famous poet friends—as well as some juicy love letters to Fanny Brawne to add irresistible sexiness to the project. His thesis was a watershed: the one extraordinary quote he'd discovered proved it beyond a doubt. If only he could find it.

"Oh for fuck's sake—where is it?" he hissed, a little too loudly.

"I don't recall Keats ever having said anything like *that!*" quipped some wag in the third row.

There was an answering ripple of giggles and a rising tide of muttered comments. Scott could barely breathe, his head pounding fit to burst. His colleagues shuffled and coughed for what to him seemed like hours before he finally recovered his thread.

"Here we are, ladies and gentlemen... thank you for your patience. As I was saying, my unique research led me to reach this phenomenal conclusion because of something Keats himself so brilliantly penned to Shelley—"

Sweat trickled down the back of his shirt.

"Uh... no, sorry. I don't seem to have it. Moving on... "

Scott's spirit was irretrievably broken. He delivered a cobbled-together version of his 'brilliant' lecture in a rushed monotone—not once daring to lift his eyes from his useless notes. He'd been pompous enough to leave the actual scanned copies of the letters and diaries behind in his hotel room, and he was damned if he could remember a word of them. The scholars crossed their arms or fiddled with their iPhones, half-listening and counting the minutes until they could escape to the nearest pub for lunch. He didn't blame them. Without a coherent argument or physical proof, why should they believe he'd been fortunate enough to stumble across these forgotten accounts? For two years, he'd gleefully hoarded it all to himself: not even Clara knew. Scott had convinced himself that if waited to reveal his findings at just the right venue at the ideal moment, it would be the making of his entire career.

As he limped through, Scott inwardly roared at himself—admonishing his stupid neglect to make a PowerPoint presentation of the first-hand scrawls of the letters between Keats and Shelley, or the outline of some truly great epic poetry, thwarted and left incomplete by the tuberculosis that had carried off his hero. No—the only real drama for today was the abject failure of his lecture. At the lacklustre conclusion, there was a smattering of polite applause. Scott didn't hang around. Instead of conducting his usual question-and-answer session—a process he'd normally revel in—Scott shoved his 'notes' into his briefcase, hurried out of a side door to the nearest off-licence, and bought some Scotch.

• • •

By the time of the farewell dinner on Thursday night, Scott had been well and truly pissed for the balance of the day. It was a state he had lovingly maintained since the delivery— or rather miscarriage—of his paper. At first he'd drifted from pub to pub; but there were too many witnesses to his downfall about, so he escaped and hid in his hotel room with his Scotch bottle, warding off the threat of sobriety's premature return. Scott had no intention of attending any of the final lectures or going to the dinner with Martin and Emma as originally planned.

At six o'clock he was waiting until the coast was clear

so he could go out and restock the hooch. The bottle he had was already nearly empty. Scott heard the couple's door close next door to his room and the muted sound of Emma's high heels on the hallway carpet as she clopped toward the stairs.

"Go on, Em—I'll catch you up out front," said Martin's voice as his footsteps paused outside of his door. Martin knocked.

"I know you're in there, Scott. Why don't you come with us to the reception?"

Scott didn't answer.

"I know things haven't exactly gone well for you this week, old man, but sequestering yourself won't solve anything. If you come along tonight and make an appearance, it'll show that you have spirit."

Scott took another sip of his drink and stared at the door.

"I understand how you must feel. Really, I do. But look at it this way: if you *don't* come along and show yourself to be a good sport, people may indeed think the worse of you."

Martin waited. He coughed.

"All right. It's up to you, but please consider what I've said. Emma and I will try to save you a place at our table. I do hope you'll change your mind."

He left.

Scott drained the last of his Scotch and set down the glass. Martin had expressed it in his usual wimpy, ultra-polite way, but he was dead right: the others would think him a coward if he didn't show up, making any future conferences pure hell. Best to go along and put on a brave face, make a little small talk, laugh at himself and show some self-effacing humour about his performance—better that he crack the jokes instead of leaving himself at the mercy of other scholar's barbs. They could be such a catty lot. The deciding factor was the urgent need to corner one of the publishers and woo them with his brilliance. Whether or not the lecture had bombed, his research was waterproof. Maybe he could chalk it up to bad nerves and still salvage his reputation with a decent publishing contract.

By the time he'd showered and made himself presentable, Scott was late arriving and there were few unoccupied seats to be found. He scanned the large room through narrowed, drunken eyes in search of Martin and Emma. It would simply not do to be forced to sit among strangers tonight. Weaving in between the chairs, he jostled into a man's jutting elbow and caused him to spill a glass of wine.

"Sorry. My fault. Here, allow me." Scott picked up a cloth napkin from the table and dabbed it on the front of the man's navy blazer.

"Not to worry. It won't show... Oh! Hello, Scott! I looked for you at the pub the other night. I guess we must have missed each other."

"Oh, it's you. Hi, Art."

Scott blinked down at the grinning American, vaguely recalling that he'd made a false promise to meet the man for a drink. "Yes, I'm sorry about that. I was—uh—delayed at my meeting."

"Aw, don't worry about it." Art patted the empty chair beside him. "Please—have a seat!"

"Well, I'd made earlier arrangements to join my friends—"

Scott desperately craned his neck and finally caught Emma's eye two tables away. Waggling *'hello'* with her fingers, she prodded her husband's arm and pointed to Scott. Martin smiled to see him, shrugging as he indicated with outstretched hands that there were no empty seats left at their table. Scott glanced down at Art's fading smile and clapped him on the shoulder.

"—but seeing as I stood you up, I'm sure they'll understand if I don't sit with them tonight."

"Good man! I never did get a chance to show off my pictures of Benjamin." Art pulled a bulging envelope out of his jacket pocket. "Gosh, but these have gotten awfully out of order. Hold on a sec… "

As Art began sorting out the comprehensive pictorial chronicles of the Life of Benjamin into their proper sequence, Scott slumped in his chair.

Jeez, how archaic. Can't he just carry his photos on his phone like the rest of the world? Scott reached into the centre of the table for an open bottle of red wine and poured a healthy glassful for himself. As he put the bottle back, he noticed a lovely blonde woman sitting to his left watching him with intent interest. Scott sat up straight and smiled.

"Hello. Would you care for some more wine?"

"No thank you. I'm fine for now." Scott felt a rising tide of lust at the sound of her sultry voice—husky and tinged with a hint of a well-bred New England accent. She proffered a manicured hand for him to shake. "I don't believe we've met. I'm Cheryl Davies, from Harvard."

"Of course—I've read your book on Shelley. Brilliant work."

"Thank you. You're very kind."

Her smile was warming his cockles.

"I'm Scott Atkinson, from Trent University."

"I know who you are. I was at your lecture."

"Oh… were you?" Scott took a hasty gulp of wine.

"Yes. I found it most… *interesting*." Turning, she rested her hand on the sleeve of the heavyset grey-haired man sitting beside her. "Darling, have you met Professor Atkinson from Trent University?"

"Who?" The man scowled at Scott from under his bushy eyebrows. "Where did you say?"

"Trent," said Scott. "It's in Ontario—Peterborough?"

"Never heard of the place."

"Well, it is rather a small university, but it's quite—"

The man had already turned away to continue his

interrupted conversation. His sexy companion smiled apologetically at Scott, then joined in the animated discussion with her brusque darling.

"Here we are, Scott," said Art, tugging on his arm. "Now, this is when Janet first went into labour. I just love the expression on her face, don't you?"

"Priceless."

. . .

Scott did not bother trying to schmooze any of the publisher's reps—they were seated at the far end of the room, and Art kept him well and truly cornered with his stack of snapshots. The Harvard snobs froze him out. Scott pleaded a headache and left before dessert was served.

Back in his hotel room, he heard low voices as Emma and Martin returned from dinner and went into their room. He took another swig of wine from the bottle he'd swiped at the farewell dinner and pressed his ear to the wall as he had the other night, using his tooth glass to amplify the sound. He heard water running in the sink in their room, the scrubbing of somebody's teeth. The wardrobe door opened and clothes hangers rattled together.

He waited, his neck growing stiff. At last, the bedsprings gave a promising squeak in the next room. Breathing quietly, Scott knelt on the bed and shifted his weight into a more comfortable position. Emma's throaty voice was murmuring what sounded like an invitation, followed by some rustling and heavy sighs. Scott closed his eyes and his shallow breathing quickened in voyeuristic anticipation as his free hand fumbled with the tie of his bathrobe.

Ah, yes…

Then, all went still.

Scott was puzzled. He pressed his ear hard against the glass until his skull ached, careful not to scrape against the wall and give away his act of eavesdropping. He could just make out Emma's words.

"Martin? Oh darling… have you fallen asleep?"

At his answering snore, Emma chuckled.

Scott felt cheated that she'd give up on sex so easily and leave him bereft of this evening's masturbation fodder. The bed squeaked again, and he heard the wardrobe being opened. A hanger clattered.

Scott slipped quietly off of his bed and went to listen at his door. Emma came out of their room pulled their door shut softly behind her. Through the peephole, he saw her clad in her dressing gown carrying a towel, heading to the communal bathroom at the other end of the hallway. A moment later, the water ran in the shower.

Scott waited. For fifteen full minutes, he listened to the muffled sound of the water cascading over Emma's body—imagining her lush skin, all wet and warm in the steam and heat. The excess of drink did nothing to take the edge off of his horniness. His cock felt like titanium.

And as for Emma… well she'd just been left frustrated, hadn't she?

The water stopped running. *Any moment now…*

When Emma left the bathroom, Scott cracked open his door and whispered to her as she passed.

"Hi, Emma."

Startling, she answered back in a conspirator's whisper so as not to wake the other guests.

"Oh! Christ, Scott. You've scared me half to death."

"Sorry." He held out the wine bottle. "Care for a nightcap?"

Emma paused, then smiled.

"Sure, why not? Martin's dead to the world anyway."

Scott stepped aside to let her into the room, took a quick peek up and down the empty hallway, then shut the door and quietly locked it. Emma hadn't noticed: she was too engrossed with squeezing the dampness out of her tumble of auburn hair with a hand towel. The sight made him swallow hard. He handed her the tooth glass full of wine, watching her sip as he poured himself a helping into a coffee mug. It thrilled him to think that she was drinking from the very instrument he'd secretly used to listen in on her most intimate moments. Scott's guestroom was too small to accommodate a chair, so they sat sprawled together on the bed in the easy manner of old friends. He was glad the light was so dim—perhaps she wouldn't notice his erection fighting to breach the gap in his robe.

Not quite yet…

Emma smiled warmly. "I'm so glad you decided to show up at the dinner."

"Well, Martin had a point. I would've looked a poor sport if I'd stayed away."

"I noticed you left early."

"Did you?"

Emma regarded him intently.

"Are you sure you're quite all right, Scott?"

"What do you mean?"

"I know the paper didn't go over anything like as well as you'd planned. Was it because of Clara?"

"Hm?" He poured more wine into his mug.

"Don't be evasive, Scott. I can tell things aren't exactly sunny between you two. I tried asking on the drive here, but you didn't seem to want to talk about it in front of Martin." She patted his hand. "It's just us now—if that makes it any easier."

Scott set his mug on the bedside table. Turning to Emma, he looked down at her hand resting lightly on his arm, then covered it with his own, glancing up at her face to gauge her reaction to the gesture. She didn't appear to mind in the least. His lips twitched as he tried to return her smile—and failed.

"Well, you're right. Things haven't been good lately, Emma."

"Poor Scott."

"But you are."

"Oh yes, we're fine. Martin and I have the odd little spat about silly things, but then I suppose all couples—"

"No. That's not what I meant, Em. *You* are good. You are a good woman." He moved his hand down and rested it on her knee. She laughed.

"And *you*, Scott, are a very drunk man. I think we should wait and talk about this in the car on the way home tomorrow. I know you're reluctant to tell Martin about your troubles, but he's your friend. He cares about you. I don't know why you men feel the need to be so macho and hide your emotions from each other all the time. It's just plain silly, don't you think?"

Scott said nothing. He held her gaze and kept his hand on her knee. Emma coughed and took her hand away from his arm.

"It's late. I should go and let you get to sleep. We have a long drive in the morning—that'll give the three of us plenty of time to come up with some strategies. These road bumps happen in a marriage, but there's always hope for you and Clara to get yourselves sorted. Never fear."

Emma drained her wine. As she leaned over to set her glass down on the bedside table, her bathrobe gaped open. Scott breathed in the irresistible scent of her freshly showered skin: a heady, warm aroma of spicy perfumed body-wash that went straight to his crotch. In one movement, he took his hand from her knee and slid it upward to cup her breast, pinching the nipple into a surprised hardness. Emma tensed.

"Look, I really don't think—"

Scott couldn't hear her over the rush of desire in his head. This was beyond his control. He pressed his mouth onto hers and forced his tongue between her lips, pushing her down onto the bed. She jerked her head aside and broke off the kiss.

"No, Scott! I know you're drunk, but please just stop. Now!"

The need to possess her was too keen to deny: he had to wipe out the day's earlier humiliation. Her hands flew up to ward him off he yanked open her dressing gown and undid the ties of his own bathrobe. At the first touch of his bare flesh pressing onto hers, Emma arched her back and forced him off with a hard shove. She leapt to her feet and glowered at him as she pulled her gown tightly closed up around her neck.

"I said 'no'! What the hell is wrong with you?"

Scott lay sprawled, shamelessly open to her view. She averted her eyes.

"Cover that up."

"Come on, Em. What's a friendly little fuck between friends? No one else ever has to know."

Emma backed toward the door. Scott stood and followed.

"Don't be so coy. I know you're up for it too—what with Martin leaving you in the lurch like that."

Her eyes widened.

"What did you just say?"

"The walls are pretty thin in this place. I could hear everything. I know he conked out on you—even after you were crawling all over him, moaning in that amazing way that you have when you need some cock."

She stared at him, frozen in place. He took another step closer.

"I could hear everything you two did the other night. Sounds like you're a lot of fun. He's a lucky man."

"You're a *sick* man!"

Emma grappled at the doorknob, panicked to find the door locked. Scott leaned his arm on the wall beside her head with his hand over the deadbolt.

"You came in of your own free will, and offered me comfort—so let's have it, Emma."

Grabbing her by the wrist, he tugged her back toward the bed. Emma brought her knee up hard between his legs. Scott doubled over. She slid back the lock, scrambled out into the hall and banged the door shut in his face. He slammed his fist into the wood.

"Cock tease!" he hissed through gritted teeth. He staggered back over to the bed and collapsed. In the next room, he could hear Emma waking up her husband. He didn't bother to press his ear to the wall this time: it was easy enough to guess what she was saying to Martin.

Through his pain, Scott's head roared with a brutal, unbidden voice.

Clara—it's all Clara's fault. Fucked up the lecture because of her... now this bullshit. Never would have tried it on with Emma if Clara had been here. The bitch is gonna pay...

Curling up into a ball, Scott pulled the pillows over his head to drown out the darkness in his throbbing skull and passed out.

• • •

In the morning, Scott's head was seized by a pain that no amount of caffeine or ibuprofen could soothe. Arriving late for breakfast, he sat uninvited at the Thornburys' table and wrinkled his nose at Martin's half-eaten eggs, sausages and fried bread.

"God! I don't know how you English can stomach eating all of that grease first thing!" He helped himself to an aluminum pot on a trivet in the centre of the table. "Is this real coffee or that instant crap like they have in the rooms?"

Emma pushed back her chair and wordlessly left the dining room. Scott slurped his coffee and grimaced, dumping an extra spoonful of sugar into his cup.

"Oh well. I guess I can't afford to be fussy this morning. Maybe we can find a place along the way back that serves proper coffee. What time are we hitting the road?"

Martin shoved aside his plate and leaned over to address Scott in an undertone, his voice shaking for control.

"Considering the circumstances, I think it's best for us all if you make your *own* way back to Yorkshire. Wouldn't you agree?"

Scott smiled stiffly at his old friend.

"What do you mean by that?"

"Don't play the innocent. You know perfectly well what I'm talking about. I don't want you in the same car as my wife."

"Hey, come on! I think you're both taking things way too seriously. Can't we just forget it ever happened? It was nothing but a stupid, drunken moment between friends."

"That is not the way Emma sees it. You were out of control—'Like a man possessed,' she said when she got back to the room. I've never seen her more shaken."

Snatching a cold slice from the toast rack, Scott buttered it thickly and took a noisy crunch. He gestured at Martin with his knife.

"Listen, pal—your wife was the one who was out of control! It hurt me to take a piss this morning. If she's ruptured something, I could have her up on assault charges. But I'll forgive and forget it if she will. After all, you and I go way back, right?"

Martin pushed back his chair and stood.

"You should count yourself fortunate that Emma didn't call the police last night to report *your* assault—and I think I've heard quite enough."

Scott tossed his toast down onto the tablecloth.

"Well? Aren't you going to be a big man and ask me to step outside? That's the logical next step for the husband in these situations—but then you always were a goddamned wimp, Martin."

Martin gave him a long, hurt look.

"Goodbye, Scott."

He turned away from the table and left the room while Scott shouted after his back.

"I see! Emma's the only one in your marriage with any guts, eh? Well, you're welcome to her, you poor sod. I don't tolerate being pussy-whipped by any woman!"

The other diners fell silent and stared. Scott met the eyes of the couple seated at the next table.

"What the fuck are you looking at? Eat your breakfast and mind your own damned business!"

Leaping up, Scott stormed from the dining room and went upstairs. Martin and Emma's door was closed. Grabbing his luggage, he thumped down to the lobby. The other guests craned their necks, peering at him from their breakfast tables as he checked out with the stony-faced landlady. He left without a word of apology for the disruption and headed back in the direction of the car rental lot.

• • •

Upstairs in their room, Emma hid behind the curtain and watched Scott march down the front walk of the hotel. As he strode away up the road, her shoulders sagged in relief.

"He's gone."

Martin was packing; double-checking the wardrobe for anything he might have missed.

"I'm pleased to hear it." His voice was uncharacteristically hard. He sat on the bed and went through the contents of his briefcase.

"Martin?"

"Mm?"

"I'm worried."

"Nothing to worry about, now that he's gone, pet."

"Not about me. About Clara."

"Yes. Poor Clara. Imagine what she must put up with at home! I hope she does the right thing and leaves the rotten bugger. I don't even recognize him any more. He deserves no one's loyalty."

"Oh, I agree… but I mean that I'm worried about her right *now*. Scott's been acting very strangely, and not just last night when he was drunk. The way he was carrying on in the breakfast room this morning! I could hear him shouting all the way up here."

Martin paused sorting papers and knitted his brow.

"What are you saying, Em?"

"I think we should stop in at the Hall on the way home, just to check that she's okay."

"How can we possibly do that? After the way he's treated you—and the way he's thrown our friendship back in my face—do you expect we'll be made welcome?"

"I don't want to be made welcome, darling. I just want to see that Clara is all right."

"Well, I don't know… I rather doubt he'd appreciate us interfering in his marriage like that. It could just make things worse for her." Martin pulled out a paperback from under a file. "Oh, bloody hell!"

"What's that?"

"It's that blasted *Yorkshire Tragedy* I found at the used bookstore yesterday. Remember the play about the Calverley murders I'd promised to lend to Clara? She seemed so keen, I thought she'd like her own copy as a keepsake. I meant to give it to Scott to pass on to her, but I didn't get the chance."

"Great! That's our perfect excuse to drop by the Old Hall."

"Emma—"

"Please, Martin. I won't rest easy until I've seen with my own eyes that Clara is going to be okay."

"I don't see how she could be, if she chooses to stay married to that man."

"I know. But let's just do what we can and check in on them, shall we? For her sake."

CHAPTER FOURTEEN

At last, Clara summoned up the strength to crawl over to her boot and put in on with difficulty, her fingers not yet fully obedient to her will. She sat catching her breath from the effort and cast her eyes blearily around the room in search of its mate. It was jutting out from under the bed. She crept over and pulled it onto her foot, her fingers regaining a little more strength with every movement. Flexing her hands, she found they ached horribly, but at least she could control them again. Her legs… well, now that was a whole other story.

Time to get up and try walking, if I'm ever going to get out of here. I can't crawl all the way into town.

Clara hauled herself onto her shaky legs and moved jerkily toward the door like a sleepwalker. Reaching down for her backpack, she yanked at it and pulled herself off-balance, catching herself from falling by grabbing hold of the doorframe just in time. As precious seconds ticked away, she blinked down at the bag and she considered what she should do. It was too much for her to carry in her present state and stay upright, but she couldn't leave behind her wallet and passport, as well as her whole life and what little existed of her work on her laptop. Everything that she needed to make good her escape was in that bag. There was no time to waste. She grabbed it by one strap and dragged it down the hallway, bumping it along gently behind her as she worked her way down the stairs. She descended sideways, one slow step at a time like an overcautious toddler, her hand holding the banister in a viselike grip.

Clara knew that speed was of the essence, but she also felt like she'd die if she didn't get a drink. She veered into the kitchen and turned on the cold water tap full force, stuck her mouth under the stream and sucked at it noisily. The cool water rushed over her face and throat as she drank, soaking through her thin cotton shirt and reviving her senses. Life pumped back into her limbs. Vaguely, she recalled once reading a caution against drinking too much too quickly after a long period of thirst, but she couldn't stop herself—couldn't seem to get it into her body fast enough. She slurped at the water until her throat backed up and water flooded her nostrils. Gasping for air, she closed the faucet and leaned against the sink weeping with relief.

Keen hunger followed. Clara ripped hunks out of the stale granary loaf on the counter and wolfed it down, barely pausing to chew and heedless of the hints of fuzzy mould.

The tinkly Westminster chimes in the living room sounded three o'clock. Clara washed down the dry bread with another hasty gulp from the tap, and then delicately heaved her backpack up onto her shoulder. This time, she kept her balance. She'd better get out and make sure she got well clear of the back lane if she wanted to avoid running into Scott.

I just hope that I don't meet their car on the road.
The road… Oh God, please let there be a road!

Clara took a quick glance out through the curtains to reassure herself that, yes, there *was* a gravel road outside along the back of the Old Hall. The row of cinderblock garages stood in plain view just like the day they'd arrived. The boxy post-war houses lined up cheek-by-jowl just as they had since the middle of the last century, with their overgrown gardens and washing lines full of clothes flapping in the breeze.

So far, so good.

Stepping up to the side door, Clara slid back the

lock, turned the knob and pulled. The door remained stubbornly shut.

Clara exhaled a long, hissing breath. She went out to the foyer and stared at the front door for a long moment. The deadbolt was unlocked.

"Okay. Here I go."

She tried the knob. It held fast. The water and bread sloshed in her stomach, threatening to spew back up as she battered her weak fists against the unyielding wood.

Clara's arms dropped to her sides. She leaned her forehead against the door in defeat, feeling her strength drain downward and out through the bottoms of her feet. Hot tears splashed to the flagstones beside her boots. Freedom was mere inches away. She could hear all the sounds of normal, everyday modern life carrying on outside; the traffic on the road out in front of the Old Hall, the shouts of children at play in their back gardens, a dog barking at a car turning into the side lane.

Tires crunching on the gravel in the yard.

An engine dying. A car door being slammed. They were back.

To hell with Scott. Martin and Emma would be sure to help her: she would leave with them. Clara straightened up and turned toward the kitchen as a single set of footsteps scuffled on the walk outside and slowly approached the side door.

Scott must have come back alone.

Clara's heart thrummed painfully fast. She didn't think she could manage to climb the stairs; and even if she could, there was no safe place to hide once she reached the top floor. Out of the corner of her eye she spotted a movement from the sitting room. A flash of blue. Clara snapped her head around to follow the motion. Lights flickered in the periphery of her vision, but she could see nothing.

The sound of keys jangling outside the side kitchen door galvanized her strength. Giving one last hopeless tug at the front door, she sidestepped into the sitting room.

The keys were turning in the lock. The kitchen door was rattling.

Clara tucked herself out of sight in the space between the bookcase and the window around the far end of the L-shaped room. It was not the best hiding spot. If anyone came all the way in she'd be cornered.

The side door opened and Clara held her breath. Slow, heavy footsteps entered the Old Hall's kitchen and stopped. Straining to hear, she could make out a distant rustle as the note she'd left the other day on the poetry book was discovered. Following a loud, derisive snort it was violently crumpled up. Clara jumped at the sharp bang as the book was flung against the kitchen wall, and clapped a hand over her mouth to suppress a cry. The calculated footsteps moved through the kitchen and into the front foyer.

Clara shrank farther into her corner and willed herself to disappear. The feet paused at the door of the sitting room, turned and began a deliberate ascent of the stone stairs.

She exhaled a timorous breath, wondering if there was enough time for her to reach the kitchen door and get outside before the upstairs search was complete. What if the door wouldn't open for her? It was a chance she'd have to take, she decided. Clara gathered herself to make a break for it once she was sure her stalker was at the far end of the wing in the master bedroom.

Something brushed against her arm.

There was a faint, swishing in the room with her— and the blue flash reappeared in the corner of her eye.

Clara turned slowly. This time, the blue figure did not vanish as she squinted to focus on the hazy image. Reaching out to grasp it, her fingers closed on nothingness and the indigo glint moved with deliberation across the carpet. Clara jerked her hand back, afraid even to blink in case she was again swept up by the force of the thing.

"Hello?"

The glint deepened in substance. As sunlight streamed through a chink in the curtain, the colours intensified, forming a translucent human shape out of the dust motes. Clara could make out a shimmer of silk damask… a flash of silver embroidery… the hint of a white lace cuff… as the Dream Woman half-appeared.

The air in the room was suddenly cool, carrying with it a mingled scent of rose-water and lavender. A pale hand materialized and pointed its forefinger down toward the throw rug beneath the diaphanous hem of the shadowy gown's skirts. Clara's stomach lurched—it was the exact spot where they'd performed Martin's drunken ritual to raise the Old Hall's spirits. A hysterical laugh caught in her throat. If she weren't so terrified, it would be funny.

Boy, Martin's going to love this story...

Above their heads, a heavy chair was overturned and kicked aside.

...if I ever get the chance to tell him.

A luminous face appeared at eye level, staring anxiously up toward the familiar clamour of an enraged husband. The visage tilted down and met Clara's gaze. Its eyes were nothing more than hollow black sockets, but Clara felt calmed by the spectre's benevolent aura. Drawn in, she took a tentative step toward the figure. Would she again be absorbed by the Old Hall's former mistress? This time, she'd almost welcome the escape.

Except that things weren't much rosier at the other end of the spectrum.

The image flickered and began to fade. As it melted away, the pointing hand hovered a moment longer before it too dissolved into thin air.

Clara knelt down and ran her hand over a bump in the throw rug. Feeling something uneven and round, she pulled the rug aside, revealing a metal ring on a square wooden door set flush into the flagstones. Her heart leapt as she recalled an open cellar in the floor of the Old Hall's derelict wing.

Upstairs, the heavy footsteps sped up as they pounded along the hallway from the master bedroom.

Clara yanked on the ring and the trapdoor opened with a blast of cold air. The blackness was impenetrable: there was no way to judge the safety of the drop, but the footsteps descending the stairs posed a far more sinister threat than the possibility of a twisted ankle. It was her only chance. A sudden rush of fearful adrenalin compensated Clara for all of her various bruises and strains and she leapt in, letting the door fall shut behind her.

Clara missed the unseen steps and landed hard on her butt, gasping at the sharp pain in her wrist as she broke her fall. Wincing, she rotated it experimentally. It was tender, but it didn't seem broken. She opened her eyes as wide as they'd go. There was nothing to see but pure black. The sparse air was stale and smelled dank and rotten. Cobwebs heavy with dust adhered to her face and hair, and her mouth tasted as if it was full of dirt. She repressed the need to cough and held herself stock-still as she adjusted to the thick darkness, listening for the sounds upstairs.

The feet entered the living room and stopped. A deep voice grunted, and the footsteps started pacing in the direction of the disordered throw rug lying beside the trapdoor above her head.

Casting about, Clara spotted murky light indicating the open gap in the floor of the Solar wing. She scrabbled toward it on her hands and knees, trying hard not to picture dead rats when her groping hand sank into something unseen and putrid. Entering the pool of dim light, she stood and peeked up between the planks covering the hole, recognizing the dull gleam of enamel on the abandoned gas stove. She'd made it through.

The cellar wasn't a deep one, and Clara easily reached the boards overhead and hauled herself up. As her strained muscles screamed in protest, the rotting wood tore beneath her grasp. A filthy splinter broke off and her struggles drove it deep into the flesh of her wrist. Wriggling her body wildly, she grappled at the dirt floor above and managed to gain enough purchase to haul herself up onto her stomach with her legs dangling down behind.

A muffled clattering noise announced the opening of the trapdoor in the North wing.

With her strained muscles screaming in protest, Clara gave a final kick and lurched up and out of the cellar like a swimmer from a pool. She needed to buy time. Dragging over some rough planks from the scattered renovation debris, she barricaded the opening as best she could: it wouldn't keep him out for long, but it would keep him occupied until she found a way to get outside. She swallowed her rising panic and whipped her head around to search for an exit.

Below, something scraped along the cellar floor.

Clara's heart gave a hopeful flutter as she spotted a doorway on the rear wall opening onto the back laneway. Darting over, she found the way barred shut from the inside by boards nailed into the wooden frame. A few frantic tugs only resulted in more splinters. She spun around to see that the doorway back into the North wing had been bricked up long ago and the dilapidated stone staircase ran only halfway up the wall and stopped dead: the upstairs floor level was gone. Even if she could get up there, each of the chamber doors into the North wing was sealed with cement blocks and mortar.

Desperately, Clara gazed upward to the large windows under the gables, but there was no way to reach them—and if she did somehow find a way up, the windows closely mullioned into such small squares that a broken pane would only yield enough space for a bird to escape.

Below, the footsteps were scuffling slowly toward the hole. Clara's anger boiled and overrode her fear. Why did he have to draw this out into a game of cat-and-mouse? Couldn't he just hurry up so they could get it over with? This agonizing stalking was driving her berserk. Clara whirled about to hold her ground, spotting movement in the shadows between the boards.

"Come on, Scott! I've had enough of this!"

She heard the hiss of ragged animal breathing as a face appeared through the gap in the slats. Eyes glared up at her in a steely, unblinking stare.

Clara froze.

It wasn't Scott—nor was it a mere collection of shadow and light as the Dream Woman had been. Calverley's gaze was not made up of hollow sockets; she could clearly make out the dilated pupils and the bloodshot veins in the whites of his eyes. Like her own, his waves of dark hair were greyed by the journey through the cellar, full of dust and clumps of cobwebs. He wiped the back of his hand across his moustache and goatee and spat away debris. Beside his apparent inability to move with any great haste, Calverley was as solid and real as Clara herself. Baring his teeth in a mocking smile, he opened his mouth in a silent laugh.

A voice echoed in the back of her skull. *At last I have you, whore!*

Clara could smell alcohol on his breath. This Calverley was not the repentant husband and father of murdered babes: this was the riotous madman, come to finish what he'd begun.

Raising his arms, Calverley grasped a plank in his dirt-crusted hands, catching his lace cuff on a rusty nail and tearing it as he impatiently tugged it free. Clara was transfixed and could not force herself to look away from those reptilian eyes as he easily heaved the boards and heaped rubble aside. Blinking away a shower of dust, he grasped the edge of the cellar floor opening to pull himself out, clutching something in his fist.

The sunlight through the dirty windows caught a glint of sharp metal.

The sound of her own scream released Clara from her trance. Her disobedient feet came unstuck from the dirt floor, and she stumbled backward into a dark corner, banging her hip against a doorknob. *A door!* She spun about to face a heavy oak door leading to the Great Hall—and with any luck, her freedom. As her fingers grappled with the latch, Calverley eased himself halfway out of the cellar and smirked in her direction. Perhaps the spirit purposely chose his eerily slow movements as he stalked his quarry: the effect was menacing and hypnotic, almost seductive. Clara fought against it. If she gave in, she felt he could hold her mesmerized—haplessly frozen in time and place, waiting for the murderer's knife to descend. She tore her eyes away and concentrated on jimmying the rusty metal standing between her and escape.

The latch gave way and the doorknob miraculously turned. Clara shoved open the door and tripped over the threshold, falling to her knees on the Great Hall's floor. She bounded to her feet and peeked over her shoulder into the Solar wing. With his twisted half-smile, Calverley leisurely sauntered in her direction, moving like someone wading through knee-deep water. He appeared unconcerned. With the smug air of a man assured of victory, he playfully dangled his bone-handled knife loosely from his right hand.

Clara slammed the door in his face and cast about for something to bar his way. The huge room was just as Martin described it: piles of stored paving stones and scaffolding from the renovation work took up most of the floor space. Clara threw her weight against a precarious stack of flagstones closest to the door, and the top half of it toppled over with a grinding crash in front of the entrance.

Clara backed away, watching the latch jiggle up and down. Calverley grunted, presumably heaving his too-too solid flesh against the door from the other side. The ancient wood groaned in protest but held steadfast. The latch rattled again. Violently.

There was a pause—then a crashing thud.

The door jolted open an inch.

Clara made a dash for the far end of the Great Hall, darting between the looming heaps of limestone slabs toward a door with sunlight streaming in from the wide gap between the wood and the floor. Unlike the other wing's doors, the way was unhindered by any barricading planks. She gave the rusty doorknob a twist. It refused to turn. Behind her, Calverley made a second tackle at the interior door. It shifted open another few inches.

Something small and black whirred by Clara's ear and she ducked, her arms flying up to protect her head.

A shrill little cry answered her shriek of surprise. Peering up at the high ceiling, Clara saw a barn swallow fluttering around in panicky circles in search of escape. It flitted toward the sunlight and battered itself against the windows nestled under the beams. She watched as the bird made a final swooping circle—then flew out through a missing pane of a large window on the back wall, high above the arch of the huge fireplace. The window's ledge was at least fourteen feet up; but if she could reach it, it seemed big enough for her to squeeze through. There was a rickety-looking scaffold beneath the window supported against what was the mother of all the Great Hall's stone stacks. Clara tested the stones with her hand. She couldn't budge them an inch. Emboldened, she shoved at it a little harder. The resulting shift was worrisome and she had a morbid mental flash of falling and shattering her bones: she'd be helplessly at the mercy of her sinister huntsman, and he bore no such humane quality. Clara had already been forced to witness his lack of pity and had no desire to permanently join the cast of the Old Hall's spectral reenactments.

Hearing a scrape, Clara turned and saw Calverley's hand appear through the opening. Even from the far end of the Great Hall, Clara could see his knuckles whiten with the intense grip on the dagger's handle. Calverley shoved his face into the crack of the door with his lips peeled back in a snarl. He didn't seem to find this game of cat-and-mouse amusing any more. Stepping back, he kicked at the now-yielding wood: a few inches more and he'd be able to fit through the gap.

Cautiously, Clara began her climb. The scaffold creaked under her weight and listed heavily to one side, causing the flagstones to scrape together. The harsh sound set her teeth on edge and she paused, inwardly praying that the pile would hold long enough for her to reach the windowsill. The wonky metal structure swayed and groaned in a sickening tilt, but there was no choice for Clara but to keep going.

A triumphant shout from the door at the other end of the Great Hall announced that Calverley had finally forced his entry. Clara refused to look back. She progressed one step at a time, careful not to make any too-sudden moves and bring the works tumbling down. Every inch of her ached and she worried that her muscles' strength might fail—but she kept pushing on, her sweaty hands threatening to slip as she gripped the dirty metal poles.

Below her, the heavy footsteps were slowly, steadily pacing toward the base of her scaffold and stone pile.

Her energy badly flagging, Clara reached up and grabbed the wide sill of the window. For the first time, she felt real hope: the broken windowpane was large enough for her to wriggle through, and there were no jagged edges. She poked her face outside. It was a long way down to the bushes growing up against the back of the Old Hall, and she wondered if they would be enough to cushion her fall if she leapt. There could be sharp branches hidden under all of those leaves—but given that her only other option was being stabbed, the decision to jump seemed the better of the two. The height was getting to her in her weakened state. A feeling of vertigo overwhelmed her senses. The lights in her concussed head were flashing like neon signs; popping and giving way to floating black spots of emptiness in the corners of her failing vision. She didn't know how she was going to make herself jump. It was all she could do to hold on to the window ledge.

Just don't look back.

But she did. Her head wobbling on her neck like an unsteady newborn's, Clara stole a glance over her shoulder down into the gloom of the Great Hall. She blinked hard to adjust her eyes just as Calverley grabbed a hold of the scaffolding.

He caught her looking. And smiled. With a jocular wave of his dagger, he began to climb.

A car pulled up the back laneway. Clara tore her gaze from Calverley, looked out and recognized Martin's Fiat coming to a stop. Emma got out of the passenger's side and started toward the kitchen door, carrying a paperback in one hand. Martin rolled down his window and called after her.

"Em, are you sure you don't want me to come in with you? Look—Scott's car is already here."

"I don't give a toss about Scott. I just want to make

sure Clara's okay, and offer her our spare room if she's not."

Martin stepped from the car.

"But what if he doesn't let you speak with her? I think I should come too. He'll have a harder time of it trying to turn us both away."

Scott's car is here? Why isn't he with them? Clara's head spun with confusion as she fought to keep conscious. *Where was Scott?*

The scaffold jolted under her feet as Calverley steadily climbed higher. "Emma!"

Stopping in mid-step, Emma looked around.

"Clara?"

"Up here!"

Martin slammed the car door and stared up at the window.

"Good Lord, Clara! What on Earth are you doing up there?"

"Please hurry! I'm locked inside... he's got me cornered—"

Her voice was raspy and thin. As Clara gave in to a fit of coughing, her head drooped forward in exhaustion from the climb and the effort of projecting her voice. Under her feet, the scaffold and the stone pile lurched back dangerously from the added burden of the Hall's master. Clara shifted her weight as far forward as she could, locking her elbows over the sill for security. The pressure on her midsection made it difficult to draw breath and the threat of a blackout pressed on the back of her skull.

"Hold on, love. We'll get you down."

Martin looked around and spotted a ladder hanging on the side of a drive shed. It was securely tied in place with twine. As he struggled with the knots, Emma stood below the window, trying to keep Clara's attention focused and prevent her from passing out.

"Don't let go, Clara. Stay with us… we'll have you down in no time."

Something brushed against the back of Clara's legs.

I've got thee now, whore—

A slow, firm grip closed around her left ankle—the coldness of the touch numbing her to the bone.

"Oh God, Emma! Hurry! He's got a knife!"

Clara shrieked as a slashing cut ripped open her calf. Blindly, she kicked out behind her with her good leg and connected heavily with the centre of Calverley's chest. Losing balance, he pitched backward, wrenching her leg and nearly dragging Clara down after him. She landed another solid kick and the icy grip vanished from her ankle. Gasping, her feet scrabbled on the stones as she battled to keep her grip on the windowsill; her legs thrashing spasmodically, until the entire stack of paving stones gave way—careening back with the scaffold and pushing it off-balance. As it collapsed with a deafening crash, Clara's limbs flailed in empty air amid the rising cloud of stone dust and dirt.

Emma screamed.

Clara pulled herself back up onto her stomach and hung halfway out the window, her eyes squeezed shut against the dust, dizziness and pain. The searing knife wound throbbed on her calf, and it was getting harder to breathe. She was dimly aware of Emma helping Martin set up the ladder before she greyed out… then Martin's warm hand closed gently over hers, rousing her back to life.

"I've got you, Clara. You're safe now."

Safe.

He helped Clara to ease herself through and twist around, guiding her feet onto the top rung of the ladder as Emma held it steady from below. The first step sent a bolt of pain up Clara's leg and she sucked in a sharp breath against the agony. Martin calmed her, and guided her patiently as she made her slow progress from the window down to the ground.

"There you go, love. I won't let you fall. That's it… just a few more steps and we're done."

Clara collapsed into Emma's waiting arms. The two of them helped her hobble between them over to the car and sat her in the front seat. Kneeling down, Martin tenderly examined the wound on her leg.

"Nasty—but it doesn't seem deep. Could've been far worse if you hadn't been wearing jeans."

Not quite whalebone stays, she thought—*but the denim served me well.*

Brushing Clara's dusty hair back from her face, Emma gasped.

"My God… what has he done to you?"

Martin stood up and saw the bruising on her head. His face was stony.

"What's happened here, Clara?"

Clara wanted to tell them… and yet she didn't dare. How could she possibly explain? She gazed at her friends for a long moment.

"Nothing makes any sense—"

Her head slumped forward and she began to weep.

"One thing's for sure," said Martin. "That bastard's still hiding in there."

Squaring his shoulders, he started around the side toward the Great Hall's exterior door.

"Door's locked," mumbled Clara thickly. She felt like she was talking in her sleep, the words came so slowly and with such effort. "Careful—he's got a knife, remember." Shivering, she gingerly poked at the gash in her calf with her dirty fingers.

"Martin, I think she's going into shock. Let's just get her to casualty and call the police to deal with him."

"He'd be long gone by the time they get here."

Martin yanked at the side door, but the lock held fast. He went into the open drive shed and started banging around—rummaging through the tools. Emma found a bottle of water in the backseat. First helping Clara to sip, she dampened some paper take-away napkins and cleaned the streaks of dirt from her face. Martin reappeared from the shed carrying an axe.

"Martin—"

"Stay put, Emma."

He strode back to the wooden door and bashed at it until it gave way. The Great Hall was filled with a haze of dust from the collapse of the stones, and he hovered in the doorway trying to peer through the gloom.

"Come on, Scott! I know you're in there—Scott?"

Clara clutched wildly at Emma's hand.

"Scott? No... it's *him*—"

"Ssh, Clara. Save your strength. It'll be all right." Her face full of concern, Emma rose to watch Martin enter the Great Hall, patting Clara on the shoulder. "Sit tight. I'm just going to see what Martin's up to."

She hurried over to the doorway.

"Martin?"

"Don't come in here, Em."

"Martin, please. Come out and let's call the police, okay? He's got a knife."

"Yeah—well, I've got an axe."

Emma hung back and held on to the splintered doorframe.

Clara sipped at the bottle and splashed a bit of water on the back of her neck to keep herself alert. Hearing a bark down the laneway, she looked up at Merlin, the would-be wonder dog, trotting toward her with his white-plumed tail waving high over his back. The little boy was nowhere in sight. Clara was glad; she wouldn't want a child to witness any of this madness. She held out her hand for the friendly Border collie to sniff. Merlin paused by her side for a moment—his tongue lapping at the salty skin and blood on her arm—before he perked up his ears at the sounds of Martin's search coming from the building. Bolting for the door, he brushed past Emma, who gave a little cry of surprise. The animal's excited barking echoed inside the Great Hall.

Clara looked around for something to help her walk. She spotted a heavy-duty umbrella lying on the floor of the backseat and used it to limp over to join Emma in the doorway. Martin was in the middle of the room staring at Merlin with bemusement.

"Where'd you come from?"

The dog was pacing rapidly up and down in front of the stack of rubble left by the collapse of the stone pile and scaffolding. Whining loudly, he started to sniff and paw at the debris. Martin followed him with the axe held aloft. The dog let loose with a volley of sharp yaps and began to dig furiously at the stones.

"What have you found, boy?"

Martin took the dog by the collar and pulled him away. As he stared, the hand holding the axe dropped limply to his side.

"Oh... Oh, Jesus Christ."

He crouched down and gently eased one of the

heavy stones aside. Clara craned her neck, but she couldn't see past Martin's hunched shoulders. She touched Emma on the arm.

"What is it?"

Emma turned, mildly astonished to see her friend standing there: she'd been so absorbed in worrying over Martin that she apparently hadn't heard Clara's halting approach. Her normally rosy cheeks were pale, and she shook her head and shrugged.

Martin struggled to keep Merlin back from his discovery. He hugged the wriggling dog to his chest and waved the two women back with his free arm, choking back the urge to vomit.

"Please... just stay outside. You don't need to see this."

"See what?" asked Clara in a leaden voice.

Martin stood up and brushed his hand off on his jeans, leaving a streak of bloody dust on his thigh. Holding the dog by the collar, he turned toward the women, his face drained of colour. Martin pushed them gently aside and emerged through the doorway on shaky legs.

"We'd better find a phone."

"Is he—?"

"The stones have crushed his chest. There's nothing we can do for him."

"Merlin! Come fer supper!"

The dog tugged free at the sound of his name being

called from the neighbouring yard and dashed off in the direction of home. Martin reached out to take Clara by the arm. His voice cracked.

"I'm sorry, Clara. It must be a shock."

Emma swooned at the sight of the blood on her husband's hand and leaned against the doorframe for support. As Martin went to her aid, Clara slipped by them and took a wavering step into the Great Hall.

"He tried to kill me."

"It's over, Clara. He can't hurt anybody now. Come on. Don't look—" Martin tried to steer her from the door, but she pushed him away with a surprising amount of energy.

"I need to see for myself!"

As Clara moved closer, she could make out a man's limp hand jutting out from the rubble. A bone-handled dagger lay on the dirt floor nearby. She hobbled a few more steps, hardly daring to breathe as she steadied herself with the umbrella and leaned in for a better look.

Something twisted in her stomach as she recognized the gold signet ring on the baby finger. The man's face was mercifully obscured from view by one of the large flat stones, but the top of his head was visible where it rested in a widening pool of dark blood. His fine blond hair was matted with gore.

Clara dropped to her knees. As she picked up the dagger, Martin stepped up, gingerly taking it from her grasp as he placed a steadying hand on her shoulder.

She reached out and stroked the familiar cuff of the red-and-blue-striped denim shirt Scott had purchased especially for the trip and the broken face of the watch she had given him on his last birthday.

STRATFORD, ONTARIO

Twenty-two months later

The front door of the B&B slammed, jolting the sleeper upstairs from her dreams.

Clara had overslept. The late-spring sun was already shining brightly through the lace curtains, forming dappled clusters of shadows across the bedclothes. Rolling over in the queen-sized bed, she groped for her watch on the side table. It was nearly ten o'clock. That meant she had missed breakfast service by an hour.

Oh well. Worse things have happened.

Clara got in and out of the en suite bathroom quickly,

performing the bare minimum of morning ablutions. She decided to forgo her shower until later: what she really wanted to do was get out for a long walk around the Avon River before the day was half over. There would be no time later. Her parents were expected by lunchtime, and they were all invited to the home of the Stratford Festival's artistic director for drinks before opening night. Maybe she'd hop off the wagon for the occasion and allow herself a glass of Champagne: it was a celebration, after all—even though it felt more like a wake. *Thank God Emma and Martin weren't able to make it over until later on in the season.* Clara didn't think she could bear seeing them: not just yet. Once the play was up and running, it would take on a life of its own and not be 'hers' any longer—then she could cope. Maybe.

Scott's parents—she could be sure—would not be attending. Heartbroken by his death, they'd cut off all contact with his widow. She'd not heard from them once since the funeral. It was a relief, frankly. Clara had been able to quietly sell the house in Peterborough and move back to Toronto without any criticism or interference from her former in-laws. It was understandable: they needed someone to blame for the death of their only son. Clara didn't mind if the Atkinsons chose to hate her. It was easier that way. They could go to their graves thinking their son a brilliant, infallible man cut down in his prime by a tragic mishap.

The truth was too horrible—and too impossible—to explain.

The real circumstances were only partly known by Emma and Martin: they'd backed Clara's story to the Yorkshire police of a terrible accident while exploring the dangerous Great Hall, and Scott's death was officially ruled a 'death by misadventure.' If she'd told them she'd killed him in self-defence, the legalities would've spun out into a protracted nightmare. As it was, her return home had been delayed by a stay in the Leeds infirmary where she was questioned daily by investigators.

She had no idea what Martin had done with the dagger. It didn't matter now—she just had to find her own way forward. One of the few mercies in all of this was that Clara had regained her freedom. Just not in a way she would have chosen.

A glance out the window revealed a light breeze rippling the leaves on the huge old maple tree out front. It was good weather for Clara's stroll along the riverbanks to her favourite cluster of willows—a sheltered canopy where she could sit undisturbed, watching the swans drift by while she rehearsed her best smile for the reception and the party after tonight's season opening.

She needed time alone to think. Feel grateful.

And remember.

Clara strained to listen for other signs of life from the adjacent suites: no muffled voices, no running water… nothing. The tourists must've already left to hit the Ontario Street shops before lunchtime. Pulling on her jeans and a T-shirt, she went out onto the landing of the Baird and Bard Guest House and called over the railing.

"Hello? Anyone here? Mrs. Baird?"

There was no answer but the stately ticking of the grandfather clock in the entrance hall. Clara descended to the kitchen in search of the coffee machine. Surely her hosts wouldn't mind if she brewed herself a much-needed pot.

Mrs. Baird had already thought of everything. Clara's designated place was set with a flowered plate, mug and linen napkin. A Thermos pitcher of coffee waited for her in the centre of the clean pine table, and a covered basket of fresh muffins with a cut-glass dish of strawberry preserves sat on the sideboard.

"Bless you, Mrs. Baird," Clara said to the empty room. She poured herself a black coffee and sat down. The local *Beacon Herald* newspaper had been set out, carefully folded open to an article for Clara to read:

STRATFORD SHAKESPEARE FESTIVAL SEASON OPENS TONIGHT WITH CLARA RAVENSCROFT'S MUCH-ANTICIPATED PLAY

'A Yorkshire Tragedie' by Canadian playwright Clara Ravenscroft will be the Festival's first offering to audiences this season. Advance buzz is already creating a groundswell

of excitement, according to the Festival's artistic director, Margot Montgomery.

"I am absolutely thrilled," enthused Montgomery in a telephone interview from her busy office. "The previews have been greeted by cheers and standing ovations, and I couldn't be more pleased for Clara. It has been a long, difficult road for her over the past year and a half, and the triumph is well earned."

Those who follow the news in the theatre world will recall the sad circumstances leading to a yearlong delay. Following her success as the recipient of the first annual Richard Monette Memorial New Play Award, Ms. Ravenscroft had accompanied her husband—the noted Keats specialist, Professor Scott Atkinson of Trent University—on a trip to England. Tragically, Professor Atkinson was killed and Ms. Ravenscroft badly injured when an accident befell the couple as they explored a derelict wing of the Jacobean guest hall they'd rented on holiday. Work on mounting the planned theatrical production was understandably postponed.

"The Old Hall in Calverley is steeped in sad history," explained Ms. Ravenscroft in a recent CBC radio interview. "While we were visiting, I became aware of a family tragedy that had occurred there during Shakespeare's lifetime, and later rediscovered an obscure 1605 play his King's Players produced, based on the Calverley story.

"I felt I'd walked—quite literally—in the footsteps of Phillipa Calverley, and wanted modern audiences to bear

witness and appreciate the extraordinary strength it must have taken for her to forgive the unforgivable."

"Was it strength, Clara—or madness?" she was asked.

Ms. Ravenscroft considered her reply.

"I think that's up to the audience to decide. One thing I've learned in the past year or two is that almost nothing is as it seems."

Box office sales have been brisk, so act fast if you want to get tickets and answer that intriguing question for yourself.

Clara set aside the paper and topped up her coffee. Despite the delicious cinnamon scent wafting from the muffin basket, her earlier appetite was gone. A folded note bearing her name was propped up against the sugar bowl.

Hi Clara!

Sorry we missed you at breakfast this morning. The couple from Michigan was looking forward to meeting you, but we all figured you needed your beauty rest before the big night. To lock up, just slam the front door behind you as you go out, and be sure to give it an extra tug. Sometimes it sticks, and sometimes it doesn't! And don't forget your key.

Mrs. B.

Clara drained the last of the coffee, and wrapped a muffin up in a paper towel in case her hunger returned on her walk. If not, she figured she'd feed it to the swans. Patting her pocket to reassure herself that she did indeed have her key, Clara headed to the front door, twisted the brass knob and pulled.

The door did not budge.

"Oh, come on—"

She planted her feet more firmly on the floorboards and gave it another yank. It remained stubbornly shut.

Her stomach gave a sick lurch, and she tasted acidic coffee rising in the back of her throat. Clara's sweaty hands slipped on the knob as she gathered up courage to try again.

This time, she ripped the door open with such energy that she almost knocked herself off-balance with the force of her own panic. She met the startled gaze of the postman on the Bairds' porch steps and gave a strange little laugh.

"Sometimes it sticks," she explained.

And Clara slammed the door shut behind her.

HISTORICAL NOTES AND BACKGROUND

The tragic events of 1605 first came to my attention as an actor in 1994 while portraying 'the Wife' (AKA Phillipa Calverley) in a production of *A Yorkshire Tragedy* with the *Poculi Ludique Societas* at the University of Toronto. The PLS has a mandate to perform plays of the Mediaeval and Renaissance periods—mostly liturgical and cycle dramas—and almost all by anonymous playwrights. This one-act play is a melodramatic and brutal account of a minor Yorkshire nobleman, Sir Walter Calverley, whose marriage to a highborn London woman produced three sons. What had begun as a relatively content arranged marriage quickly degenerated.

By all accounts, Sir Walter was an erratic and unhappy man, given to licentiousness, drink and gambling. Sir Walter's behaviour grew ever more irrational. Despite his own infidelity, he took to accusing his pious and loyal wife of being a 'strumpet' and pronounced their sons 'bastards'. The family fortune was soon in ruins. Sir Walter's younger brother, William, was imprisoned and held in bond for his sibling's debts. The utter hopelessness of the situation drove Sir Walter over the brink. Rather than doom them all to a degrading life of penury, he attempted to murder the entire family. After killing two of his three sons and leaving his wife for dead, the madman was apprehended before he could reach his third child who was staying close by with his wet nurse.

The story gripped the public imagination at the time. In lurid tabloid style, pamphlets relating all of the gory details were widely circulating throughout England even before Sir Walter's case came to trial at the Autumn Assizes in York. It was as great a sensation in its day as the O.J. Simpson trial was to the Americans in the 1990s. *The King's Players*—William Shakespeare's own acting company—cashed-in on the scandal by hastily producing a script, and performing *A Yorkshire Tragedy* at the Globe Theatre in London in 1605. The authorship of the play has never been satisfactorily authenticated, although the title page of the first printed edition in 1608 declares it as 'Written by W. Shakespeare'. It is a potboiler, intended to shock and horrify the audience into pity for the saintly wife. It doesn't seem possible that it is entirely the work of the Bard, who was at the peak of his powers during this time with such masterpieces as *King Lear* and *Macbeth*; but there are a few good moments and flashes of eloquence. I have paraphrased here and there—the drama has become too strong a voice to exclude from *Base Spirits*.

The PLS revival of this rarely performed piece caught a fast hold of my imagination. To play the part,

I had to walk in the shoes of a brutalized wife who witnesses her children murdered by their own father. The most difficult challenge of the role was the final scene of forgiveness in which the wife literally gets down on her knees to beg for the life of the 'base spirit' who has committed the foulest of crimes. According to the contemporary records, she did indeed forgive him, and tearfully begged for his life to be spared. It is difficult—if not impossible—for most of us to understand how she could find such compassion for her husband. Was it shock? Battered-wife syndrome? Perhaps it was a case of 'better the devil you know', as she was a woman stranded hundreds of miles from her London origins. She might have been too fearful—of him, of her own feelings, of God—*not* to forgive. There also seems to be an honest belief, as portrayed in the writing of their farewell scene, that he was possessed by the Devil and not responsible for his own actions. Whatever her reasons, it is enough (I hope) to show that forgiveness was unconditionally granted.

The production was remounted for the 1995 Summerworks Theatre Festival in Toronto. During the rehearsal period, I had occasion to visit Leeds and I knew that the village of Calverley was nearby. Curious, I took a local bus out into the countryside. Not only was Calverley Old Hall still standing, it was divided up into private residences and a holiday rental accommodation. Parts were derelict and awaiting restoration: though the chapel had been restored, the Solar wing and the Great Hall were in terrible disrepair, full of rubble and—yes—stacks of flagstones. It is a friendly village, and I was directed to the home of Edward Garnett, the local historian. He gave me a tour of the Hall and a copy of his book *The Calverley Murders: A Yorkshire Tragedy*.

The gripping historical account gave me a more complete insight into the characters and the status of a woman in the confines of Jacobean marriage, as well as the circumstances of their arranged union. Sir Walter's father had died while his eldest son was still a minor, and as a Ward of the Courts he did not have control over his own destiny. His wayward nature and tendency to be a chronically unlucky gambler sealed his doom. Garnett also gives a harrowing description of the method of Sir Walter's execution—'peine forte et dure,' or pressing—through a contemporary account of the death of Catholic Saint Margaret Clitherow, who was also pressed to death in 1586 in York. This method of death was an agonizing ordeal to be sure: one inflicted on those accused who refused to enter a plea. Without one, a trial could not proceed by law. Pressing was employed to compel the defendant to plea (as in being 'asked the pressing question'). In Saint Margaret's case, she refused in order to keep her family clear of implications in a time when being Catholic was deadly dangerous. I suspect the less-than-saintly Sir Walter's silence was to ensure that his little remaining property would be kept from falling into the hands of the Crown. I also chose to interpret his submission to such torture as his final act of penance.

Phillipa was eventually remarried to Sir Thomas Burton of Stockerston in Leicestershire. She bore him three daughters, and died shortly after giving birth to the third in 1613. The surviving son, Henry (the 'brat at nurse') eventually built an addition to Calverley Hall in the 1640s or '50s: the wing today available as holiday accommodation through the Landmark Trust. It's not *that* haunted! (http://bookings.landmarktrust.org.uk/BuildingDetails/Overview/144/Calverley_Old_Hall). I could find no account of the fate of William, who was gaoled for his brother's debts. I can only assume that there must have been enough capital—or pity—to free him from his bonds.

I chose not to write a purely historical novel because I wanted the circumstances of the spousal abuse not to be removed at a 'safe' distance. One of my early beta readers questioned the situation of the modern Clara, finding it hard to believe that a well-educated woman and an academic could find themselves engaged in the age-old sick dance of marital violence. Unfortunately, it does happen with alarming regularity in all sectors of society. The original frontispiece of the 1608 printing bears the legend 'Not so new as lamentable and true', and we have only to open a newspaper to find a contemporary Calverley story on an almost daily basis. To be blind to this sad fact only gives these situations the room and privacy needed in order to flourish. The silence and denial often prove a deadly combination. By naming demons, we can hope to exorcise them.

Sources and Further Reading:

Garnett, Edward *The Calverley Murders: A Yorkshire Tragedy*, Margaret Fenton Ltd., 1991.

Walker, Peter N. *Murders and Mysteries from the Yorkshire Dales*, Robert Hale Limited, 1991.

Sturgess, Keith *Three Elizabethan Domestic Tragedies*, the Penguin English Library, 1969.

Cawley, A.C. and Gaines, B. *A Yorkshire Tragedy*, the Revel Plays, 1986.

ACKNOWLEDGMENTS

I am grateful to the Poculi Ludique Societas at the University of Toronto for introducing me to the play, *A Yorkshire Tragedy*, and for casting me in the role of Phillipa Calverley. Many thanks to the people and parish of Calverley in West Yorkshire for their kindness and generosity of spirit on my several visits. Especial thanks to Edward (Ted) Garnett, a local historian, who gave me a private tour of Calverley Old Hall and a copy of his book *The Calverley Murders: A Yorkshire Tragedy*.

I'd like to thank the invaluable 'team' who helped me put the final version of this novel together: my excellent editor Heather Sangster at Strong Finish (http://www.strongfinish.ca/) (and thanks Kevin May, for making it possible), my splendid cover artist Neil Jackson (http://www.pigandcowdesign.com) and the dynamic formatting duo of Amy and Rob Siders at 52 Novels (http://www.52novels.com/). Author's jacket photo by Laird MacIntosh.

Other, more personal thanks are due to my good friends and family who have seen me through it all. To my ever-expanding circle of writer friends: cheers for all the support and encouragement. A tip of the hat to the wonderful creative community in my adopted hometown of Stratford, particularly The Network Gals!

I cannot possibly single out and name every individual who deserves praise, but my particular thanks go to Stephen Ayres for always believing, and above all, to Craig Williams for keeping me on course and cheering me on through the darkest of times, and ensuring that I'd be here to tell the tale.

If you enjoyed my work in e-book format, please feel free to leave a review on the site where you made your purchase.

And thank *you* for buying my book. I hope you'll be back for more.

ABOUT THE AUTHOR

Ruth Barrett was born in Pointe Claire, Quebec and grew up in Barrie, Ontario. She attended Trent University in Peterborough where she studied English Literature, and began her love affair with the United Kingdom during an exchange year at the University of Leeds. After earning her B.A., Ruth returned to England and studied Classical Drama at the prestigious London Academy of Music and Dramatic Arts (LAMDA).

In her years pursuing an acting career in Toronto, Ruth performed onstage, in television and radio, and eventually specialized in voice-over work—most notably as the voice of 'Creakie' (a domineering little blue monster!) in the Treehouse TV show, WEE 3.

Always a storyteller, Ruth honed her skills as a writer through further training at George Brown College, and the Humber School for Writers correspondence program under the enthusiastic mentorship of Booker Prize-winning author, Peter Carey. Ruth went on to publish several short stories in anthologies and literary journals, earning a few awards and a Toronto Arts

Council grant along the way.

In her 'day job,' Ruth applies her background in both writing and television as a writer of descriptive narrative TV and film scripts for the visually impaired and blind. In April 2011, Ruth was tasked with co-narrating the royal wedding of Prince William and Catherine Middleton with the CBC and the Accessible Channel in a six-hour marathon of live improvised description.

These days, Ruth resides in the beautiful town of Stratford, Ontario—home of the world-famous Stratford Shakespeare Festival.

COMING SOON

SPIRITED WORDS BOOK CO.

Look for the following books from Ruth Barrett and Spirited Words Book Co.

Short Story Collections

Those Ills We Have—Twisted stories of urban lust and loss.
Tales Unfolded—A chilling world of deadly deeds and unearthly tribulations.

A Novel of a Revenant Spirit

The Rake's Chronicles—A fatal mélange of sexual obsession, untimely death and supernatural revenge set against the tidy backdrop of Victorian England. ('The Tell-tale Heart' meets *My Secret Life*.)

And in the fullness of time…

THE DEAD DRUNKS: a series of quirky, character-driven mystery novels. Follow the unlikely investigative team of wigmaker, Teddy, and ex-cop, Winston as they track down murder most foul in the world-famous theatre community of Stratford, Ontario: small town, big politics. Things behind the scenes are definitely not what they seem…
Keep an eye out for book one—*In the Bag*.

Please join me on-line for all the latest 'spirited' news and gossip, and announcements of my new releases:

http://ruth-barrett-spiritedwords.blogspot.com/

http://twitter.com/#!/LadyCalverley

https://www.facebook.com/pages/Spirited-Words-Book-Co/101014656667433

Or drop me a line at: spirited_words@yahoo.ca